Murder Richly Deserved

by

Roxanne Dunn

Cover Art by *Lisa Dawn MacDonald*

The Wild Rose Press, Inc.
PO Box 708
Adams Basin, NY 14410-0708
Visit us at www.thewildrosepress.com

Publishing History
First Edition, 2024
Trade Paperback ISBN 978-1-5092-5557-3
Digital ISBN 978-1-5092-5668-6

Published in the United States of America

Dedication

To my husband, family, and friends; far, near, and always in my heart, with a heaping bushel of love and gratitude.

Praise for Roxanne Dunn and *Murder Richly Deserved*

"…Set in a world of opulent wealth, greed and duplicity, Dunn paints marvelously detailed scenes, taking the reader on a fast-moving, tension-filled ride…"

> ~*Brian Anderson, the Lyle Dahmer mysteries*
> ~*~

"…a classic jewel theft story with a twist, made stylish, witty, and entertaining in the hands of talented writer Roxanne Dunn."

> ~*ML Barrs, author of Parallel Secrets*
> ~*~

"…Dunn follows her first two thrillers, *Murder Unrehearsed* and *Murder Undetected* with a nimble heroine and a nasty villain, engaging characters and yes, even a dog. Dunn has given readers another entertaining adventure…"

> ~*Jeffrey D. Briggs, the Seattle Waterfront Mystery series*
> ~*~

"…In this compelling read, the author takes the reader on a ride through the streets of Paris to a castle in the Pyrenees…"

> ~*Linda Norlander, the Cabin by the Lake Mystery series*
> ~*~

"…a delightful caper-murder mystery with a touch of romance in this page-turning story that transports you to world of intrigue…"

> ~*Charlotte Stuart, the Discount Detective Mysteries*

Chapter One

There hadn't been a single diamond, emerald, or ruby big enough to bother stealing since Christmas, so I hadn't jumped from one rooftop to another or short-circuited an alarm system for three months. As I followed the server to my favorite table at the *Cochon Qui Rit*, I was starting to worry that I would lose my edge.

"Chloe, so good to see you." The head chef, in her crisp white coat, placed a flute of champagne in front of me, tiny bubbles sparkling in the candlelight, and I looked up to thank her.

That's when I saw it. The Queen of Persia diamond. Set in a heavy twenty-four carat gold band and surrounded by lesser stones, each worth more than all but the most expensive baubles sold at Touché or any of Paris' other exclusive jewelers.

It winked at me from the pinky finger of a man with a dapper white goatee, a round face, and a shiny bald spot surrounded by curly gray hair. He wore a maroon brocade dinner jacket, a pink shirt, and a silk tie in shades of vanilla and dark truffle.

Outrageous. That diamond belonged in Alexander's Museum of Antiquities in Istanbul. I know because I took it from there myself. That was seven years ago when I was nineteen and added it to my secret stash in the safe in my mother's wine cellar. Two years later, someone—I never found out who—stole it. Who would have known to search the dimness behind all the wine bottles in the quaint seafront town of Sterling, Washington? Between Seattle and the Canadian border, the petite tourist destination had to be the tiniest dot on the map.

In the cadre of jewel thieves, there is a certain amount of recognition and respect. Generally, when something is stolen, if I know what was taken, when, and how, I can guess who might have pulled off the robbery. But my ring had disappeared without a clue—and ended up on the other side of the world, on the finger of a man completely unknown to me.

Halfway across the restaurant and seated facing me, he gazed around with a smug little grin, as if daring everyone to run over and ogle his ring.

The *Cochon Qui Rit* is a famous, or should I say infamous, restaurant a hop and a skip from the Eiffel Tower—a place where, at certain times, one can feel the pulse of the underworld, strong and steady.

It's famous because the all-women crew serves up lunches and dinners that have earned the place three Michelin stars for the last four years. Infamous because the head chef, Viane Thibaudet, was convicted— wrongly, she claims—of murdering her own father, then her husband's parents, one after the other, and attempting to murder her husband. Infamous secondly, because she and all the women who work there return every night to prison.

I admire Madame Thibaudet. It took charismatic charm to persuade a judge that teaching other inmates to work in a high-end restaurant would rehabilitate them.

Personally, I prefer to sleep where I can watch the

lights on the tower from my soft, cozy bed. And share it when I wish with the new man in my life, whose *je ne sais quoi* between the sheets always amazes me.

My heart beat triple time as I dragged my eyes away from the diamond. I could not let the man wearing it catch me gazing at it, even though other diners were pausing in their conversations, raising their eyebrows, and nodding discreetly in that direction.

Either he was fat or wearing clothing that made him look fat. That round red face could have been faked, too, along with his jolly expression. In fact, he could have stepped right out of a production of Shakespeare's *Henry IV*. Fat, jolly, hedonistic Sir John Falstaff. I had to find out who he was and why he'd chosen to reveal himself to me. Until I knew more, I'd call him Falstaff.

Another man sat at the table with him, his back to me. Lean, with dark hair that swooped back over his ears, he wore a black suit tailored to fit perfectly across his broad shoulders.

Without a smidgeon of doubt, Falstaff meant for me to see the ring. He had managed to plant himself right smack in my line of vision, and although he gazed around the room, smiling and occasionally nodding at the other diners, he avoided looking at me. Each time I glanced at it, my pulse kicked up a notch. Game on! The Queen of Persia belonged to me. All I had to do was figure out how to get it back.

Just before the server brought my dinner, I took my compact from my bag and pretended to powder my nose while I used the camera hidden inside the compact to shoot several pictures of him, then zoomed in on the ring itself.

The familiar thrill, the adrenaline pumping through

my veins, enhanced everything—the deep red of the roses in the center of each table, the rich but subtle decor, the laughter of the guests, the whole ambiance of the dining room. It made everything better. It elevated the breast of duck with green peppercorn sauce, which always tasted superb, to the level of divine. I would have loved extra slices of baguette to mop up the creamy juices, but I didn't want to linger. I had to prepare for what might happen next. While my brain whirred, I ordered a quick dessert: a single scoop of lemon sorbet.

When his server brought him a single scoop of lemon sorbet, mimicking mine, I signed my bill, slipped into my leopard-print trench coat, tucked my signature red clutch bag under my arm, and left. The desire to get a close-up glimpse of the Queen of Persia almost overwhelmed me. After all, she belonged in *my* treasure chest. But I didn't even glance in that direction.

As I hurried toward the nearest taxi stand, I pulled the combs out of my hair, releasing it from the French knot. It tumbled to my shoulders, and I fluffed it around my face. I put on a pair of large, ugly, pink plastic glasses that I carry in my handbag, turned my coat inside out to show the nondescript black side, and pulled a dowdy knit hat out of the pocket and jammed it down on my head. My red clutch went into a grocery carry bag that lived in another pocket. I didn't have an alternative for the red stilettos.

Just down the street, before I got to the taxi stand, a cab stood at the curb, vacant. No lights were on, but a man wearing a leather bomber jacket leaned against it, one foot crossed over the other, smoking. "Are you available?" I asked.

He shook his head. "It's not—"

I held out a fifty-euro bill.

He looked me up and down and grinned. "Sure."

"I'll be across the street from the *Cochon qui Rit*. Please wait until I signal, then come and pick me up."

He shrugged and took the money. "*Merci*." Again, he flashed a big smirk.

I ignored it and hustled back. Three minutes later, Falstaff and his friend stepped outside. From the alcove of the apartment building across the street from the restaurant, I snapped a series of photos with the camera in my compact. I only needed one, actually, but the man with Falstaff begged the perfect photo. In the camera's night vision view finder, his eyes were deep indigo, set in a rectangular face with a perfect nose and mouth. His tailored suit screamed *ex-pen-sive* London tailor, perhaps Tristan Dakota on Savile Row. He'd unbuttoned his starched white shirt at the collar and undone his black bow tie. The cufflinks that gleamed below his sleeves sent brittle rainbow shards into the night.

A shining, pearl-gray car with a hood a mile long, one of those fearfully expensive antique imports from England, glided to a stop in front of the two men. As a chauffeur wearing a uniform crusted in gold braid got out, marched around, and opened the rear door, I waved at the taxi. The men climbed in, and the chauffeur closed the door with a discreet, classy, thump. Seconds later, I slid into the cab and instructed the driver to follow them.

We turned left where rue St. Dominique intersects the street right in front of Les Invalides, the giant complex with the glowing golden dome over Napoleon's tomb. By then, they were two cars ahead. Perfect. We turned left again beside the Seine and headed toward the Eiffel Tower. Piece of cake. You could see that car a mile away. I rested back in my seat.

The driver gazed at me in the mirror.

I knew those eyes.

He grinned. "Chloe?"

I caught my breath.

"Nice glasses, Chloe Eugenie Duval."

The rich, deep timbre of his voice made my knees wobble.

Chapter Two

It came to me in a flash that I hadn't met Honoré St. Lazarre, the new man in my life, by chance. I leaned forward. "You're driving a cab?"

He shrugged. "Hey, this is an expensive place to live, so I drive a couple of nights a week."

"Who was that guy I gave fifty euros to?"

"What guy?"

"The guy who was leaning on this car, smoking."

"I have no clue. You gave money to some random guy?"

"He wasn't random. He was leaning on this car, and the light wasn't on, so I asked if he was available and he said 'sure.'"

"I have no clue who it was. Sounds like you gave good money to some random guy who happened to be leaning on my car." He started to laugh. "So that's why you jumped in when I had to stop for traffic." He laughed some more, as if it was the funniest thing he'd ever heard.

I wanted to smack him. And I had the disquieting sense that when he signed up for the baguette baking class where we met, he knew I would be there.

So who was he? Friend or foe? Or both? An enigma. Best of all. A totally delicious thrill ran up and down my spine. I felt the way I did in that heart-stopping moment before I stepped, uninvited and unsuspected, into someone else's apartment. No amount of dark chocolate, champagne, or caviar would ever equal the kick I got. No wonder I had never considered giving it up.

I pulled in a deep breath. *Underestimate me, Honoré, my love. That will be fun.* Sooner or later, I'd find the truth about the man driving my taxi. But right then, I needed to keep both eyes on the gleaming silver car ahead of us.

We blazed through a red light amid shrieking brakes and blaring horns and before reaching the Eiffel Tower, squealed around a corner onto a bridge. By the time we crossed the river, the other car was four vehicles ahead of us. Honoré darted between two other taxis and a bus with less than a hand-width space on either side, and we plunged into a narrow street clogged with traffic. We slowed to tortoise pace, then turned onto an even narrower, more congested street that doglegged off in a different direction. I was having a hard time staying oriented, but so far, we seemed to be headed vaguely toward the Arc de Triomphe.

I said, "That car doesn't exactly melt into the crowd. It practically equals a written invitation to follow them, so why do they seem to be trying to shake us off?"

"I have a better question. Why are you following them?"

"Maybe because they stole something from me."

We roared into the next intersection, which had five roads leading into it and was jammed with buses. Honoré glanced back over his shoulder and reversed, but stopped when a car pulled up behind us. He rolled down his window, leaned out, and peered in both directions, then sat back with a crooked grin and drummed the steering wheel with his fingers. "Ah, so," he said.

The silver car had disappeared by the time we finally

squeaked through the intersection. Honoré wriggled down one street after another, one hand steering and the other blasting the horn, until we reached one of the wide boulevards radiating out from the Arc de Triomphe. We turned toward it, and I spotted our quarry. "Did you know where they were headed?"

"How could I know?"

"I think you know more than you pretend."

He dashed into an opening barely two inches longer than the taxi and a few minutes later joined the crush of vehicles streaming around the giant traffic circle at the Arc. A quarter of the way around and two lanes over, the magnificent old car pulled to the curb. It stopped for a moment, and then glided away. I caught a glimpse of Falstaff's portly figure heading toward the Metro station.

"Stop," I yelled. I blew Honoré a kiss, jumped out of the cab, and ran, praying I would not get run over—or break my neck in my stilettos.

In the station, I slid my Metro card over the reader, shoved through the gate, and joined the jostling crowd streaming through the tunnel. Falstaff was well ahead and seemed to be following the arrows pointing to Line One eastbound. He glanced back over his shoulder as he started down a long flight of stairs, then pushed past a couple holding hands and sped ahead. I heard the train whoosh to a stop as I ran down to the platform. He boarded the second-to-last coach. As the doors started to close, I leaped onto the end car.

I stood beside the door so I wouldn't miss him if he got off. As the train swayed and rattled down the track, I clung to the handrail and peered into the car ahead, but a lot of people were standing, and I caught only glimpses of the back of his head. We rattled and hissed through three stops, halting at each one long enough for passengers to hop off and on, but Falstaff stayed put. At each stop, more people piled on, until the car was so full that I lost sight of him.

When we pulled into the Concorde station, hordes of people disembarked. The coach ahead was nearly empty. My neck began to prickle. Falstaff didn't get off, but he wasn't inside either.

I stepped off and fought my way through the crowd waiting to board, then scanned the throng streaming in and out of the platform. People rushed in all directions. This stop had multiple tracks, tunnels, exits, and entrances. The perfect place to disappear.

I turned my coat back to the leopard print side, tossed the carrier bag, stuffed the ugly hat and glasses into my pockets, and tucked my red clutch purse under my arm. Then I strode through the station. As I started up the stairs to the exit, a Metro security officer planted his feet and spread his arms a few steps ahead of me, blocking the way.

On the landing above and behind him, a man in a pink shirt sprawled across the stair, one arm dangling down and dripping blood. He groaned and lifted his hand to his face. I recognized that hand.

The Queen of Persia ring had disappeared.

Chapter Three

My heart pounded. It looked as if Falstaff, whoever he was, played in a tough league.

I had to get out of the Metro. Glancing over my shoulder every few steps, I hustled to the next exit, ran up the stairs, and marched out into the damp night air. I covered a block, then two blocks, as my heart rate slowly returned to normal.

I'd resigned myself to the fact that most likely I'd never see the Queen of Persia ring, my all-time favorite prize, gained by my all-time favorite caper, again. Then, out of nowhere, it was right there in front of me. I had no clue how Falstaff knew I'd want it, but obviously, he did. And he wasn't ready to let me have it, which meant he wanted something in return. So, he'd begun a flirtation, as if we'd been guests at a dance. As if our eyes met across the room, but we danced with other people, all the while sensing each other's presence and knowing that when the time was right, we'd be dancing together.

Assuming he was still alive, the problem was, I danced solo. I avoided teamwork. I didn't collaborate with other people. I preferred to go alone into empty hotel rooms and apartments where I knew the owners were out for the night. This reduced the risk of exposure and the threat of bodily harm to near zero. As long as I'd adhered to this rule, I'd done well.

In following Falstaff, I'd taken a step toward

bending that rule, and no question, seeing him lying on the stairway had alarmed me. I'd run. I hadn't stopped to wonder whether he'd slipped and fallen or if someone had attacked him, or whether he was dead or alive. I'd scrambled to get away. It wasn't like me to feel fearful, but I kept looking over my shoulder. I stayed as far away as possible from other pedestrians.

There was something reassuring about stepping onto Pont Neuf. This old bridge had witnessed pestilence, revolution, and two major wars, and still it stood, solid and safe. I began to feel I could breathe again, and the fact that I cared more about the ring than the man who'd been wearing it crept into my consciousness. How could I be so shallow, so callous?

Pushing the thought out of my head, I crossed the river and continued straight onto rue Dauphine. I had to stay focused. In the middle of the first block, I paused in front of a bookstore as if to gaze at a window display and studied the reflection of the street behind me. Cars streamed by at a steady pace, and on the other side, two couples strolled, their heads close together.

A few steps farther on, I came to a shiny black door embellished with gold script that read, *Chez Celeste,* and underneath that, in French, *Fashion Meets Affordability.* I keyed in the code on the number pad beside the door, stepped inside, and locked it behind me. For several seconds, I stood there, leaning against the door and chiding myself for getting spooked.

The scent of sandalwood lingered in the air. Tiny star-like lights cast a soft glow down on the room. An antique, jewel-toned Persian rug covered the uneven stone floor. Old-gold silk shantung panels stretched along both sides and across the back, hiding crumbling plaster walls and lending the room a patina of luxury.

Aunt Celeste meant it to feel luxurious, exotic, and subtly masculine, like a sheik's tent in some magical, far-away place. Although the boutique catered to chic but budget-conscious women, the customers who kept her coffers brimming were well-heeled men with expensive tastes. Those she let into her back room could count on finding rare and beautiful baubles, either for themselves or for the special people in their lives.

I walked between racks of party gowns and dinner jackets to the fitting rooms and entered the cubicle on my right. I slid my hand behind the gold shantung panel on the back wall, flattened it against a cool, smooth security pad, and waited for it to read my fingerprints. A portion of the wall pivoted open, and I entered Aunt Celeste's back room. Silently, the panel closed behind me.

Floor lamps cast a puddle of light over three chairs stationed around an oblong glass coffee table. A huge bouquet of red and white tulips sat in the center. The only other light came from the security system in the work area where she designed and made her own line of hats and dresses. A pair of shoji screens separated the work tables, sewing machines, and bolts of fabric from the cozy sitting area.

Aunt Celeste was stitching a hand-made silk rose onto a wispy, broad-brimmed hat. "There you are!" She rose from a chair with deep red velvet cushions.

Picture a hummingbird. A tiny, curious, friendly creature darting about, flashing iridescent emerald, sapphire, or crimson feathers. Pausing only long enough to suck up sweet nectar. Exotic. That's Aunt Celeste Bertrand.

She claims to be my father's sister on the flimsiest

evidence: a grainy black and white photo of a man she states is her brother—I can't quibble with her on that—and a slender, petite, young woman she identifies as my mother. In the photo, they face each other, leaning in as if about to kiss. The background, a gigantic brick building, suggests the Chateau Frontenac in Quebec City. My mother scoffs at this. She denies that she ever visited the Frontenac and insists that she doesn't know who my father is. Whatever. Aside from my mother, Aunt Celeste is the only person who has ever wanted to be a member of my family, and I adore her.

She wore a vintage tango dress, a black, body-hugging silk sheath with a fantail at the back, a deep vee neckline, and long, sheer sleeves. A sequined black and silver fascinator hat tilted over one arched eyebrow. "I had a feeling I would see you tonight." I'm only five and a half feet tall, but having kicked off her high-heeled black and silver sandals, she had to stand on tiptoes to kiss each of my cheeks.

My black and tan dachshund, Baguette, offended at being left out, leaped onto the chair she had vacated and gave one short, sharp bark. His jacket, as I expected, matched the fabric of her dress and a black beret with a silver band perched on his head. I leaned over and scratched his ears, which mollified him. Actually, Baguette doesn't care all that much about me when Aunt Celeste is around, and in fact, he spends most of his time with her. But he thinks he should be the center of attention.

She took my hands in hers. Tipping her head to one side, she gazed at me, her dark brown eyes alert and lively. A wide smile curved her bright red lips and revealed small, perfect, white teeth. "I heard a rumor about your favorite ring."

"It's not a rumor."

"Wait. Don't tell me. I must pour champagne." She went to the wet bar that ran along the side of the room and poured two slender crystal flutes brimming full.

I regarded the tiny tornado of bubbles swirling up the center of my glass. It transported me back to the *Cochon Qui Rit*, to the moment I looked up and saw my ring on Falstaff's finger.

She lifted her glass. "To the Queen of Persia."

We touched our glasses together, sipped, and then stood there for a minute, grinning at each other; and I knew both of us were remembering the day I walked out of the museum in Istanbul, my hand in my pocket, clutching the ring.

I sucked in a breath. "I'll tell you everything."

We leaned against the bar and she listened without interrupting. Then she said, "What if the ring you saw was a fake?"

I pulled my compact out of my purse, found the photo, and handed it to her. "It wasn't."

"Exquisite." She held it close to her face and squinted. "No matter. If it were fake, the real one would not be far away." She looked at me, dark eyes twinkling. "Pour us more champagne, darling, while I look at the rest."

She scrolled through my photos, pausing to tap a long red fingernail on Falstaff's companion. "Ooh-la-la. Do you think you took enough shots of this one?"

I grinned. "You wouldn't ask if you'd seen him."

"Be still my heart." Her hand fluttered above her chest. "Any idea who he is? Or his chubby buddy?"

"None."

She smiled. "I expect they will be in contact with you soon."

"If Falstaff isn't dead."

"You had only a brief glimpse of a man sprawled on the stairway above you. Are you certain it was him?"

"My gut tells me it was."

"We must find out. And let's hope he had sense enough to leave the Queen of Persia in the car with his friend. But first—" nudging Baguette off her chair, she waved a hand at a matching red velvet seat and sat down "—sit."

I sat and Baguette settled on his wicker bed beside her.

"I have a question," she said, giving me a look that told me she was serious and concerned. "What do you know about this delectable Honoré St. Lazarre who was driving the taxi and who turned up in your life exactly three weeks ago?"

A tremor shook my heart. There had always been a whiff of mystery about him. And now, it seemed as if there was also a whiff of danger. "Why do you ask?"

"Why are you avoiding the answer?"

It was one of the things I loved about her. She preferred the truth, no matter what it was. "I'm beginning to think he's not who he says he is."

"You are fond of him." She raised her glass. "In the event that Honoré is not his true name, I offer a toast to Pierre, Luc, Jacques, or whomever."

I got up and paced the tiny sitting area.

She picked up the sunhat she was working on and pushed her needle through the pale-yellow silk rose, then pulled the thread tight, anchoring it at the base of the crown. "You've been alone a long time, darling. You need to be careful."

I wanted him to be the research scientist he claimed to be. I didn't want him to be Pierre, Luc, Jacques, or whoever. I loved his name, the very sound of it. Honoré. I loved the way those three syllables rolled out of my mouth. The way they tumbled around in my head at all hours of the day. They had a sweet, gentle rhythm all their own. Honoré. Honoré St. Lazarre.

Please, God, if he isn't who he says he is, don't let him be a cop.

"If you were a cat, your tail would be swishing. Please sit. You're making me dizzy."

I let out a big sigh, then plunked into a chair. "I can think of three possible explanations for his behavior tonight." I held up a finger. "One, he was trailing Falstaff and his companion."

"A taxi is a great car for that. No one pays any attention to them."

"True." I stifled a sigh. A flic would know that. But so would anyone else. "Anyway, he had parked the taxi and was lurking nearby so he could see them when they left the *Cochon Qui Rit*."

She nodded. "Possibly, but not necessarily because of the ring."

I put up another finger. "Two, he was following me."

"You were on foot, so it seems unlikely he'd have a car waiting."

"Or—" I put up a third finger. "It was a coincidence. He just happened to see me and decided to surprise me."

"I'm suspicious of anything anyone calls a coincidence."

"But I like that idea best."

"Of course you do. You're as romantic as your mother."

She got up and crossed to the bar. An espresso machine sat on the counter. Bolted in place, it hid the touch pad that unlocked the entrance to a secret room. Reaching behind the machine, she pressed her palm to the screen, and I heard a click. She placed a hand on each side of the machine and pulled, backing slowly away as the entire counter, along with the wall behind it, pivoted toward her. An opening showed up, just big enough for each of us to slide through when we turned sideways. We squeezed inside as overhead lights came on and the fan that circulated the air began to hum. The wall closed behind us.

We were in a space five feet wide and fifteen feet long. The people who owned the building during the second world war hid whole Jewish families in there until they could smuggle them out of the city. Whenever I went in, I felt as if we were standing on sacred ground. I drew a deep breath and thanked God that neither the brave folks who lived there nor the ones they hid were ever caught. I gave thanks that my grandmother escaped the Holocaust when she was a child. She'd seldom talked about it, but occasionally, her bitterness had spilled out, and gradually I learned how she'd watched her parents and brother grow weaker and weaker and how one day, when she'd returned to the cold, barren barracks, she'd found herself alone.

I took a deep breath and glanced around. Aunt Celeste had fitted the far end of the space with shelves and drawers which held the jewelry she discreetly acquired and sold.

Near the entry, a super-secure, super high-speed

computer, a printer, and a scanner stood on a French Renaissance desk. We settled on chairs with spindly legs and faced the computer. The camera at the top of the screen took a shot of her face, and the machine began to whir. She dragged the scanner toward me. "Now, darling, shall we find out who these men are?"

I scanned two photos each of Falstaff and his buddy, and in a moment, all four shots appeared on the screen. "And your Honoré?"

I felt the blood rush to my cheeks. "I don't have a picture of him."

She gazed at me. "I think I'd better meet him."

"I did check to see if he worked at the Darwin Center, and their website identifies him as a biology researcher."

"And he also drives a taxi?" The way she raised her eyebrows made it clear that Aunt Celeste thought I should have dug deeper.

"Part time." I hadn't *entirely* taken him at his word when he told me he was a research scientist, but I had, from the beginning, wanted to believe him. And why might he not drive, too? Research scientists aren't wealthy.

She was right, of course. I had not been careful enough. I'd learned the hard way that misplaced trust carries the risk of long, disapproving stares from a judge and even longer nights locked up in a cold, gray, concrete cell. I did not need to repeat that experience.

The only good thing about it was that when I was a child, my mother taught me to look for the silver lining in any cloud, and sure enough, when I was "inside," I found one—a tiny handful of likeminded people. For the first time, I had the luxury of discussing knowledge and skills of my chosen craft, the way people with ordinary professions, like doctors and dentists, do.

Which is why, when I moved to Paris, I was happy to meet a couple of Aunt Celeste's friends. The four of us bonded and formed our *Société de Voleurs de Nuit*, an exclusive trade guild for burglars. Sort of. If you get my meaning.

Clearly, Honoré was hiding something. I couldn't, even for a moment, let myself believe that he just happened to be driving that car at that moment in that place.

Just as clearly, the four of us had a better chance of discovering what he was up to than I did by myself. She waited for my decision; hands poised over the keyboard.

I sighed. "I'll get a photo. In the meantime, let's ask if anyone knows anything about him."

She typed a couple of sentences, then shut the machine down. "Now, we wait."

As I removed the storage disc from my camera, Aunt Celeste started the program that wiped the computer's hard drive clean. I opened a desk drawer and set the camera disc on a powerful magnet, erasing the photos I had taken that evening.

The *Société* would look at the photos, then erase them. We never stored information in a traceable form any longer than necessary. That was one of our strictest rules.

When the computer stopped whirring, we returned to the sitting area. I kissed my aunt, scratched Baguette's ears, and went back out through the shop. By that time, it was eleven o'clock and traffic had diminished, so I snagged a taxi without difficulty, and in fifteen minutes, stood at the entrance to my apartment, listening. I pressed my ear against the door but heard nothing.

The only other person who had a key was Aunt Celeste, who lived one floor above me, but that didn't mean much in my world. The door was locked, and the tiny, knee-level rectangle of paper that I always leave between the door and the jamb was still there, at exactly the right angle. I unlocked both locks and stepped inside. Again, I listened. Absolute stillness. I was alone.

The sudden emptiness left me feeling like a deflated birthday balloon. I needed some endorphins. I needed to run.

I flung my coat, hat, and purse on a chair in the salon, turned on the overhead light, and started toward the bedroom to change into my running gear, then stopped. *Voila*! My silver ice bucket sat in the middle of the glass-topped coffee table. Rivulets of condensation ran down the sides into a neatly folded white napkin. It contained a bottle of the champagne I buy only for special occasions. Honoré! But he had never sneaked into my apartment, and why would he leave and put the paper back in the door?

Nonetheless, I tiptoed to the bedroom and peered in.

On the bed, right in the middle of the puffy white duvet, stood a large shopping bag. Inside, neatly folded and wrapped in tissue paper, I found the maroon jacket Falstaff had worn at dinner.

Somebody else had been in my apartment, and the champagne and jacket were messages. The champagne told me whoever it was knew a lot about me; the jacket, hmmm. Maybe it meant Falstaff wanted to bargain for the Queen of Persia. If so, what might he want in exchange?

Someone rapped on the door. I stuffed the jacket back in the bag and shoved it into the back of my closet.

Chapter Four

Honoré St. Lazarre propped himself up on one elbow and brushed his fingertips down my arm. "You are not sleeping."

"No." It was nearly one A.M., and I hardly ever slept between midnight and three, but he'd never stayed all night before, so didn't know that. Nor did he need to know. Not when I knew so little about him.

His fingertips smoothed my hair back off my face and his breath whispered across my cheek. "A problem, perhaps?"

"No." The fact was, I felt more alive after midnight than at any other part of the day. Especially tonight. I'd found the Queen of Persia, or it had found me. And disappeared again. Where was it now? Who had left Falstaff's jacket in my apartment and why? I had to find the key to the puzzle. I would not sleep soon.

"Financial difficulties?" He dropped a kiss on the end of my nose. "I can understand. It takes a large amount of money to maintain an apartment, especially one so spacious, with such a view."

I turned onto my side, my back toward him, to hide my smile. "Honoré, you are fishing."

He draped an arm over me. "Fishing? Is that an American term? Canadian, perhaps?"

I laced my fingers through his. "You know perfectly well what I mean." He spoke French beautifully, but if he was Parisian by birth, as he claimed, so was the man in the moon.

I, at least, was French Canadian. My mother came from a small, very French village south of Montreal. As a teenager, she was so thin that a man with normal-sized hands could span her waist, and she had a slight limp, which made her an unlikely suspect when guests at big conventions "lost" their jewelry.

At the age of thirty, single, a talented cat burglar with a young daughter and the Quebec police hot on her trail, she took a job at a private museum on Vancouver Island; about as far away from Quebec as she could get without leaving the country. She married an American dentist she met in the gift shop and moved to Washington State, taking along a suitcase full of purloined diamonds, sapphires, and pearls.

I inherited her willowy frame, her large brown eyes, dark, wavy hair, and her passion for beautiful things. While my stepdad was at the office, grinding some poor soul's molars, the two of us would parade around the house decked out in glittering jewels. By the time I was four, I knew I would follow in my mother's footsteps.

Honoré nuzzled my neck. "You wound me, Chloe Eugenie Duval."

"*Désolée.*" Not. Not sorry.

At that moment, thousands of lights, glittering like diamonds, began to dance up and down the Eiffel Tower, filling my window. I pointed. "I never get tired of watching."

Honoré was right. It takes a lot of money to maintain a large apartment with such a great view. But all that sparkle breathes life into my soul. It inspires me to stay on top of my game. When the lights subsided, Honoré rolled me over to face him. "I have had a miraculous recovery of my strength."

Did he know how irresistible he looked, his chestnut hair all tousled, his chocolate eyes unfathomable in the soft light from the lamp on the nightstand? Never mind the rest of his well-muscled, not-quite-six-foot body. I put a finger on his lips. "Impossible."

"Perhaps I shall surprise you."

And he did.

****

I waited until he fell asleep, then got out of bed, slipped my arms into his shirt, which he had discarded in a heap on the floor, picked up his pants, and carried them into the salon. His leather wallet had molded to the shape of his butt, and showed the kind of wear that only comes with time, but all the cards inside, including his driver's license, were bright and shiny—new.

So who was Honoré St. Lazarre? Did he actually moonlight as a taxi driver, and if he did, why did he insist that he just happened to be driving my taxi? Could that possibly be the truth?

The first lock clicked, then the second, as it often did about that time if my lights were still on. The front door opened, and Baguette, still looking splendid in his black jacket and silver-trimmed beret, trotted in and sniffed at my ankles.

Aunt Celeste had donned a red cape and a black feather boa over her tango dress. She hung her cape and Baguette's lead on hooks beside the door and tossed the boa over one shoulder. "I see a frowny face. Do I detect a disturbance in the force?"

I showed her the cards in my hand. "All brand new."

"Ahhh, I see."

I slid each of them into the correct slot in the wallet, then tucked it back in the pocket I'd retrieved it from.

Baguette stopped sniffing the sofa and dragged Honoré's shoe out from under it. He tossed it aside and ran to the bedroom door and began to growl.

Aunt Celeste's eyebrows disappeared under the veil of her fascinator hat. She gazed at the bedroom door for a moment, then back at me.

The door opened.

Honoré, totally naked, stared at Aunt Celeste for a long moment, then smiled at me. "A party? Give me a moment to slip into something festive." He stooped to let Baguette sniff the back of his wrist.

Aunt Celeste unwound her feather boa. "This should cover it." She strode over and draped it around his neck, then stepped back and looked at him, all the way up and all the way down. "It suits you perfectly."

Well, it did hide some impressive features.

"*Merci*, Madame Bertrand."

I sucked in a breath and held it. He knew her. Why hadn't he told me? Why hadn't she?

He sauntered to the sofa, sat, then arranged the boa. He crossed his legs at the knee the way ladies do in pre-impressionist watercolor paintings, when they're about to have tea.

I looked from one to the other. "You two are acquainted?"

Aunt Celeste sat in a wing-back chair, which on her, looked like a throne. "Under a different name. Olivier St. John, I believe." She winked at Honoré. "Where did you think he got the cufflinks you're wearing?"

I didn't want to admit it, but she was way ahead of me. I hadn't even noticed them. I held the pair side-by-side and stared at them: lovely gold rectangles with softened corners. Like the path of planet Earth around the sun, clear Burmese rubies formed an elliptical ring around large emerald-cut white diamonds. They were gorgeous. Crafted in France in the eighteenth century, they had once belonged to a descendent of the Hapsburg family.

I knew exactly how they got from that person's hotel room to Aunt Celeste's back room. I could guess how they got from there to here.

I sank down on the floor and pulled Baguette onto my knees. I couldn't believe I'd been so focused on discovering his identity that I hadn't recognized them.

Aunt Celeste had gone to the coffee table and was twisting the cork out of the bottle of champagne as if she hadn't a concern in the world. She shook her head so slightly that only I would notice, and her forehead puckered in a worried little frown. "You're slipping, darling."

Chapter Five

I used to think Italian men were la crème de la crème. But then I decided there was nothing more enticing than the *savior faire* of the Parisian French.

In my day job, I work for Rhineland Bankgruppe, a German investment bank headquartered in Brussels. The engraved brass plate beside my door proclaims me Chloe Eugenie Duval, Wealth Management Advisor. I had the requisite MBA, but the fact is, I eased past fifteen other candidates for the position because my first language, even before French, is money. I love the stuff. I love making it.

My job suits me perfectly. All I do is sit behind a polished maple desk in an office muted by thick, muddy-purple carpets and decorated with good watercolor prints, and chat with well-heeled men about their stock portfolios. Women are assigned to one of two tall, suave men with touches of gray at the temples.

The morning after the Queen of Persia diamond came back into my life, my calendar showed an eleven o'clock appointment with a new client, Zachary Le Noir. His name had been all over *Paris Financial Times* lately. According to them, he'd grown rich by buying gold whenever the price dropped a fraction of a euro and selling it whenever it went back up. Neither a conservative investment strategy nor a game for the faint hearted. But if you have great quantities of a highly valued commodity, even a few pennies' increase in unit price can yield a big profit.

The rumor that accompanied the freshly brewed espresso and chocolate croissants in the common room that morning was that my boss, a gruff, solidly built man with a thick accent and a thicker mustache, tried to talk Monsieur Le Noir into going with one of the senior partners—those who deal with the richest of the rich. However, he insisted on having me, a mere advisor, manage his portfolio. This tickled me right down to my bright red toenails.

I only half listened to my colleagues' conversation as it swirled around me. I was hoping for a message from Aunt Celeste, telling me she had info about Falstaff—what happened in the Metro; who the heck he was. And something—anything—about his buddy. And Honoré, of course. But by 10:45, I'd heard nothing from her, and it was time to go to my office and get ready to welcome Monsieur Zachary Le Noir.

On work days, I wind my hair up in a French knot and put on one of my tailored-but-feminine black suits, a white shirt open at the neck with only a hint of décolletage, a subdued silk scarf, and small gold earrings. So, for our first meeting, I was, as corporate policy dictates, the picture of trustworthy. Right on the hour, I opened the door to admit him.

Zachary Le Noir walked in. The man who'd been at the *Cochon Qui Rit* with Falstaff. Whatever game the two of them were playing, they were keeping the ball moving.

My heart started to beat triple time, but I kept my smile cool and my greeting professional.

Equally reserved, he took the chair across the desk

from mine.

I managed to get through the usual pleasantries about the weather, then turned the monitor on my desk so we could both see it.

The security staff watching the screens in the shadowy green room in the basement would never have guessed we were connected, or that our connection was a priceless twice-stolen ring.

His portfolio contained a lot of manufacturing stocks, all good, all seriously boring, and all at odds with his reputation as a commodities trader. I pointed at the screen with a slender Venetian glass pointer. "Let's talk about a more aggressive selection."

He smiled his megawatt smile. "Mademoiselle Duval, I find discussions of stocks tedious. Please, I have researched your reputation, and I trust your judgement. I leave the selection to you."

The sparkle in his eyes took my breath away.

Leaning across the desk until our noses were only inches apart, he spoke very softly. "I am certain you know more interesting ways to make money."

As if we were forbidden lovers plotting a rendezvous, our secret vibrated in the space between us.

He sat back and adjusted his cuffs to display gleaming gold cufflinks. Each had a two-carat white diamond in the center. Like a starburst, progressively smaller stones reached out to each corner. I had never seen them before, and I didn't like them as well as I liked Honoré's, but they were, all the same, quite wonderful, and I knew I would find a way to acquire them.

I pretended not to notice. Instead, I glanced at my watch. "I had no idea it was so late." A little lie, often useful.

The corners of his lips turned down. "But we have not had a chance to become acquainted." The spark of mischief in his eyes belied his tone of disappointment, confirming my belief in the urbanity of the Parisian male. I loved it.

My appointment book lay open on the desk. I ran my finger down the page, then closed it. "The chef at Chez Gaspard has just won his third Michelin star, and I have a standing reservation on Tuesdays." Actually, I didn't, but Robbie Gaspard, the chef and owner, always made room for me. He was, after all, a member of our *Société de Voleurs de Nuit*. And after seeing the photos Aunt Celeste sent out, he'd find it intriguing to see Zachary Le Noir in the flesh.

"I've heard of it."

I shifted my gaze to the dark, two-day growth on his rectangular jaw and those blue-violet eyes. "It's only a short walk from here, and I'd be delighted to have you join me."

Zachary Le Noir held my sober black wool coat for me while I slipped my arms into the sleeves. On the way to the restaurant, with elegant and amusing old-fashioned courtesy, he insisted on walking on the outside of the sidewalk, next to the street. I believe the custom is meant to protect a lady's skirts from water and mud thrown up by the wheels of passing carriages. Although anachronistic, it is a courtly, gentlemanly gesture, and I enjoy this sort of attention to manners. When he offered his arm to cross the street, I tucked my hand into his soft, warm cashmere sleeve and he snugged it in against the solid muscles of his chest.

Moments after we opened the door and walked into the heavenly smelling, wood-paneled restaurant, Robbie

Gaspard, in his stiff white coat and tall white hat, appeared from the kitchen and greeted me with a kiss on each cheek. He escorted us to a corner booth upholstered in quietly expensive gold and black stripes, and a minute later, set glasses sparkling with champagne on the starched white cloth in front of us. "Would you prefer the menu today, mademoiselle, or shall I choose for you?"

"We are completely in your hands, Robbie."

"*Bien*. I shall not disappoint you." He bowed low, took my hand and kissed it, then hustled away.

Zachary's mouth curved into a wicked grin. "And I, Mademoiselle Duval, am completely in *your* hands."

"Monsieur Le Noir." I gazed over the rim of my glass at him. "To a successful investment partnership."

He lifted his drink and rainbow-hued shards of light danced off the diamonds at his wrist. "While I appreciate your advice about my portfolio, that is not what I wish to discuss with you."

"Shall I assume that you also do not want to talk about gold bullion?"

"You shall."

I couldn't stand it any longer. "Perhaps you are interested in gemstones." I reached over and tapped the cufflink closest to me.

He grinned. "As long as my heart beats, I shall wear diamonds." He unfastened it and tucked it, warm from the heat of his body, into my palm.

I ran a fingertip over the surface, starting with the lovely round-cut center stone, then each of the smaller ones. I tipped it from side to side, watching how the refracted light changed with different angles of incidence. The diamonds were of such brilliance and clarity that they probably came from India before the mines were exhausted; set in eighteen-carat gold. I turned it over and found the mark of an early-nineteenth-century jewelry maker in Luxemburg. It was typical of his work around 1800 to 1815. I could barely breathe. "It's lovely." Finally, I reached out to give it back.

"Please," he said, smiling and holding out his wrist.

My heart rate kicked up a notch. A person could get lost in those violet-blue eyes, but I wasn't that foolhardy. I repressed a sigh.

Better to stay focused on the diamonds. His shirt had the silky feel of fine Egyptian cotton. The cufflink slid through the buttonhole with ease, and I had to admit that it would never look better anywhere. Except maybe on my own wrist.

He adjusted the sleeves of his jacket, partially hiding them.

They would become part of my forever treasure trove.

He said, "As fond as I am of precious gems, I'm here to ask for your help in recovering something even more valuable. May I expect that you will guard what I am about to tell you in the strictest confidence?"

A shiver of anticipation ran down my spine. "Of course. Whatever you say to me is confidential. My own word as well as the privacy rules of Rhineland Bankgruppe guarantee that."

A server, long white apron over sharply creased black pants presented us with an appetizer of roasted baby artichokes stuffed with fennel and herbs and topped with béchamel sauce. He poured a pale, straw-colored wine and withdrew.

Le Noir took a bite. "Ambrosia." Slowly, as if savoring each one, he ate all his artichokes. Then, as he mopped up his plate with a piece of baguette, he said, "I come from a family with an unbroken line of succession from the seventeenth century until the present day. Our ancestral home is in Bulgaria, and my cousin, Baron Petar Ivanov, and I are the current custodians of various treasures which came to our family many years ago.

"Such as?"

"A talisman that belonged to Charlemagne, a tiara of clear, pure, Burmese rubies and sapphires, a three-thousand-year-old golden sun bowl used in parts of eastern Europe in ancient ceremonies, and much more."

"Including the Queen of Persia ring?"

He sat back a moment, a broad smile on his face. "Not many people recognize it for what it is."

"I saw it in Alexander's Museum of Antiquities in Istanbul."

"Ah. You knew it from there."

It was my turn to smile. "The man you dined with last evening was your cousin?"

"Exactly."

So Falstaff was a baron. He looked like one. Baron Petar Ivanov.

He raised one eyebrow. "He did not expect you to follow him."

I concentrated on finishing my artichokes. "Is he well?"

"He will recover."

All my senses were on high alert, but I had to ask, "Wasn't it foolish to wear the ring in the Metro?"

"He is not a foolish man." Zachary patted his breast pocket. "The ring is safe." He sipped his wine, as if waiting for me to make the next move.

The server showed up to remove our appetizer

plates, giving me a minute to think. I am not an impulsive person. You might be surprised to hear that. But although burglary is often the result of impulse, it is not an impulsive act. Any successful attempt requires logical thought and careful planning. At the moment, I needed to learn all I could about my companion and his cousin, what they did, and why.

When we were alone again, Zachary Le Noir said, "As you may know, the 1878 Treaty of Berlin made the north half of Bulgaria a vassal state to Turkey and the south half a semiautonomous body within the Turkish Empire. The Turks used their power to steal most of our treasures." He gazed at me for a moment. "Including the ring."

"But you have it now. How did you retrieve it?"

"Ah! Long story. My cousin found it in Alexander's Museum of Antiquities in Istanbul, and we sued the museum for it. We lost, incidentally. But during the trial, we were allowed to have it examined and discovered that what they had was a replica."

Of course. When I took the real one, I'd left a replica in its place.

He said, "It was a good one—a very good one—but a fake nonetheless."

That fake had cost me a lot of money. I did my best to look surprised. "Seriously?" I loved that the museum hadn't realized what it was.

Le Noir nodded.

"So what happened?"

He gazed at me for a moment, and the corners of his lips twitched up. "When we revealed the deception to the museum, they offered a handsome reward. Five years ago, an agent recovered it."

"For the reward, I assume."

"He intended to return it to the museum, but we were able to persuade him to give it to us instead."

I shivered. Persuaded? How?

Fortunately, Robbie Gaspard appeared beside us and took my mind off the possibilities. "Today, I have made for you a filet of Dover sole and medallions of lobster in champagne sauce, accompanied by asparagus grilled with raspberry vinaigrette." He set shallow, fish-shaped bowls in front of us. "You will not find better anywhere."

I breathed in the delicate scent of parsley, butter, and lemon. "Heavenly."

"*Bon appétit*." Robbie headed back to the kitchen.

As I broke into the golden crust on the fish, Zachary said, "Forget about the ring for a moment. I want to tell you about something that belongs not to us, but to a Jewish family that worked on my cousin's grandfather's estate."

He'd promoted their ancestral home to an estate. A still-existing estate in Bulgaria shouldn't be all that hard to find. And its history shouldn't be hard to trace.

His fork stopped halfway to his mouth. "You are familiar, I assume, with the tapestry at Bayeux."

"Yes, of course."

"The family I'm speaking of once was wealthy and owned a similar tapestry, but in the years leading up to and during the two world wars, they lost everything, simply because they were Jews."

He'd played a sympathy card. Was it sincere, or was he just trying to hook me? Did he know my grandmother lived through the Holocaust as a small child? Did he know her parents and grandparents had been robbed of all their art and jewelry after the Nazis invaded Austria?

"Charlemagne commissioned the tapestry sometime around 800. Created by monks at the monastery we now know as Mont-Saint-Michel, it depicts the story of Moses leading the Israelites to the Promised Land and other stories. When the Vikings attacked the monastery in 847, the monks fled, taking the unfinished tapestry with them. Much later, it showed up at a cathedral in Germany, where it was displayed off and on for many years."

"If it has been well preserved, then it would have extraordinary value."

"Even in poor condition, it would be priceless."

"True."

"In the seventeenth century, the church sold it to finance a new roof, and the family, having a lot of money at the time, bought it."

"And now?"

"It was stolen at the outset of the war in 1939. Hitler's government cut it into seven segments and gave the pieces to various favorites. My cousin's father recovered five, but died without obtaining the remaining two. Petar and I have tried. We know where they are, but we've exhausted all legal avenues."

"I see."

"We still feel an obligation to return it to the family."

"That's very good of you." His tale had the ring of truth and it tugged at me. If my grandmother had been able to retrieve some of her family's possessions, perhaps she wouldn't have grown up so alone and afraid. Perhaps she would have been less bitter.

Robbie Gaspard showed up to ask if we enjoyed our

meal.

Zachary Le Noir speared a medallion of lobster. "It's genius."

Robbie loved to hear that his cooking made people happy. His hazel eyes sparkled and danced. "Monsieur, you are talking too much." He tried to hide a giant smile by brushing his fingertips across his salt-and-pepper goatee. "*Manger*! Eat." He winked at me and stalked away to create more splendid food.

The fish tasted fresh, delicate, and was perfectly cooked. We did not resume our conversation until it was nearly gone. Finally, Le Noir looked up. "I have forgotten everything in the delight of this meal. However, during the second world war, an officer of the Vichy French army promised to guide Jewish families across the mountains into Spain and pledged to keep their valuables safe. He led them to a castle in the Pyrenees, in a region sparsely populated and seldom travelled. The woman who owned it provided food and shelter while they rested overnight, and when the refugees went on their way, she told the Nazis where to find them. As a reward, each of them received a piece of the tapestry. After the war, they married and filled the castle with the treasures of the people they betrayed."

"People like that deserve to burn in hell."

I might be a thief, but I would never steal from a fleeing refugee. It's different when wealthy people leave their baubles lying around. The fact is, people generally insure their jewelry for more than it's worth, so it's a win-win type of situation. And if they don't, *tant pis*. It's not like anyone needs diamonds or sapphires or rubies.

Le Noir leaned across the remains of Gaspard's excellent fish. "*D'accord*. If there is a God, then hell is where they are."

"They died?"

"Disappeared, vanished, in 1953."

"Revenge?"

"No trace of them has ever been found, so no one knows."

"And now?"

"They had one son. He died, and his son owns it now."

I held up my hand. "The grandson of the Vichy French officer and the woman in the castle has the two pieces of tapestry?"

"Correct."

"Who is he?"

"Count Maxime Charpentier, as much a thief as his grandparents."

"I've heard of him."

"Everyone has. Maxime the playboy. Ski bum in the winter and yachtie in the summer. And a life-long friend."

"Seriously?"

Zachary nodded.

Count Maxime's scandalously lavish parties fueled all sorts of rumors and filled gossip columns from Nice to Paris to London. I would have loved to be invited, for more reasons than one. First, just to be part of the spectacle. Second, because the count's friends would be wearing some spectacular gemstones.

"But business is business, so my cousin and I brought suit against him for the return of the tapestry. He argued that it was bestowed as payment to his grandparents, and therefore, rightly belonged to him. The court decided in his favor."

We waited while the server removed our plates and placed the dessert menu in front of us.

"And you are telling me this because?"

"We still need to set a grievous wrong right."

Should I believe him? If he had a reputation as a philanthropist, wouldn't the *Paris Financial Times* have mentioned it? I shook my head. "I don't see how a financial advisor can help."

He grinned. "I believe you have other talents, and only someone with your abilities can retrieve the two remaining pieces of the tapestry."

"Monsieur Le Noir, you mistake me for someone else."

"The Queen of Persia will be yours if you help us repair this injustice."

I could hardly breathe. I grabbed a piece of baguette and mopped my plate to avoid looking at him. Did I dare believe him? Okay, so he had buckets of money. So did his cousin, most likely, so they could afford to give me the ring. But why did they want me to get the tapestries?

My companion slid a hand inside his jacket and my heart skipped a beat. I thought he might bring out the Queen of Persia ring, but instead pulled out a map which he opened and laid on the table between us. "Maxime's château is here." He pointed to a circle drawn in red ink, south and east of Toulouse, in the mountains not far from the Spanish border.

I pulled in a deep breath. The Pyrenees, in my opinion, were about as far from civilization as Mars is from Jupiter, so the château had to be remote, perhaps almost inaccessible. "Why would anyone want to live there?"

"Only a caretaker actually lives there. But my

nephew will marry Maxime's daughter in the chateau next weekend, and I am invited to bring a guest and stay for the weekend. If you would come as my date, I'd be honored."

Chapter Six

Three wily, exciting, enticing men had stormed into my life. And it seemed they all knew more about me than I knew about them.

In order of appearance: Honoré St. Lazarre, whose wallet contained a shiny new driver's license and credit cards. I had to admit to the tiniest chance that I'd fallen in love with him, and—just my luck—his real name, for all I knew, might be Ted, Bill, or Larry. If it were, that alone would be reason enough to fall out of love, if, in fact, I *had* fallen. If it were Olivier St. John, as Aunt Celeste had first known him, then I could live with that. Probably. Depending on his reason for using a pseudonym. At least it had a certain rhythm to it.

Second, portly Falstaff, aka Baron Petar Ivanov, who moved more athletically than many heavy people do, so might have been wearing a disguise, and who waved my Queen of Persia ring around as if he owned it, which he didn't.

Third, his cousin and my new client, Zachary le Noir, who played on my sympathy to get me to steal an ancient, priceless tapestry.

A prudent person would have distanced herself from all three.

But no one ever accused me of being prudent.

On the way back to the office after lunch, my phone buzzed repeatedly. I was dying to look at it, but Le Noir insisted on escorting me, so I had to wait. I only half listened as he promised to pick me up at the train station near the count's château on Friday evening. In the lobby of Rhineland Bankgruppe's building, he kissed both my cheeks and finally, I was alone.

I hustled to my office, closed the door, and pulled out my phone. Aunt Celeste's message was right there on top.

—*After the rain stops, it should be nice enough for a stroll in the garden this evening. Care to join me?*—

I answered at once.

—*Perfect! I'd love to.*—

The garden she referred to was the Luxembourg Garden, one of the places our *Société* met, and our normal time was between six and seven in the evening. We'd gather at the pond, then wander through the park until we found a quiet place where we could talk. I'd go early and see how many people were there.

In a few days, I'd attend the wedding. I'd spend a weekend at a remote chateau with Zachary Le Noir. Not with him as in the same bed, of course, but with him. It would give me a chance to find out who he and his cousin, Baron Petar Ivanov, really were, the name of the game they were playing, and what they knew about me—why they had chosen to contact me.

My first question was, if they had managed to get their hands on the Queen of Persia ring, why did they think they needed me to retrieve the alleged tapestry? Second, was their story about the Jewish family true, and did they actually plan to return the tapestry to them? If so, and if I helped them, could I trust them to give me the ring? Third, even if their motive was purely philanthropic, and even if my grandmother might have approved of their returning it, why wouldn't I go straight for the ring instead?

Le Noir and his cousin, how they'd found me, and how they got the Queen of Persia were mysteries to be solved.

It's true that in the entire world, the number of burglars who specialize in gems is relatively small, and no two people conduct a caper exactly the same way. Each of us has a signature style, like the fist of an old-time telegraph operator. If you know what to look for, it's almost as clearly identifiable as a fingerprint. But when the ring disappeared from my mother's wine cellar, there had been no fist, no fingerprint. And there was no trail leading from the wine cellar to Baron Ivanov's finger.

I booted up my computer. Rhineland Bankgruppe's team of investigators vets potential clients before accepting them. I'd skimmed the evaluation team's report on Zachary Le Noir earlier, but now I read it critically. And gained nothing. I could have learned as much from reading back issues of *Paris Today,* the gossipy society rag that specializes in dirt on rising entrepreneurs, *faux pas* of social luminaries, and snarky tidbits about people who've made it to the top.

I realized I'd been doodling while I read, writing Honoré's name over and over on my notepad—Honoré St. Lazarre—and embellishing it with scrolls, flourishes, and tiny rosebuds. I went to the credenza behind my desk, crumpled the sheet of paper, lit it on fire, and dropped it into the antique Tuscan funeral urn that I keep for this purpose. I watched until the flames died, then put the lid back on so the smoke alarm wouldn't go off.

How the heck did Honoré fit into the puzzle? New

credit cards and driver's license would have made sense if he'd lost his wallet, but then the wallet would have been new as well. And it wasn't. And he'd met Aunt Celeste using another name. Plus, I couldn't swallow his part-time taxi driver story. I wished I thought I was imagining things, but he must have been following either me or Le Noir and Ivanov when he showed up in that cab.

The prestigious Darwin Centre, where Honoré claimed to work as a researcher, is a non-profit organization funded by wealthy donors who want to find ways to protect endangered species. Scientists apply to come and work for a period of time in the center's state-of-the-art labs. I pulled the website up again and sat there and stared at the screen.

The day I met Honoré in baguette class, while we kneaded the dough and shaped it into loaves, he'd told me this: "The goal of my project is to identify the snippet of genetic code that allows certain species of fish to thrive in warm water, then splice that code into salmon who only exist in colder waters and are threatened by rising ocean temperatures."

In Sterling, Washington, where I grew up, the decline in the salmon population and risk to the orcas was a major concern, as in the orcas were not getting enough food. It tickled me to think there might be a solution. "So," I'd said, "if you're successful, then the salmon would be able to adapt to warmer water, produce healthy, vigorous offspring, and repopulate."

"Exactly. And that could save several pods of Pacific Northwest orcas, who eat only Chinook salmon, from extinction."

We'd chatted about his interest in the orcas, but in

my world, things are not always what they seem to be, and I'd gone right home and looked him up on the Darwin Centre website. It identified him as a conservation biologist with expertise in gene splicing, which he'd acquired at Oxford, just as he'd told me.

So I'd taken him at his word.

But now, like the persistent moan of the early-morning foghorns that cut through damp, cold, fall air back home on Puget Sound, warning boaters of hazards ahead, a question pulsed in the back of my mind: Did I know for sure he was who he said he was? The answer: absolutely not. Anyone could, with very little education, know about the plight of the whales. And he could have guessed that I'd care about them and connect with him on that basis.

When awakened by the foghorns, I'd pull a blanket up over my ear and go back to sleep. But to ignore this question would be reckless. Even though the Darwin Centre was, as far as I could tell, totally reputable, I had the unshakeable feeling that I couldn't trust what I saw on the screen.

Chapter Seven

It rained periodically during the afternoon. But as I left the office and headed home, the clouds were drifting off to the east, leaving behind puddles, awnings that dripped cold water down your neck when you walked under them, and a chilly breeze to shake the leaves.

Perfect. We wouldn't have to worry about being overheard. If it had been a warm, sunny evening, hundreds of people would be heading toward Luxembourg Gardens to watch toy sailboats bob across the pond or lounge in a green chair and indulge in everyone's favorite pastime, eavesdropping.

I tugged on black tights, a knee-length, belted, camel-colored coat, and cheetah-print ballet flats. I added a cheetah-print scarf, and voilà! I looked like half the young moms in Paris. I'd blend right in. There'd be a dozen lookalikes at the big pond in front of the palace.

My red scooter, Poppy, is as close to a magic carpet as you can get. I pulled the cover off, hopped on, and buzzed between lanes of gridlocked traffic. I parked on Boulevard Saint-Michel, walked into the park, and arrived at the pond a tiny bit early. A fine mist hung in the air, softening the edges of the stately stone palace and lending a dreamy, watercolor look to the flowerbeds and long rows of trees.

I headed straight to the concession stand where my

favorite sailboat, her brave French flag fluttering, waited on the top shelf. About a foot and a quarter long, she had a weathered white hull. The navy and red stripes below the gunwale and a red boot stripe were also worn, and her name was partly missing on the port side, but still visible on the starboard bow: *Diamant*. A brand new, sparkling white sail flew from the main mast, and a smaller sail stretched out over the stern. I knew I should remember if the boat was a ketch, a yawl, a sloop, or something else entirely, but that kind of detail never stuck in my head. I paid an hour's rent, and the gangly, college-aged kid managing the concession handed it over, along with a long wooden baton. And a big grin, as if he knew I was one of those adults who had never grown up.

I leaned over the wide concrete rim, lowered *Diamant* into the water, and pushed her away with the baton. She struck off bravely, straight toward the middle. Then the breeze filled the mainsail, and she veered off to the left, slotting in between a couple of other boats that were headed that direction. I joined the kids running after them, and waited, laughing and cheering with them, until she bumped the edge.

As I reached out to turn her around, a man wearing a black trench coat stepped up beside me. I caught my breath, thinking for half a second it was Honoré. He dropped a boat with new, shining white paint into the water, then straightened up and grinned at me. He was about the same size as Honoré: six feet tall, medium build, and he had the same wavy, medium-brown hair. It ruffled in the breeze. "Want to race?" He sounded as eager as a little kid.

My antennae went up, but I grinned back. "Okay."

Who *was* this guy?

"I must warn you that my boat has new paint. A smoother hull means it will go faster." He spoke French with a slight, but unmistakable, American Midwest twang.

"Theoretically," I said, wishing he'd bug off. "*Diamant* is a valiant little boat, in spite of her scruffy appearance."

"You'll see," he said. "Ready?"

"Ready." I'd show him. Seriously, the *Société* was not going to meet if he kept hanging around. "*Bonne chance.*"

We pushed them off; the breeze caught their sails, and they bobbed away with mine half a boat-length ahead, making steady progress toward the opposite shore. Along with a handful of kids, we jogged to the other side. Our boats bumped into the rim of the pond at the very same moment, and we shoved them off again.

This time, as we ran after them, I dropped behind him and looked around.

I spotted Aunt Celeste strolling along the path in front of the palace with Baguette at her heel. André Dubillard, computer genius, the fourth member of our *Société*, followed a discreet fifty feet behind. Neither of them looked in my direction. Obviously, they knew exactly where I was, but would not risk meeting as long as the American was hanging around.

I hustled to catch up with him. Who was he, and what was he doing here? Why didn't I think he just happened to be there?

"Brava!" he said, as *Diamant's* bow bumped the edge.

Without waiting for his boat to come in, I leaned

down, pushed her off again, then followed. I scanned for Aunt Celeste. She was disappearing behind a row of trees, heading toward the tennis courts. André, still fifty feet behind, still looking straight ahead, followed.

We were going to plan B. They would exit on the side closest to Chez Celeste. I knew that if I looked around, I would see Robbie Gaspard, chef extraordinaire, making his way toward a different exit.

The air vibrated with tension, and I was dying to know if they'd learned anything about Petar Ivanov or Zachary Le Noir, but at that point, my job was to stay put and look as boring as possible. I drifted away from the American, and when our boats came close together a couple more times, I stuffed my frustration down, smiled, and said, "*Bonne chance.*"

After half an hour, when he didn't try to engage in conversation, I decided he just happened to be there. I lifted my boat out of the water and took her back to the rental cart. While the concessionaire returned her to her lofty perch, I refreshed my lipstick and focused the camera in my compact on the American. He was picking up his boat. One photo caught him from the side, and in the other, he was looking straight at me.

I took my time replacing my compact and lipstick, then strolled to the exit. When I got to Poppy, I pulled out my phone. Aunt Celeste had sent a message.

—*So sorry to miss walking with you, darling, but something came up. Kisses.*—

—*No worries. It's still chilly anyway. Hugs.*—

I pulled on my helmet and was about to get on when he caught up with me. A frisson shot through my chest.

"Nice bike," he said, and with a little wave, walked on.

I wished I knew for sure that was the last I'd ever see of him.

Chapter Eight

Aunt Celeste was the most risk-averse person I'd ever met. The fact that she'd cancelled our meeting didn't mean we had a problem. She was merely being prudent, and I had to agree with her. After all, three men had recently appeared in my life. How were we to know the American wasn't a fourth?

I scoffed at myself for thinking he might be interested in me, but just in case, I kept an eye on my mirrors. Poppy, a racy red scooter in a city with a million black bikes, couldn't have been easier to follow. No worries, though. When I rode away from Luxembourg Gardens, no one shadowed me.

He was probably a businessman, a lonely advertising executive from Chicago or Boston or San Francisco—nothing more—enjoying Paris after a long day of meetings. Maybe he'd been hoping to meet someone for a drink or dinner. If I'd flirted a bit, we'd have been sitting in front of a glass of champagne by then, exchanging titillating tidbits about ourselves.

I drew in a deep breath, relaxed my grip, and zoomed across the bridge that came out on L'île de la Cité at the back of Notre Dame. I made a left turn to run along the side of the church, past the scaffolding and cranes where men were climbing up and down, working to restore the damage done by the big fire. When I buzzed by the courtyard in front of the cathedral, I spotted Robbie Gaspard sitting on a stone wall, playing one of his long, slender, black-and-silver bagpipe chanters. So far, so good.

I crossed back over the Seine, parked Poppy in a totally random spot halfway between Notre Dame and Aunt Celeste's shop, and moseyed back, stopping at a newsstand to buy a newspaper. I sat down beside Robbie and began to read the horoscopes for that day.

"Zachary Le Noir," he said, without looking at me. "Thanks for bringing him to lunch today. I think he liked the fish."

"How could he not?"

Out of the corner of my eye, I caught his quick grin.

He said, "Full name, Zachary Sebastian Le Noir. Adopted at birth by a Portuguese mother and French father. Raised in Brazil. No siblings. Both parents deceased. Zachary inherited their enormous coffee plantation. Good employer. Provides housing for workers, medical care, and education for the children. The enterprise is run by his wife while he galivants around the globe, collecting art and nubile women."

Robbie played several bars of "Scotland the Brave," tapping his dress Campbell tartan sneaker to keep time. His father was Parisian French, but his mother descended from a Clan Campbell chieftain, and while he was growing up, he spent summers at their castle in the Scottish Highlands. The only thing he liked better than creating delicious food and charming the socks off the clientele at his restaurant was playing the bagpipe in the Paris Highland Marching Band. And occasionally fencing an exotic bauble or two.

He rested the end of the chanter on his knee for a moment. "Besides trading gold, as advertised by *Paris*

Today, Le Noir owns art galleries in New York, Amsterdam, and two here in Paris. One on Île Saint-Louis. And he plays the horses."

More tartan sneaker tapping and a few more bars. "Here's the good part. There's a rumor that he occasionally buys and sells very rare, very valuable pieces of art that are never seen in public."

I stared at my paper. "Never seen because they're hot, I assume."

"What other reason would there be?"

"Paintings, sculptures?"

"All of that and more."

"Diamonds?"

"Not generally. Just museum quality items."

"So why the Queen of Persia?"

"Good question."

A middle-aged couple wearing sensible walking shoes and all-weather jackets sat down next to me and huddled over a map. "Scotland the Brave" picked up where it had stopped, full volume. I couldn't help grinning when, a second or two later, the couple got up and moved to the very end of the wall.

I turned a page in the newspaper. "Did you notice his cufflinks?"

Gaspard played a few more bars, then, "Do dogs have fleas?"

"Any guesses about their provenance?"

"Designed by Pierre Emile Kohnen, mid 1800's, most likely 18 carat gold."

I repressed my smile and pretended to read.

He lifted the chanter to his lips, then paused. "Am I right?"

"Do dogs have fleas?"

He said, "I recognized them. I sold them to a very good client in 2009, and they were stolen a couple of years later. In fact, they've been missing from his home in Zurich since late 2010."

He started playing "Danny Boy," one of those lovers' songs that sets my teeth on edge. I wondered if he knew how irritating I found the lyrics. Who could ever think Danny Boy, whoever he was, was going to return, all loving and faithful? I gritted my teeth, turned a page, and waited a couple of beats before asking, "Anything else?"

"Not much about his cousin. His name is Baron Petar Ivanov; goes by Petar Ivanov. He was attacked in the Metro last night, but is recuperating in a private—I mean very private—hospital. The two of them own several valuable Paris properties, including the Saint Francis Hotel. Of interest is the fact that in the city records, the owner of the Saint Francis is a charitable organization, which probably exists only on paper."

"A shell corporation? A money laundry?"

"What else would it be?"

"I love that hotel." I knew from experience that floors four, five, and six had large, luxurious suites. Prices for those hovered around two thousand euros a night.

"Le Noir and Ivanov occupy the top floor. Each of them keeps a penthouse suite up there."

I'd heard that the seventh floor had two palatial suites. "Robbie Gaspard, you are a treasure."

"I know that, too. And you need to go. I have to get back to the restaurant."

"Got it." I folded my paper and got to my feet.

He nodded. "My love to the enchanting Celeste."

"Scotland the Brave" followed me as I wandered out of the courtyard.

Long rays of evening sunshine sneaked in under the last of the afternoon clouds and warmed my back as I walked over the Seine. Tourists, a veritable cloud of locusts, hovered around the old green bouquiniste stalls along the river, buying souvenirs and shooting selfies. I mingled with them long enough to peruse old comic books at one stall and vintage posters at another. No one was paying any attention to me, so I wandered on to Île Saint-Louis.

The street the gallery was on was only two blocks long, and even though the shop was just a couple of doors down from the main street on the island, few people walked about. So it was no surprise that the sign on the door said *Fermé*. Closed. I peered through the wide front window. In the center, soft lights shone down on half a dozen large, abstract sculptures. One had a great long neck, so I supposed it might be a giraffe.

A shadow drifted across my reflection in the window. I held my breath.

I waited several seconds, then retraced my steps and turned onto the main street. Just around the corner, a man wearing a knee-length trench coat and a wide-brimmed hat turned his back to me and studied a display of women's hats and handbags. Okay, so maybe he was just a guy shopping for a gift for his wife, but I felt almost certain he was the American from the pond. All he would have needed to do to alter his appearance was add the hat. How hard is that?

I walked straight on to the end of the street and slid into a seat at an outdoor table where I had a clear view of passing pedestrians. I ordered a glass of champagne, and it came with a strawberry perched on the rim of the glass, which made me hungry, so I ordered crème brulée to go with it.

As I cracked the lovely brown crust and scooped sweet, sinfully rich custard into my mouth, I scrutinized the people walking past. By the time it was all gone, the man who'd been looking at women's hats and handbags had not come by and was nowhere to be seen. I needn't have worried.

Excellent! The Queen of Persia was calling me.

Chapter Nine

I still needed to touch base with André Dubillard and Aunt Celeste, so I hustled back to my scooter, and in the light from the streetlamp, did a quick visual inspection. Poppy wasn't new anymore, but she looked new, and I wanted to make sure no one had scratched or dented her while I was gone. Then, as I opened the compartment behind my seat and got my helmet out, André Dubillard showed up on his big, black, spookily silent, all-electric motorcycle. If I hadn't been facing the street, I wouldn't have known he was there. He lifted a forefinger to his lips and dismounted.

Quickly and lightly, he ran his hands over Poppy's front fender. Then he moved to the back and with a wink, stooped and reached up under the rear fender. When he straightened up again, he held a disc the size of a two-euro coin between his thumb and forefinger. "American," he said.

A bug. The image of the man at the pond popped into my head. If he had planted it, he wouldn't have needed to follow Poppy closely enough for me to spot him.

Just then, a stocky man in leather pants and jacket stepped up to the scooter parked next to mine. He tipped his head toward André's machine. "That your bike blocking mine?"

André nodded. "I'll be on my way in a minute."

"Appreciate it." The guy opened a saddlebag and removed his helmet. As he slid it onto his head, André dropped the bug into his saddlebag.

André got on his bike and backed it out of the way. "No problem."

The man started his machine, touched a couple of fingers to his helmet, nodded, and headed toward the Seine.

André said, "Better saddle up."

I started Poppy, and we watched the departing bike. Seconds later, after the guy passed through the first intersection, a motorcycle came around the corner and fell in behind him.

André grinned. "It won't take them long to realize they're following the wrong person."

I pulled Poppy out and turned the opposite direction. He came up beside me. "Where are we headed?"

So the American, whoever he was, had bugged my scooter. No reason not to look at the Paris homes of Le Noir and Ivanov. "The Saint Francis Hotel."

"Thought so."

"If the Queen of Persia is still in Paris, most likely that's where we'll find it."

"I'm your wingman."

Dodging a couple of cars, he followed me the wrong way down the one-way street. After another block, we turned off and picked up speed. I took a right, then a left, then a right again before heading toward the Saint Francis, a twenty-minute ride away. André stuck right behind me.

I was dying to get into Le Noir's and Ivanov's seventh-floor penthouse suites. However, no one, not even the Pope, could just hop into an elevator and go all the way up there. In fact, security was tight in the Saint Francis. You couldn't just hop on an elevator. Period.

Guests on the six lower floors were issued key cards which allowed them to use the elevators that went as far as the sixth floor. André had made one for me, so I could get that far, and had done so several times.

The suites on floors four, five, and six were favored by young, *nouveau riche* honeymooners, many of whom carried a truckload of precious and semi-precious baubles with them and thought the safe in the closet was a good place to lock them up.

I had the proper maid's uniform for those floors, and thanks again to André, an ID badge. With a couple of fresh towels over my arm, I looked like I belonged there. And the closet safes were about as difficult as a grade-school cake walk.

One evening between Christmas and New Year's, I'd walked into a corner suite, turned down the bed, placed a couple of chocolates on the pillows, and walked out with an emerald pendant on a platinum chain that once belonged to the Russian royal family. The fifteen clear, one-carat diamonds that surrounded the emerald paid my rent for a year all by themselves. The emerald was worth a lot more. Aunt Celeste had offered the necklace to one of her contacts, and in addition, I'd ended up with enough cash to add a bouquet of AAA bonds to the cushion I was accumulating at Rhineland Bankgruppe.

But getting to the seventh floor was a challenge. I'd thought of it before and decided that rappelling down from the roof would be possible, but risky because a ring of lights ran all the way around the perimeter, and they stayed on all night, so it was never dark.

Inside, there was one elevator, a big glass bubble, that ran from the sixth to the seventh floor. A staircase, also enclosed in glass, spiraled around the elevator. Both had retina scanners and were accessed via a door with another retina scanner. Motion-activated cameras captured everyone who came and went as they were coming and going. And, whereas the women on the lower floors wore a classic black dress and white apron, the maids—and there were never any men—who served that floor were distinguished by beaded, sequined, flapper-style dresses and headbands.

For someone with André's ability, bypassing a retina scanner wasn't a huge problem, and Aunt Celeste wouldn't have any trouble replicating the flapper uniform. But allegedly, the security system on the seventh was foolproof. Although I'd never met one I couldn't defeat, a flutter in the bottom of my stomach reminded me that there could be a first time.

The blare of traffic faded as I led the way down a long slope occupied by a wide, green park. The Saint Francis Hotel, a square, solid, solemn pile of limestone, sat at the bottom. A little way behind it was the Bois de Boulogne. So we were in a low-density neighborhood that lacked the usual tangle of vehicles.

We swept past the stately front door with the French tricolor fluttering bravely above. Light poured out of the lobby onto a doorman standing at attention and dripping gold braid from his black epaulets. Three blocks farther down, we tucked our bikes in against the curb, walked back, and sat side by side on a bench in the park across the street. For several minutes, we merely breathed in and out and absorbed the ambiance.

For me, this was always the first thing to do. Even

though parts of the building were familiar, I never went in thinking I knew it. Before I could plan the retrieval of my ring, I needed to get a sense of the place, to recall the mannerisms of the staff, to feel as if I were part of it.

André, too, had learned not to rush into things. A computer genius by the time he was in junior high, he got busted for blackmailing politicians in his home state of Illinois, using information he found in their private e-mail accounts. By the time he got to high school, he could hack into any database in the world, and he'd learned to mine more profitable sources. He graduated with honors and went on to MIT, where two shockingly indiscreet high-ranking national figures paid his tuition plus a generous stipend in return for keeping their secret.

By the time I met him, André Dubillard was a cybersecurity consultant with a purposely nerdy appearance and lucrative contracts all over Europe. If anyone could make getting into those penthouse suites easy, it was my self-proclaimed wingman.

"Stay here," he said, getting to his feet and picking up the square black case he'd brought from his motorcycle. He strolled away, deeper into the park. A few minutes later, a drone passed silently over my head. It hovered above the front of the Saint Francis at a height a little above the seventh floor, then turned and disappeared down one side. When it reappeared on the other side, I got up and strolled back to Poppy.

Chapter Ten

André was already tucking the drone into a saddlebag when I got back to our bikes. "Dinner *chez nous*," he said. "Lamb tagine tonight." André himself couldn't put together a ham and cheese sandwich. His wife, Suzanne, however, was an excellent cook.

I liked them both. Dinner sounded great, And I was dying to know what the drone picked up. But they acted as if they were still on their honeymoon, and I didn't think I could stand a whole evening of blatant domestic harmony. "Thanks, but I need to touch base with Aunt Celeste." Truth. We needed to catch up.

"She's already there."

"I need to feed Baguette."

"He's there, too."

"Okay, then." *Darn!* "I'll stop and get a couple of bottles of wine." I would need it.

"A dry, fruity red would be good."

"Right." So I was no wine expert, but he didn't have to be bossy about it. Okay, I admit it. I was feeling sorry for myself. Seeing them so happy together left an empty ache in my heart.

André lived one long block from me, on the fourth floor of a red brick building directly facing the Eiffel Tower, so I tucked Poppy in for the night and walked over. By the time I got there, the scents of cumin and turmeric had drifted all the way down to the entrance on the ground floor. Even the elevator, which generally carried a faint odor of old rubber boots, smelled foreign and exotic.

It turned out that Suzanne had been called back to the hospital to perform an emergency orthopedic surgery and left the tagine on the stove, ready to eat.

André opened the bottles of wine to let them breathe. I'd followed his advice and chosen a couple of Valpolicellas. He glanced at the labels. "Excellent choice."

I couldn't help smiling. If I'd had a brother, I'd have wanted him to be André.

I cleared books and newspapers off the table in front of the big front window. André's apartment was cozy to begin with, but then Suzanne moved in, and they'd crammed it full of souvenirs of their honeymoon: ebony figures and enormous wood masks decorated with shells from Africa, prayer bowls from Tibet, rugs and hangings from Turkey, even a quarter-size replica of a Chinese warrior. Only the kitchen escaped the clutter. Suzanne kept everything in that tiny alcove sterile and white.

Aunt Celeste was in there, whisking up a salad dressing. "True or false? The man you call Falstaff; he's a Bulgarian Baron named Petar Ivanov."

"True, according to Robbie Gaspard," I said.

Aunt Celeste poured the dressing over a leafy green salad. "It gets better. Your Zachary Le Noir is actually his brother."

I looked up from the table, where I was setting three places with dinnerware the honeymooners had brought home from Morocco. "He says they're cousins."

She cut a baguette and heaped the chunks in a basket. "They're both. Actually, they are twins, orphaned almost at birth and adopted by sisters, so, raised as cousins."

André elbowed in beside her, bent over the stove, lifted the lid off the pot, and stirred the tagine. "My turn. True or false: Our friend Ivanov faked his attack in the Metro."

"False," I said. "Robbie says he's in a private hospital."

He set the tagine on a hot pad in the center of the table. We filled our plates and raised our glasses and chorused, "*Bon appétit*." Baguette, ever the diplomat, settled halfway between my feet and Aunt Celeste's.

"Let's be clear," Aunt Celeste said. "We don't know a lot about them, and Le Noir hooked you by telling you they plan to return the tapestry to the rightful owners. I did a search on the web, and there is an estate in Bulgaria belonging to a Baron Petar Ivanov, but I couldn't find any records of families who lived on the estate or worked there, so who knows what they're up to?"

I said, "Let's say they really want to return the tapestries, as Le Noir says they do. Am I crazy to think they will give me the Queen of Persia if I do?"

André pointed his fork at me. "You're crazy. Totally. Absolutely. Without doubt. I don't trust them. Le Noir apparently has buckets of money, so why does he need your help? There's something fishy about that." He scowled. "Forget about making a deal with them. Just go for the ring."

I said, "I'll know a lot more after I go to the wedding this weekend."

"I'm worried about you going, darling," Aunt Celeste said. "We don't know enough about them."

André raised an eyebrow. "I have a feeling a sane

person would stay far away from both of them, but I don't see you doing that."

"If it looks like they really are trying to right a wrong, why wouldn't I help them?"

He said, "Fine. You aren't going to change your mind. But Celeste is right. I'm not going to let you go alone."

We finished eating and stacked the dishes in the kitchen. André set the drone on the table and plugged it into a laptop. Aunt Celeste prepared coffee, and I rummaged in the cupboards until I found a box of dark chocolate truffles.

André tapped a couple of keys. "First time I've used my new drone." He grinned. "It's got high-resolution cameras which are able to operate in low light, both wide-angle and zoom. It also has thermal imaging, and the latest in electronic sensors. Let's see what it picked up." He pulled two chairs close, one on either side of his. "Sit down, you guys."

I sat on his right. "I need a Chez Celeste original to wear to the wedding."

"Of course you do, darling." Aunt Celeste reached across André and patted my hand. "I have just the thing in mind. You will sparkle and shine and dazzle the world."

André split the laptop screen in two. On one side, we saw an image of the park where we'd been sitting, and on the other side, long strings of what looked like computer code. "That's the electronic surveillance data," he said, pointing at the code. "I'll analyze it later. It should tell me what kind of security system they're running."

He minimized that part. The video took over the

whole screen again, and we were flying seventy or eighty feet above the park. There I was, sitting on the bench. We slowed down as the drone went higher, floated over the street, and hovered above the hotel's top floor.

On the side overlooking the park, a terrace ran the full width of the building. A row of potted shrubs divided it in the middle. The two halves mirrored each other, with clusters of chairs grouped around low tables and a bar and a fireplace on each side. Through the sliding glass doors that led inside, we could see oval dining tables, the same on both sides, with huge bouquets of flowers in the center.

On the left side of the terrace, a fire blazed in the fireplace and about twenty people milled about, drinks in hand, the men tall and elegant in dark suits, the women thin and sophisticated in long, glittering gowns.

Well above the party, the drone went off to the left, turned the corner of the building, and zoomed out for a shot of that whole side. There were three large, widely spaced sets of windows, each with flower boxes full of red and white geraniums. Then it dropped down and zoomed in. Through the first two windows, we could see the same dining table with a small kitchen behind it, then a living area with a sofa, several chairs, and a couple of coffee tables. Through the last window, a sumptuous bedroom with a spacious bathroom and dressing area. The whole place looked pristine. No books or papers, no shoes lying around or pajamas hanging on the back of a door. "Do they actually live there? Does anyone?" Aunt Celeste asked.

I shrugged. "Remember those top-floor maids in their flapper dresses? They have to do something all day."

At the back of the building, the drone captured two semicircular balconies, one for each suite, each rimmed with pots of geraniums and furnished with lounge chairs, low tables, and soft lights. The wall of another building loomed just a few feet away—a disappointing view.

The room off the second balcony was dark and the drapes were closed. As the drone passed by, however, the drapes glided slowly apart. The drone stopped and went back. I held my breath.

Light filtered in from the ring of lights on the edge of the roof, and we looked into a bedroom identical to the one on the other side. But in this one, a large packing crate stood near the foot of the bed; a smaller one right in front of the window. A figure dressed from top to bottom in black, including hood and gloves, walked slowly around the larger crate, as if inspecting it, then the smaller one. He photographed two sides of each. Then he pointed a remote control at the window and watched the drapes close again.

His eyes were the only part of him I could see, but I didn't need to look twice. I felt certain it was Honoré.

Chapter Eleven

Cutting through morning traffic, I buzzed across the Seine and up the Champs-Elysées. My boss, bless his stuffy soul, had gotten used to my arriving at work on bright red Poppy, although it was clear that, in his opinion, a scooter was not respectable. After a long lecture about the importance of conveying rock-solid reliability to Rhineland Bankgruppe clients, he'd agreed that it was okay as long as our clients didn't see me. But if he heard even one complaint…

I'd kissed his cheek and he'd huffed and puffed as he wiped lipstick off with a crisp white handkerchief. The starchy old guy was a living, breathing anachronism, as lovable as any museum piece.

I drove up onto the broad sidewalk and stopped facing a pair of mighty fifteen-foot-tall carved wood doors, then pressed a button on my handgrip. The doors swung inward at a stately pace, and I drove into a short passageway where marble columns soared above a patterned, polished marble floor to support an arched ceiling. I stopped again and waited until the doors closed behind me, then drove on into the courtyard and past a dozen parking spaces reserved for customers.

As terrified as he was about the possibility of a client seeing me arrive on Poppy, my boss was even more horrified by the thought that they would see me parking her on the street as if I were a barista in a coffee shop. So he'd hired a team of carpenters to construct a miniature garage just for me in the farthest corner of the courtyard, with a roof to keep Poppy respectably dry and clean.

I didn't linger in the common room. I grabbed an espresso and headed straight to my office. I needed to know—the day before yesterday—who Honoré was and if he worked at the Darwin Centre or not, and André had come up with a brilliant scheme to check out his alleged workplace. The city inspects Parisian buildings every five years. If anything needs painting, refurbishing, or repair, then up go the scaffolds, and the work gets done. So André hacked into the city records and discovered that the building housing the Darwin Centre was past due for inspection.

In case Honoré was there, I couldn't pose as a building inspector myself, so André agreed to do it. Having lived through a recent upgrade to his apartment building, he had no doubt he could pull it off. By the time I got to my office, he had downloaded the records of previous inspections and sent them to me. I booted up my computer.

A five-story traditional limestone constructed in the mid 1800's, it sat in the middle of a block in the Marais, the old Jewish quarter. The Darwin Centre office and labs took up the first three floors. The two upper floors had apartments, all leased directly from Darwin, with preference to visiting scientists. Balconies on floors two through five were marked for re-inspection—the perfect reason to go in and take a look at them.

Andre added a note: "The building and The Darwin Centre itself are wholly owned by Pearl Samantha Elena Aragon and her brother Raphael Greenbank Aragon. When you read this, call me."

I picked up my phone. André answered at once. "I prefer not to commit some things to writing," he said.

"Tell me."

"The Aragons are remnants of a semi-famous, enormously rich family left over from middle European aristocracy. They sponsor good causes, they have a huge network, and they have their fingers in lots of juicy pies, some of which are clandestine."

"Good clandestine or bad clandestine?"

"Don't try to sidetrack me. I'm telling you that Raphael Aragon is nobody's fool, and with him in charge of Darwin Centre security, I promise you, Honoré will have an impenetrable identity as a researcher. Sorry I suggested it. We'll be wasting our time. We won't know any more than we do now."

"I'll think about it."

"That's what you always say." He huffed out a breath. "Why do I think that's a lie?" He hung up.

I phoned the Darwin Centre to set up an appointment and requested the next day. "Tomorrow?" The young man who identified himself as Raphael Aragon's assistant sounded astonished. "Usually, we wait weeks."

I laughed. "We are trying to repair our image." Then I called André back and told him.

The next morning, at eight o'clock, the hour at which I normally opened my eyes, I slid into a chair at a sidewalk café across the street and half a block down from the Darwin Centre, where I could see the entrance. I ordered a *café crème*, then checked in with André.

His voice came clearly through my earbud. "I don't know why I let you talk me into this. I'm less than a minute away." Seconds later, he strode past the café dressed in a navy suit with an official-looking badge on his breast pocket. He'd slicked his hair back, added a phony mustache, and carried a beat-up attaché case. "Turning on the camera," he said. "How's the picture?" The camera in his jacket button began sending images to my smartphone—the bakery he walked past, the cheese shop, the entrance to the Darwin Centre.

"Looking fine." I wished I were going in myself. I hated sitting outside and waiting. It was almost as bad as sitting in the corridor outside the principal's office when I got caught for passing notes in third grade.

He opened the door and stepped into a corridor paneled in dark wood, walked several feet forward, then turned into an office with an open doorway. His voice came clearly into my right ear. "Jerome Bremmer from the city."

A strong bass voice responded, "Raphael Aragon."

André had to be as surprised as I was that Aragon himself was waiting for him, but his tone didn't show it. "*Enchanté*, Monsieur Aragon."

On the screen on my phone, Aragon rose to his feet and stood behind his desk. A tall, square-shouldered, square-jawed man with thick black hair and a black goatee, he wore a double-breasted dark suit with a fine pinstripe, like a gangster from the 30's. "Monsieur Bremmer, I find this very odd. The city, and department in particular, is known to be the slowest in the universe. A next-day appointment is unheard of. In fact, last week, we scheduled an appointment two months from now."

André didn't miss a beat. "*Desolé*, monsieur. I will make sure that it's cancelled. I am a new addition to staff. The budget has been increased, and we are trying to improve our image."

"Well, that explains it." His grin made me wonder if he was buying it. "Be my guest. You'll find an elevator at the end of the corridor. Let me know if you have any difficulties."

André found Honoré's name on a mailbox beside the elevator on the ground floor and again beside a door to a lab on the second floor. The signs consisted of a wooden bar at the bottom and another at the top. He demonstrated that names and photos could easily be slipped in and out of the space between.

Although he wasn't allowed in the lab, he could see someone working there through a large window. He or she was about Honoré's height, but wore a full white isolation suit, including hood and face shield. It could have been anyone.

Chapter Twelve

It's a wedding. What could go wrong at a wedding?

As the TGV hurtled south out of Paris Friday afternoon, I settled into my first-class seat in the upper deck, opened my laptop, and began to work on my weekly report for my boss.

Tuesday, the day after our lunch together, Zachary Le Noir sent a bouquet of tulips and daffodils, along with a formal invitation to the wedding and a handwritten note begging me to attend. He needn't have begged. Even if he hadn't dangled the Queen of Persia in front of me, I'd have had to be crazy to turn down a chance to attend one of Count Maxime de Charpentier's fabled parties. And since the bride was his daughter, this one would be epic.

André Dubillard and I argued after I'd told him I wanted to check out the château's security system and see if I could find out where the tapestries Le Noir wanted me to steal might be stored.

"What you're planning is risky, sweet pea," he'd said. "We really don't know anything about these guys."

When he insisted on coming, I scoffed, but felt relieved all the same when he made plans to fly to Toulouse, rent a car, and stay at an inn near the château.

At the station in Toulouse, I transferred to a local train that headed southeast into the Pyrenees. By the time I arrived in the little town of Rénard, the sun had dropped below the mountains on the west. Zachary Le Noir was waiting on the platform, his smile just right—not too eager, not too bright, just a delighted-to-see-you-again sort of smile. The chauffeur took my bags, and I took Zachary's arm.

I needed to learn more about Zachary, too. Was he a globe-trotting art dealer with a coffee plantation in Brazil—nothing more? Just a savvy, dashing man with lots of money who traipsed around the world doing good deeds, a philanthropist who wanted to return an ancient tapestry to the descendants of the family that once owned it?

That image had a certain appeal but sounded a little too sweet. A steady diet of such niceness could sort of stick in your throat. You'd be going around humming *Somewhere Over the Rainbow* all day, every day; secretly, desperately wishing for something exciting to happen. Somehow, I couldn't see myself doing that, and I didn't see him doing it either. And what about his cousin, Baron Petar Ivanov? Theatrical, yes. But an over the rainbow kind of guy? Not. Over the rainbow kinds of guys don't get attacked in Metro stations.

It tickled me that the car was the same one I'd chased through the streets of Paris five days before, still elegant, still immaculate, still with a hood half a mile long. An angel perched way out there on the front, wings spread, as if blessing us and promising a safe journey. The chauffeur closed my door with a discreet, expensive thump. Zachary slid in from the other side. "Comfortable?"

We glided away from the station in cushioned comfort, and in less than a minute, we'd left behind the village with its single row of steeply pitched tile roofs and red geranium window boxes. Bare trees hung early-budding limbs over the narrow, pitted road. A deer strolled across in front of us, causing the chauffeur to stop. She gazed toward us for a moment, then turned and slipped away into the brush under the trees, head high. Queen of the forest. After a moment, I couldn't see her.

Our road grew even more narrow. We switched back and forth, climbing steeply. As the glow of sunset faded from the sky, tall conifers replaced deciduous trees. Finally, we reached a clearing. The car stopped. Zachary opened his door and got out. "Come here," he said, holding out his hand. I scooted across the silky soft leather, took his hand, and stood beside him. He said nothing, but pointed at the sky.

The stars glittered like the diamonds in his cufflinks that first day I met him—so many of them, almost close enough to touch. They demanded silence, even reverence. The Big Dipper. Orion. The Milky Way. I wished I knew more names.

Shivering, I slipped back into the car. Zachary followed and touched a button over his door, and warm air began to flow.

"Magic," I said. "*Merci!* That was magical."

"I'm good at magic." His voice sounded more seductive than ever, and I felt myself leaning toward him. Not physically, of course. But leaning. Not a good idea. I pulled myself back. I needed to stay objective.

Soon we stopped again. We had reached a flat, open spot dominated by a rambling three-story structure, half-timber in style. Soft yellow light spilled out large ground-floor windows. It was an inn and had to be where André had reserved a room, and he should have arrived a couple of hours earlier.

"Now we walk," Zachary said.

A short, stocky man wearing shorts and a sweatshirt with cut-off sleeves appeared, grabbed my suitcase out of the trunk, and bounded away up a precipitous, curving path.

We started up after him. Low to the ground, lights shone on rough, uneven flagstones that led upwards.

The path reminded me of a trail to an ancient monastery in Ireland, a place one can only attain by a single route. I'd been there on a tour with my high school teacher and a dozen other fifteen-year-old kids. I hadn't liked that there was only one way to get out. It made me feel so claustrophobic I'd hyperventilated. Later, I'd been forced to spend months upon months in a cheerless cell with only one door, a locked door. Standing there, looking up the winding track, I could hardly breathe. "Is this the only way to get there?"

"The château is on a little plateau. It's this or a helicopter."

Okay, so I did things that scare a lot of people silly. Things most of them would never consider doing. But I always had a way out.

"Or I could carry you piggyback."

I took a deep breath. I could do this.

For several minutes, we climbed irregular, softly illuminated stone steps flanked by scrubby trees and bushes. The night closed around us like black velvet. There was no sound except for our footsteps. My enigmatic companion followed me, saying nothing, but occasionally grasping my elbow when I stumbled on a rock, or when the next step up was extra high.

It seemed as if we might go on forever, and then suddenly, we stood on a grassy plateau. The château, a huge, heavy stone building three stories high and anchored at each end by a round tower, stood about half a city block away. It was the kind of castle that most people surrounded with formal gardens and illuminated with soft white light. But Count Maxime de Charpentier wasn't everyone. Bold blue, gold, and lime-green laser beams zoomed, bounced, and swirled back and forth across the immense façade. Surrounded by darkness, it appeared to be floating in space.

Zachary pointed to the right. "The count keeps his treasures in a secret room in the east tower. Allegedly."

The lasers created sudden eclipses—dark, then dazzling bright, then dark again. In the flashes of light, I could see that the towers were not identical. The west tower, on our left, had a large door at the base and many windows all the way up, but the east tower had none. Both had a row of narrow slits circling the top, the type that would allow archers to rain arrows down on an invading army.

"I don't see an entrance to the tower with the alleged treasure room."

"During WWII, Maxime's grandmother had the door and all the windows sealed over. Now, the only way in is through those archery openings at the top or via a secret passageway from somewhere in the main part of the building."

"Hidden behind a bookcase, I assume."

He grinned as he nudged me toward a broad terrace with steps leading up to the main entrance. "Behind a bookcase, a statue, a fireplace, or God knows what. The place is a maze. There could be all sorts of hidden passageways."

"How do you know?"

"When I was a kid, my family visited from time to

time. Back then, Maxime and I spent hours searching, but we never found it." He took my hand and squeezed it. "Now you know why I say we need a person of your talents. But be careful. The château has eyes and ears. Legions of eyes and ears."

Chapter Thirteen

Mammoth urns overflowing with pink and white roses marked the perimeter of the welcoming flagstone terrace that ran the width of the building. "The wedding will take place here," Zachary said, "tomorrow at sunset."

We crossed the terrace, climbed broad stairs under an arched stone entrance, and faced a heavy, carved, wooden door three times taller than my companion. At the top, the sharp metal teeth of a portcullis hung down, as if ready to fall and skewer unwanted guests. I pointed at it. "Does that work?"

He grinned. "Sure does."

"But no moat? What's up with that?"

"No need. A moat would be redundant. We're on a tiny plateau. Sheer rock walls drop off on all sides. That's why the trail we came up on is the only way. When you see it in the daylight, you won't believe how narrow it is."

I expected a butler to fling the door wide and stare down his nose at me, but Zachary opened it himself. The oval foyer, with a white marble floor and walls, all gleaming under crystal chandeliers, could have accommodated Cinderella's carriage plus horses and footmen. But except for us—two tiny people—it was empty. Long, wide marble hallways ran off to the left and right. I had to tip my head back to see the ceiling.

With fluid grace, Zachary escorted me up a wide spiral staircase to the third floor, where it ended in a gallery with a chest-high railing. We gazed down from our lofty aerie into the foyer for a moment. Then, halfway down the right-hand hall, he opened the door to a spacious bedroom furnished in tones of cream, gold, and white. My bag rested on a stand beside an ornate, gilded armoire. An antique armchair upholstered in pale gold silk sat close to a gas fire burning in a wide fireplace, as if inviting me to sit down with a cup of tea and a book.

"Tonight, only seventy people are invited, so dinner will be served in the small dining room. I'll come for you in half an hour."

"Thanks. I have a feeling I'd need help finding it."

"If you need *anything*, my room is opposite yours." His lips twitched into a grin, as if to tell me that he was mine if I wanted him, but he would not come begging.

The sparkle in his eyes, so close I could see flecks of violet in their indigo depths, made it hard to breathe.

****

The small dining room was the size of two side-by-side tennis courts. Bustling waiters served drinks to women in beaded gowns and men in black tie who appreciated good champagne and a new face to flirt with. My floor-length, off-the-shoulder, sequined black dress with a wide ivory sash hugged me like a second skin and fit right in.

Even a foodie extraordinaire like Robbie Gaspard would have approved of the dinner menu. When dessert had disappeared, Count Maxime de Charpentier stood and called over the din of conversation, "Follow me." He led the way to the room next door, where roulette wheels were spinning and dealers stood behind blackjack, baccarat, and craps tables. "Put your own money away. Each of you gets a ten-thousand-euro stake. Have fun."

Midnight came and went. Monaco had nothing on this remote casino. I played blackjack, then tried my luck at roulette, then went back to blackjack. I'd grown up playing the game with my grandmother. "Learn some simple rules," she had told me over and over, "and you'll never have to go without shoes."

She'd meant that literally. The family that had taken her in after the Holocaust hadn't had much money, and she'd helped put food on the table by gambling with the men in the town square. So, at two o'clock, when Count Maxime closed the games, I still had most of my ten thousand euros, unlike most of the guests.

In the pitch-black night, a helicopter landed on the lawn and began to ferry guests who couldn't be accommodated in the château's thirty-four bedrooms down to the inn at the base of the hill. Five minutes after it lifted off, it came back again. From the terrace, Zachary and I watched the last ones leave, and then he escorted me back to my room. He bent and kissed both cheeks. "Sweet dreams," he said, and gave my back a little pat, as if dismissing me.

What was up with that? Did I have bad breath? I would have said no, of course, but it would have been nice to be asked.

****

I chatted briefly on the phone with André Dubillard who had set up his equipment in his room at the inn. Then while I waited for the château to rest quietly, I pulled on black leotard and tights, slipped into my ballerina-style flats with soft, flexible soles, and tucked my tools into a belt at my waist.

At three-thirty, his voice came clearly through my earbud. "Not a creature is stirring up there. Ready?"

"All set," I said.

"Let's do a little reconnaissance."

I tugged on black gloves, pulled my hood up over my head and hid my face under the attached mask. Only my eyes were not covered. I opened the door. Spaced about fifteen feet apart, small downlights cast a soft glow over the carpet. I peered both right and left, and listened. Hearing nothing, I stepped out and eased the latch into place without a sound. If Zachary Le Noir was right, and the building had legions of eyes and ears, I wanted to know what kind and where they were. Up-to-date security devices could easily be hidden in the paintings that hung along the hallway. Sticking to the shadowy edges of the corridor, I walked to the gallery at the top of the stairway that went down to the foyer, then all the way to the end of the hall and back.

I stopped to gaze at a large modern abstract right in the middle, near my door, and hummed a few bars from "La Mer." It was the perfect place for surveillance cameras, one facing in each direction. I would have loved to run my fingers around the back of the frame and find the wires I felt certain were there, but tucked my hands behind my back.

"Bingo!" André said. "You picked it. It's the only surveillance gear in this hallway, and it's both audio and video. I'm erasing you and looping their recording from the last half-hour, so you're good to go."

I walked quietly to the far end of the corridor, to a door locked with a good, but far-from-wonderful deadbolt. It took only an instant for my lock picks to defeat it, and I found what I'd hoped for: a servant's stair that ascended from basement to attic. I shone my flashlight just long enough to see that I was right, then eased the deadbolt back in place. In total blackness, I felt my way up to the fourth floor, easing my weight from one tread to the next to avoid the inevitable creaks of ancient wood risers.

"No eyes or ears on the stairway," André said as I reached the top, "but it looks like this floor has the same cameras as the third so I'm looping that footage, too."

Faint moonlight spilled into a long, gloomy corridor running from one end of the building to the other. The air smelled hot and dusty. Tiny bedrooms opened off both sides, some with doors ajar and dormer windows letting in the light. Actually, it was an attic, the original servants' quarters, and nothing like the sumptuous rooms on the floor below.

"Uh-oh," André said. "You're about to have company."

Below me, I heard the stairway door open, then close. A light came on above the stairs.

André said, "Either hide in a closet or get out onto the roof."

Footsteps started up toward me.

"I need to back out and restore their system. Wait 'til I tell you it's safe to come out."

I dashed into one of the tiny rooms, closed the door, and took a quick look around. It contained a single bed, still covered with a duvet; a chest of drawers, probably empty; a chair with worn upholstery; and a small, open closet, abandoned except for one worn plaid shirt hanging on a peg. No place to hide, and I didn't want to, anyway. I pushed the dormer window open, creaking and groaning on rusted hinges, and a moment later, tested my shoes' grip on the roof tiles. "I'm out."

"Excellent. They won't have any reason to suspect anything. I've restored their video and audio feed."

"Keep me posted." I climbed to the peak of the roof.

"Will do. There are two men."

The mountain air wafted around me, cool and fresh and fragrant, and I tingled from head to foot. I was itching to send my cable to the top of the tower and climb up there, but a light came on in the nearest dormer window and moments later, I heard the unmistakable sound of a garage door opener. Then low voices came from somewhere below me. I crept to the edge of the roof, lay flat on my stomach, and looked down on the two men—Zachary and Count Maxime.

They had opened double doors that had to be at the end of the fourth-floor hallway, and a platform supported by cables on either side now protruded from the building. Soft light poured out, illuminating them. A mini crane stood at the end of the platform. They attached a sling to it, swung the arm around until it hung out over the edge, and lowered the sling.

A couple of minutes later, it came back up. They swung the arm around and, grunting with effort, lifted out a crate about the size of an under-counter refrigerator and set it on a handcart. Count Maxime pushed the cart inside while Zachary sent the sling back down.

This time, the crane brought up two flat boxes and a square one, a cube big enough to contain a soccer ball. They carried them into the château, then secured the crane and its arm with straps. The garage door opener pulled the platform back in, crane and all, and everything went silent.

I crouched beside the window with the light on. It was barred and shuttered on the inside. I put my ear against it, but could hear only a vague murmur of voices.

I backed away and spoke softly into my mic, "They brought some crates like the ones we saw in the penthouse suite at the Saint Francis Hotel up from the ground and took them inside. We need to look at the footage from your drone again."

"Your Honoré was in that room at the Saint Francis. How is he mixed up with these two?"

"He's not *my* Honoré, and I only said it *might* be him." Actually, I was positive it had been him. But clearly, he wasn't working with them. Either he'd been spying, stealing, or looking for evidence. The question was why? Please, God, don't let him be a cop.

The window went dark. I sat beside it and waited. A minute later, I heard creaking hinges, and a hand pulled shut the dormer I'd climbed out of. I waited a good five more minutes, and when nothing else happened, crept back and peered inside. The room was empty; the window firmly latched. So, there I was, outside. Just me and the trees.

I got to my feet, swept my arms up overhead, and drew in a long, grateful breath, then lowered my hands and rested them on my heart. It had been too long since I'd stood like this, as high as the treetops, alone, quiet, with an excellent puzzle to solve. I'd not accomplished what I'd set out to do. But what I'd seen was amazing.

The tower tugged at me. I gazed at the crenellated top. It would have been super easy to climb up, as planned, and see if I could find an opening in the roof. Unfortunately, the last clouds had straggled away, allowing the full moon to shine brightly. Earlier, I would have blended into the shadows of the trees. I'd have been virtually invisible. I could have peered down inside and been back in a couple of minutes. Heck, in a few more minutes, depending on what I found, I might have been able to locate the treasure room.

I itched to take a peek, and another five minutes passed before prudence finally won out. Clearly, the night had eyes.

I tiptoed along the roof and tried each of the dormer windows. They were all locked, so I crept down to the front of the château, lay flat on the edge, and counted windows to make sure I was above my bedroom. I unwound a thin, military-grade cable from my waist, looped an end around a chimney a little higher up, and tugged to make sure I'd pulled the slack out. All I had to do then was clip it to the harness I wore over my leotard. "André," I whispered, "I couldn't get back into the attic. You're done for tonight."

"Sure. Talk tomorrow."

Ten seconds later, I sat on my windowsill, behind the drape. A gentle purring sound came from the direction of the bed.

I pressed the remote release on my cable and wound it back around my waist, then pushed aside the drape. In the dim light from a pair of wall sconces, I saw a long, lean, distinctly Honoré-shaped lump in my bed. I was only half surprised to see him, but still, I sat there, wondering why. Who was this man? Obviously, our meeting in the baguette class had not been a coincidence.

Although I'd barely made a sound, the purring stopped, and although he didn't move, I could tell he was fully awake, spying on me.

Well, let him. I crossed the room into the bathroom,

shrugged off my tool belt and harness, and tucked them under a pair of thick, fluffy bath towels on a shelf beside the shower. He still hadn't moved or made a sound, so I climbed onto the bed, knelt facing him, and poked him in the ribs with a finger, wishing my fingernails were longer and sharper.

"Ow." He propped himself up on his elbows. "About time you got in."

"What are you doing here?"

He sat up. "Here, as in here in this bed, or here, as in here in the infamous count's castle?"

"Both, and technically, it's a château."

"Château, castle, house, hovel, call it anything you like. What are you doing here, flaunting your feathers like a peacock? Why do I get the feeling that you're going to ruin months of hard work and planning?"

"Don't be ridiculous." I pulled off my leotard and tights and dropped them on the floor. "It's a wedding. Weddings always take months, and there is no way I can ruin it." I slid under the covers and stretched out and commanded my fingers to stay put. To not reach over and touch him.

"There's a lot more than a wedding going on. So why are you here?"

"I was invited."

"By one of the most dangerous men in the galaxy."

"Ooh. Scary."

"Look, if you keep hanging around with Zachary le Noir, you are going to get hurt."

"What *is* it about men? You don't own me, you know, just because I appreciate you in certain circumstances."

"I want you to pack up first thing in the morning and

get yourself back to Paris."

I rolled onto my side, my back to him. "It's already first thing in the morning, and I'm not going anywhere but to sleep."

He put a hand on my shoulder. "Listen to me, Chloe. Your friend Le Noir is not who he seems to be."

I pushed his hand off. "He's not my friend. He is merely an acquaintance. And he's taking me on a helicopter tour at eleven, which is only seven hours from now."

"Please look at me."

I rolled onto my back. I wanted him to cover my face with kisses. I wanted him to make love to me. And I wanted to punch him in the nose. Why couldn't he be an ordinary guy I just happened to meet?

"He's not exactly a law-abiding citizen, either. He traffics stolen cultural properties, and he is way out of your league."

"What do you know about my league?"

"I know who you are, Chloe Eugenie Duval."

"So who are you? You're not a cop. You're here to find something you couldn't find in Ivanov's suite in Paris."

"I'm not even going to ask where you got that idea. It is none of your business. What I'm here to do has nothing to do with you. And I warn you that if you are thinking of going along with Le Noir, you need to stop. Get out. You're playing with fire."

"*You* listen to *me*, Honoré. I may have been stupid enough to believe you signed up for that class because you wanted to make baguettes, but I'm not stupid enough to believe everything you say."

"You have to trust me." He rolled away, off the

other side of the bed.

I sat up and threw my pillow at him, and it hit him on the back. "Ha! I'm not going to make that mistake again. No way. Nada. Nope. Never."

He threw the pillow back. "And I was stupid enough to think you might listen."

I hugged it to my chest and pressed my hands over my eyes. When I opened them again, he was gone. Good riddance.

So why did I have a great, gaping crater where my heart was supposed to be?

Chapter Fourteen

I slept like a rock until ten the next morning when someone knocked. I wrapped a sheet around myself and went to open the door. Zachary Le Noir stood there in a taupe silk dressing gown and nothing else, as far as I could tell. My eyes opened wide. Honoré claimed he was dangerous. He didn't know the half of it.

He handed me a tray with one red rose, two small silver pitchers, one steaming with coffee, the other with hot milk, and a basket of croissants. "Good morning."

A person could get used to having her breakfast delivered that way.

As I took the tray, the sheet slipped off my shoulders and he smirked. "See you at the helicopter in one hour, sleepyhead."

I felt a little disappointed that when he closed the door, he was on one side and I was on the other. Even if that was better.

****

Compared to the boxy, black helicopter that had ferried guests down to the inn the night before, the one waiting for me was a jaunty red and white with just room enough for two people, the sports car equivalent in choppers. Zachary grinned like a kid with a new toy as he held the passenger door for me, then went around and climbed into the pilot's seat.

"Does this belong to you?" I asked.

"For the next five hours, it belongs to you. I'm just

the chauffeur."

He started the engine. "Voice-activated headphones," he said, handing me a headset, then putting one on himself. "Where would you like to go?" His voice transmitted clearly in spite of the noise.

"First, I want to see how we got here last night."

We took off. The ground fell away abruptly, as if a giant cleaver had sliced the rock away. "You can see—" he tilted the nose down "—there's the inn and the trail we climbed last night." I gasped and grabbed his arm. I'd never been afraid of heights, but this was different. The glass went all the way to the floor.

He patted my hand. "You can relax the death grip. You won't fall out."

"That's exactly what it feels like."

"If you do, it will be a first."

"Are you sure you've done this before?"

"Many times."

"It's pretty warm today," Zachary said, "and we're already up in the mountains, so I want to gain some altitude before we head out." He circled a couple of times, giving me a clear view of the château. It perched on top of towering, craggy rock, hundreds of feet above the valley floor. From above, it looked like the head of a dragon, and the road we'd driven, the dragon's long, narrow, serpentine tail. The inn, where we'd left the car, stood on the only flat spot for miles. The trail we'd climbed in the dark was steeper than I'd realized and no wider than an average city sidewalk.

"See why it doesn't need a moat?"

"Got it."

"The Cathars built it originally, during the Inquisition, as a stronghold. A handful of archers could hold off an entire army by picking the attackers off one by one as they came up the trail."

"I get it, but I don't like that there's only one way in. That would have terrified me if I'd been led here to escape the Nazis during the war."

"You would have been so tired, cold, and hungry that you'd be grateful for any shelter. Besides, while they were here, they were safe."

"Then she betrayed them."

"After they left."

My great-grandparents might have been among them if they had managed to make it to the south of France before they were captured. They could have been there in the château believing that in one more day they'd be able to breathe freely again after many days and nights of fear and deprivation and hardship. They would have told the kids not to worry. They would have set off full of hope, expecting to cross the border into Spain. The cold hand of dread squeezed my heart. It would have been doubly cruel to be taken at that point. "What kind of person would do that?"

"A greedy one, eager for stolen loot." He gazed at me for a moment. "Makes you angry, doesn't it? Do you see why I want to get the tapestry back?"

"I do." If I helped return it to the rightful owners, I'd feel that I'd paid back some of the suffering my great-grandparents endured as Holocaust victims.

But Honoré's warning bumped around in my head. Could I trust the man beside me? And even if I could, should I? Those crates Zachary and Count Maxime had brought up to the fourth floor the night before must have contained some kind of stolen property. Why else would they do it at night? I had the uneasy feeling that Honoré was right: that they were cultural treasures. Stuff worth millions. Stuff people sometimes died for.

"Think about it." Zachary scanned the sky all around. "In the meantime, we've plenty of altitude now. Want to take the controls?"

I was only too happy to think about something else. "Do mice like cheese?"

Zachary stayed on the pedals and cyclic stick with me while I got the hang of it, then gave me control. I flew straight and level, then turned from side to side. I loved how the machine responded to my wishes, as if it were an extension of myself. "I want one of these."

He laughed as he put his hand over mine on the stick. "I'd better drive." A flock of hang gliders with red, blue, and yellow wings dipped, climbed on rising thermals, and soared all around a ruined castle perched on a high outcropping of rock. "I don't want to run over those guys."

"They look so free." I could imagine the warm, midday air rushing past their faces. "Have you ever tried it?"

"Sure. When Maxime first came to live here, we used to do that all the time. Sometimes we'd lose the thermals, end up in the valley, and have to walk all the way back up to the château. That's a hungry, thirsty climb."

"You've known him a long time?"

"All my life. Maxime's mother was the old Baron Ivanov's mistress. She and Maxime lived in a cottage on the estate."

"The estate in Bulgaria."

"Correct. The baron's wife, the Baroness Ivanov, was my adoptive mother's sister. She didn't mind having

Maxime and his mother around to take some of the abuse he lavished on her. In fact, they became friends. But the baroness wanted a child of her own. And she adopted my cousin at the same time my mother adopted me."

"So how did Maxime become the Count de Charpentier?"

"His mother left the baron, married the old Count de Charpentier, and moved here to the château. The baron was furious with her. He disowned Maxime, whom he had previously acknowledged as his son.

"But the three women remained friends?"

"Correct."

We dropped down to Carcassonne for lunch, so by the time we returned to the château, it was mid-afternoon. And I needed to talk to André.

But Zachary said, "I must show you something." He led me into a room three times the size of the room we'd dined in the night before. Women in black pants and white shirts were covering round tables with white cloths and setting bouquets of pink roses in the center of each. At one end, a pair of men dressed like stagehands at a theater were hanging a twenty-foot-long, two-foot-high tapestry on the wall behind the long head table.

Zachary urged me forward—not that he needed to—until we stood right in front of it. "This is one of the two pieces of tapestry Maxime refuses to give up," he said. "Priceless. Irreplaceable. Embroidered with woolen thread on a linen backing. Almost a thousand and a half years old."

It was so beautiful I couldn't speak. I wanted it. I wanted to hold it. If it had belonged to my family, I'd have done anything to get it back.

The colors had faded in places, especially the blues,

but all the same, it was stunning—a story told in thousands of tiny stitches for people who probably couldn't read. Starting on the left, it pictured Moses leading the Israelites through the Red Sea. Long lines of people followed, then chariots with horses rearing as the water started to wash over them. Later, Moses came down from a mountain with stone tablets clutched to his chest. At the right end, an army marched around a walled city as trumpeters lifted their gleaming gold instruments skyward.

Zachary let me look at it without interrupting until I said, "It's right out of the Old Testament in the Bible."

He smiled. "You must have attended Catholic school."

I nodded. It was one of the sisters' favorite stories in grade school. For some reason, they thought Bible passages about enduring forty years in the desert gave them permission to smack my hand with a ruler. "How many monks did it take how many years to embroider those millions of minute stitches?"

He gazed at me, an appreciative smile on his face. "A lot."

I wanted to touch it, but, of course, no one should touch a piece that old, especially with bare hands. And they'd placed it high enough that no one could. Should I believe Zachary and his cousin would return it to the rightful owners if I did decide to get it for them?

"You can see why I want it."

"Let me see if I understand. You've been friends all your life, but you sued Maxime for it. You lost the suit, so now you want me to steal it from him."

He stared straight ahead at the tapestry. A muscle twitched in his cheek. Finally, he turned to face me.

"Exactly. We do business together. Sometimes business and friendship don't mix."

"I see." How much of that should I believe? When it came to disputes over precious things, every hundred-thousand euros of value multiplied rivalries, skirmishes, and ulterior motives exponentially.

Zachary glanced at me with an ironic grin. "I'll say this for Maxime: He takes good care of it. As soon as dinner is over, his caretaker will put it away in this special storage box again." He pointed to a large wooden box that looked like an old steamer trunk with metal straps and corners and leather handles on each end.

"With the other one. In his famous treasure room in the impregnable tower, I assume."

Zachary frowned. The muscle in his cheek twitched again. "Of course."

From what I'd seen so far of the tower, unless there was a trapdoor in the roof, which didn't seem likely, I'd have to get in through the archers' slits. But the wall hangings would be too bulky and too fragile to go out that way. I'd shred them dragging them through those narrow stone openings. I'd have to use the alleged secret passage. I could probably find the entrance inside the treasure room. That shouldn't be too difficult, but where would I end up? What obstacles might I face on the way out, and how would I get two of them out of the château without being discovered?

And finally, was I really that crazy? Some things were better left where they were. After all, there was probably an easier way to get the Queen of Persia back.

****

As the first streaks of orange appeared in the western sky, I rested my hand on Zachary's arm and floated down the grand staircase to the foyer. Aunt Celeste had designed the perfect outfit. A fascinator hat with three long, blue, arching feathers hid my earbud. A chaste, high-necked, long-sleeved peacock-blue unitard glittered and gleamed and fit like a second skin. The skirt, which wrapped over the unitard and fastened on with a wide silver buckle, billowed around me in a froth of midnight blue shot with silver, hiding the climbing harness and tool belt that clung to my hips. I thought I looked like a peacock, and actually, I did, but Aunt Celeste's sense of fashion was right on. I fit right in with the women who fluttered around Count Maxime's elegant black tux, laughing and chatting and pretending not to criticize each other's gowns.

Thousands of tiny lights twinkled above the huge flagstone terrace. On the far side, ranks of chairs faced an arbor covered with creamy white roses. Near the entrance, tall round bar tables decked with white cloths and bouquets of more pink roses offered places to set down empty glasses. Waiters wearing jewel-toned brocade jackets circulated with trays of champagne and hors d'oeuvres. At least a hundred and fifty people strutted about, flirting with themselves and each other. Count Maxime de Charpentier was giving his daughter a lavish wedding.

The men wore black tuxes. Except for one. His jacket was sunshine yellow, his shirt lime green, and his tie a bright, multicolored floral. He sat in a wheelchair with his leg elevated and strapped into a brace. A tall blonde woman in a strapless black dress handed him a glass. She tipped her head back and laughed at something he said. White gauze wrapped his head, mummy-like, covering all but his mouth, nose, and one eye. The Queen of Persia diamond twinkled and gleamed at me from his pinky finger. My heart did a little flipflop. I raised an eyebrow at Zachary and nodded in his direction. "Is that your cousin?" As if I didn't know.

He gazed at me for a moment. "It is."

"What happened to him?"

He avoided looking at me by snagging a couple of glasses of champagne from a passing tray. "Aside from his usual theatrics, he's recovering from an attack in the Paris Metro."

A helicopter hovered over the château. The whup-whup-whup reverberated off the face of the building, making conversation impossible. It landed near the top of the path we'd ascended the night before. Judging by the acres of white visible through the window, the bride, Abigail de Charpentier, was making her entrance. Bully for her.

The rotors stopped turning and, in the silence, Maxime strode to the aircraft with his long, graceful stride, followed by four little girls dressed in bubbly pastel dresses. He opened the door and lifted Abbey, followed by miles of white lace, to the lawn. The girls hovered around her, straightening her train and lifting it off the ground. Maxime settled the veil over her face, and they all started toward the terrace.

My earbud crackled and André murmured, "Oops." More crackling. "Sorry."

I cupped my hand over my ear as Zachary bent down and said, "I must excuse myself. It's time to go stand beside the groom."

Guests filed into the rows of white, beribboned chairs. I claimed the outside seat in the last row, the one farthest from the ecstatic couple. Church bells drifted up from the valley below, chiming the hour.

It was the bells that got me; transported me back to the vestibule of the little white church with the tall steeple in Sterling, Washington. I stood there, wearing the strapless white wedding sheath I'd thought looked so perfect. The bells in the tower began to chime. My mother kissed my cheek, then settled the veil over my face and walked up the aisle toward the front. My best friend handed me my bouquet of white orchids and after a minute, followed my mother, doing that odd hesitation step we'd practiced to perfection. The strains of the "Wedding March" soared to the ceiling of the church and billowed out into the foyer. I took my stepfather's arm. He patted my hand. "Breathe, Chloe."

I'd been that close to walking to the altar when they arrested me, thanks to the loose lips of the man I loved. I hadn't been inside a church or attended a wedding since. I gripped the back of the chair in front of me and closed my eyes. My heart hammered at my ribs and cold sweat beaded my forehead. I wanted to run as far and as fast as I could.

I can't say I don't believe in God. I might. But I knew she wouldn't mind if I skipped the kneeling and praying and took a little peek inside the east tower. So, when the bride started up the aisle and everyone turned to ogle her, I backed away from the crowd and whispered, "André, I'm going in."

"Got you covered. I'm looping all the CCTV feeds. Eighteen minutes, remember. Three to get to the roof. Five to get into the treasure room, five to look around, and five to get out. And don't get too excited. Recon only."

"You know me."

He chuckled. "Like I said. Recon. Only."

I strolled back into the castle. It looked as if everyone was outside, but just in case, I kept my pace slow as I walked past my bedroom, then all the way to the end of the corridor. In fifteen seconds, I'd picked the lock and entered the back stairway. I ran up to the fourth floor and across the hall into one of the old servants' bedrooms.

With one click of the belt buckle, my skirt came off. I hung it, along with the fascinator hat, on a peg in the closet. I pulled on a pair of gloves with nonslip palms, then listened for a moment at the door, and hearing no sound, opened the window and stepped out onto the roof.

"Three minutes gone," André said. "Fifteen left."

I unwound my cable from my hips, shot it up to the top of the tower, and tugged to make sure the arrowhead had penetrated the stone. I attached my new, specially made hand ascenders, and in a few seconds, sat on the crenellated top, praying that if anyone happened to glance up, my blue unitard would be invisible against the deepening blue of the sky.

"Fourteen left."

I surveyed the flat roof, hoping for a trapdoor, but found nothing, so I rappelled down the back side, the side away from the wedding, to the archery slits.

"Thirteen minutes left."

They were about three feet high, wide on the outside and narrow on the inside, as expected. I gazed at the closest one. It looked too narrow to let me in. I'd get stuck, and I'd be very hungry before I got skinny enough to get out again. I pushed off and swung over to the next slit, then the next, then decided just to give it a try. I cleared away spider webs, gripped the top edge, pulled my feet up, and slid them in. I twisted sideways and my hips went through. I blew out all the air in my lungs and slithered my chest in, and finally my head, one ear at a time. I landed on the platform the archers would have stood on and peered around in the dim light. "I'm in." Did they feel as invincible as I did at that moment, when they looked down on approaching enemies?

André's voice in my ear: "You're getting behind. Eleven minutes remaining."

Where the tower abutted the main building, a narrow stairway spiraled downward. Leaving my cable in place, I unclipped my harness and started down. Uneven, roughly hewn blocks of stone, each about a foot high, formed the steps.

I counted eleven before I came to a flat landing with a thick wood door. It hung open on hinges that were so rusted they refused to budge. I slid sideways into a round tower room that was vacant except for a drift of old, dry pine needles and a squirrel-sized skeleton. It had three windows, one looking to the front, one to the back, and one opposite the stair, all bricked over, but leaking a little light. I imagined sentries watching in each direction, prepared to run to the platform above and rain arrows down on invaders or pour oil down on troops attempting to scale the tower.

"Nine minutes, thirty seconds remaining."

Little light filtered down from the arrow slits. I put on my headlight, turned it on low, and hurried on down. Every eleventh or twelfth stair, I came to another landing, each one about three feet square, and another room about thirty feet in diameter.

When I came to the fourth landing, there were two doors, one positioned like the ones leading into rooms in the tower on the floors above, and the other in the wall of the château itself. Both doors looked sturdy and new. Each had an alpha-numeric keypad beside it with a steadily glowing red light. My heart beat faster. The tower room had to contain Count Maxime's stolen treasures. And the other door had to be the entrance to the secret passage. I pressed my ear to each door in turn and heard nothing. "I'm there."

"Eight minutes, twenty seconds left. Place the scanner over the keypad and hold it steady."

I removed André's code scanner from my belt, held it over the face of the keypad, and turned it on. First, numbers scrolled by, too fast to read, then the alphabet, until it stopped at G. Then 8. Then 2. Then H. E. L. L. "Gate to hell," I said.

"Cute."

I entered the code on the keypad. It beeped and the light blinked green. Holding my breath, I opened the door and stepped into a spotless, cool, clean-smelling room. On the wall near the door, a gauge showed fifty-nine degrees Fahrenheit and thirty percent humidity. The door closed silently behind me. The inside keypad flashed red and started beeping. I re-entered the code. The beep stopped, and the light turned green.

I gazed around. "No cameras. Nothing." I'd expected better security—heat sensors or laser beams at least, but apparently Count Maxime de Charpentier thought his tower secure without any of those things.

"Lucky for you. Seven minutes and ten seconds left. That means only two minutes inside, sweet pea. Max."

Soft lights shone down on an array of paintings and sculptures hanging or standing around the perimeter of the room. In the center, a waist-high counter displayed two tall, conical gold hats covered with rows of symbols and a large, battered, embossed gold bowl. Priceless. I could barely breathe. On shelves below the counter, an array of gold Celtic torcs, bracelets, and other small gold pieces gleamed in the soft light. Each of them irreplaceable. Invaluable.

"Ten seconds. Then get out."

"Just—" The trunk I'd seen in the dining room, the one the men had removed the tapestry from, stood beside the door.

"You promised. Get out now."

For some reason, I flipped the lid of the trunk open.

Zachary's cousin, Baron Petar Ivanov, still in his yellow jacket, stared up at me with his one unbandaged eye. I didn't need anyone to tell me he was dead. Someone had removed his leg brace and tucked him in with his knees on his chest and his arms crossed. Whoever had folded him up had also taken the trouble to make sure his shirt lay smoothly across his belly and his tie was straight. And the Queen of Persia had been removed from his finger.

"Chloe! Move!"

I dropped the lid. My hands shook as I keyed in the code, then keyed it in again on the outside panel. I scrambled back up the steps. *Holy shit. Falstaff. Dead. Murdered.* I wriggled through the slit and rappelled back down the side of the tower to the peak of the roof. I forced myself to go slow, to take care not to slip.

"A minute and a half behind. Three minutes, thirty seconds remaining." André wouldn't sound so cool if he knew, and I wasn't about to tell him. I tried to block Falstaff's image as I retrieved my cable and wound it around my hips. There was nothing I could have done for him.

I'd be fine. I just needed to be careful, to be sure no one could know I'd been there. I started across the roof and my heart jumped to my throat. Thirty feet away, a man sat in the shadow of the dormer I'd climbed out of, his back against the window, blocking my way. It took a couple of seconds to recognize the American from the pond in the Luxembourg Gardens in Paris. He patted the roof beside him. "Have a seat."

He didn't know. He couldn't know what I'd seen. "No. Thank you."

"But it's so refreshing to find a fellow American this far from home."

"Sorry. I'm Canadian."

He folded his arms on his chest. "Adopted at age five by an American residing in Sterling, Washington. Therefore, also American." A note of impatience had crept into his tone.

I crossed my arms and glared at him. "And that gives you leave to follow me around and obstruct my path?"

He got to his feet. "It does, actually."

I pulled myself up tall. If he thought I'd be intimidated by his broad shoulders and half-a-head advantage in height, he could think again.

He pulled a wallet out of his pocket and flipped it open. "Stan Gibson, FBI."

"An FBI agent in France?" It was getting dark under the trees that hung over the roof. I squinted at the badge he held. "Come on. The FBI has no jurisdiction here, Stan Gibson, or whoever you are."

He grinned. "*Au contraire*, as they say around here. I'm a member of the Art Crime Team."

Thank God he wasn't talking about murder.

"Therefore, you hang out on rooftops."

"Guilty as charged."

"And pretend to sail boats in the Luxembourg Gardens. And bug my scooter."

"I wasn't pretending any more than you were."

Since I hadn't managed to find anything to steal since Christmas, whatever his reason for following me, it couldn't have been something I'd done.

André's voice, urgent in my ear. *"What the hell? Shove him off the roof and get going!"*

I put one foot on the windowsill. "Move, please. I'm allergic to cops."

Gibson didn't budge. "I've heard a rumor that there's a room full of priceless loot—stolen cultural artifacts and treasures—in that tower."

"I wouldn't know. Besides cops, I'm also allergic to weddings, so I came up here to avoid watching the blissful couple say their I do's. But now it's time to meet my date."

Stan Gibson got to his feet. "Zachary Le Noir is a dangerous man."

I caught my breath. Another man who knew more about me than I knew about him. And a cop.

"Chloe, get out! Move."

Chapter Fifteen

Stan Gibson, the FBI Art Crimes Team agent, climbed through the window and disappeared into the dim attic corridor. I had one leg in and one leg out when André's voice sizzled in my ear, "For God's sake, hurry! We've got company. Someone else is in the system. Get yourself out of there as fast as you can."

I yanked my harness off and stuffed it in my tool belt, snatched my skirt off the hook in the closet, swirled it around my waist, and clicked the buckle. Through my earbud, I could hear André typing. "Keep moving." His voice had the edge of a competitor in a fierce competition. "I need to shut down. They're probing—searching for my computer."

With shaking hands, I jammed my fascinator hat back on. I glanced at it in the old, cracked mirror above the chest of drawers to make sure the feathers hid my earbud and headed for the door.

"Who do you think it is?"

"Interpol," he hissed. "Got to be."

I ran across the hall and started down the dusty, dimly lit servants' stairway. "How about the FBI?"

"Don't talk. Go. I'm backing out. The stairway is okay. You need to go all the way to the main floor and exit into the kitchen."

"What if the door's locked?"

"It's not." He still sounded tense, but the sharp edge

was gone from his voice. "The cooks are using it."

I bunched up the yards of iridescent metallic fabric in my skirt and held it in both hands as I raced down. "How will I know which level to exit on?"

"I'll tell you."

"You can see me?"

"I'm André Dubillard, remember?"

I couldn't see the stairs over the froth of fabric in my hands. Plus, it was dark. I had to trust my feet to find the steps. For nearly a minute, the only sound was my soft-soled shoes landing on creaking wooden treads.

"Next landing, you're there."

"How do you know where I am?"

"Your earbud—on a holographic model of the building."

The door to the kitchen squeaked like a rusty gate when I pushed it open. I stepped away from it as fast as I could, not wanting to be seen before I had a chance to orient myself.

Half a dozen men wearing striped pants, white jackets, and tall white hats bent over flaming grills, a bank of ovens, and a long, gleaming, stainless-steel counter. They scrambled around each other, barking orders while a dozen more sous-chefs swarmed madly around them. Only one of them looked up.

I whispered, "André, did Interpol—or whomever—find you?"

"Nope. I escaped." He sounded like a kid who'd just beat a deadly rival in a foot race.

The man who'd looked at me was stacking gougères, puffy, golden-brown pastries, in a pyramid on an oval silver tray. I pulled in a long breath, then marched over and took one.

He jerked up straight and glared at me over the top of half-moon glasses.

"May I try it?" I took a bite.

"Well, you can't put it back." He sounded like my third-grade teacher, a nun who I'm sure had inflamed bunions.

"Yum! Stuffed with lobster salad. It's epic."

His gaze traveled from my fascinator hat to the bottom of my ebullient skirt, then back up. I could see him thinking I was a spoiled, empty-headed socialite.

I sent him my best smile and practically cooed, "I'm starving, and the Count sent me to check on the dinner." No lie, I *was* starving. Something about danger made me hungry, and opening trunks containing dead guys definitely smacked of danger.

I felt confident that I'd left no trace in the treasure room, and André had made sure the security system hadn't been able to see me, but all the same, my heart continued to race.

The cook grunted and went back to his task.

My best bet was to act like the social butterfly he thought I was. "I'd better try another." Nibbling the second flakey nugget, I strolled through open double doors into the huge dining room full of round, white-linen-covered tables, each with a bouquet of pink roses in the center.

André said, "You are incorrigible."

"I try." So who had done Petar Ivanov in? And who had the Queen of Persia? And why was the FBI and Interpol—or whoever—snooping around in the château's security system?

Bartenders stood behind bars that lined three sides of the perimeter, heads down, slicing lemons, setting out napkins, and digging olives out of wide-mouth gallon jugs. Frosty bottles stuck out of buckets of ice that stood like soldiers beside ranks of shining glassware. I begged a glass of champagne at a bar near the wide doors onto the terrace and wandered outside. The wedding seemed to be progressing very slowly.

"What's happening?" André asked.

"It's all good." My knees had stopped shaking. "The sun is setting, and the bride and groom are kneeling in front of the priest—repenting for the major error they just made."

And thanks to all the good in the universe, I'm standing here with a glass of champagne in my hand in spite of the fact that a man named Baron Petar Ivanov is dead. And the fact that Stan Gibson from the FBI Art Crimes Team is here, which means someone is trafficking illegal cultural goods in or out of the USA. And the fact that Interpol seems to be involved. All of which means, I'm not touching anything in that tower. Ever.

"We must talk."

The pressure eased off my chest. André had that effect on me. "Come on up. No one is going to notice one more person."

I wandered over and slipped into my back-row seat and scanned the crowd. Count Maxime, as father of the bride, sat on the center aisle in the first row. No one sat beside him. Apparently, she did not have a mother. Of the six groomsmen, Zachary stood fifth in line.

With every other man dressed in black, Ivanov's bright yellow jacket would have been easy to spot. I knew he wasn't there, but I looked for him anyway, wishing I were wrong. That trunk someone used to stuff

Ivanov into was the same one Count Maxime used to store the tapestries. Someone who knew how to get it from the dining room to Maxime's treasure room in the tower. If the secret passage was as secret as Zachary said it was, then that narrowed the possibilities to the count himself or someone close to him. So the big question was, who wanted him dead?

Zachary had been with me until he joined the wedding party, so he couldn't have done it. And I was pretty sure Ivanov was still sitting there in his wheelchair when the helicopter delivered the bride, so Count Maxime was probably off the hook. For personally committing the crime, anyway.

As I scanned the assorted guests, I noticed vaguely that the priest finally allowed the blissful couple to get up off their knees, and they stood there, facing each other, holding hands, her veil covering her face until he lifted it and kissed her.

God's representative here on earth droned on for another fifteen minutes about marital love. But I saw no one who looked guilty of murder. Nor was I able to identify anyone who looked like an Interpol agent.

The evening breeze picked up, and I could see goose bumps on the arms of the woman in front of me before he pronounced Abigail De Charpentier and Bristol Kozlec man and wife.

The congregation stood. Some smiled and waved, some cheered, and some wiped tears away. The bride and groom, four flower girls, and six bridesmaids clinging to the arms of groomsmen made their way down the aisle and headed into the château.

When they reached the entrance, Zachary dropped out of the bridal procession and strode over to me, where

I waited like a well-mannered guest for my row to be allowed to empty out and follow. He took my hand, which, by then, was freezing, tucked it into the warmth under his elbow, and led me into the dining room. "I must show you the other tapestry."

We stood in front of the head table again. The second piece of tapestry hung to the left of the one we'd looked at earlier. Not quite as long as the other, it depicted Noah herding animals into the arc, the flood waters, the dove coming back bearing an olive branch, and finally a glorious rainbow.

It was as beautiful as the first, especially the rainbow, which glowed in jewel-toned colors. I stared at it, barely registering the familiar scenes, biting my tongue to keep from asking, "Do you know your cousin is dead?"

If he knew, Zachary gave no sign. He raised my hand to his lips, bent, and kissed it. "I should rejoin the wedding party, but we must talk."

Over his shoulder, a pair of chocolate brown eyes glowered at me through tortoise-shell-framed glasses. My knees started to shake again. Honoré balanced a tray of *gougères* on one hand. Who was he, anyway? He waited until Zachary strolled away, then offered me the tray.

I pulled in a deep breath and murmured, "Nice glasses, my love. And cute moustache. You should wear it more often."

His expression stayed cool and pleasant. Only the edge in his voice betrayed aggravation. "We must talk." He turned his back and left me there, staring at the crunchy pastry in my hand.

What was this? *Must talk to Chloe night?* I strode

back to a spot near the entrance where I could watch everyone.

Count Maxime flitted about, joined off and on by the tall blonde in the strapless black sheath, the one who had given Petar Ivanov a drink before the wedding. She wasn't just tall. She was statuesque. Maxime ranged here, there, and everywhere, greeting guests; the ideal host, kissing women on both cheeks, shaking hands with the men, and leaving everyone smiling rosy smiles.

So who had a motive, the means, and the opportunity to spirit Ivanov away from the crowd and do him in? With vision in only one eye and impaired mobility, he'd made an easy target. Anyone could have walked up behind him in his wheelchair and wrapped a garrote around his neck. A minute later, he'd be dead. That didn't require much strength, but getting him into the trunk—that was a lot for one person to manage unless he or she was exceptionally fit.

I felt some comfort in knowing it couldn't have been Zachary. As I watched, he held a chair for the bridesmaid who'd been clinging to his arm, then sat beside her, and, as if glued to it, stayed put, chatting, with an amiable smile on his face. He didn't just look innocent. He was, at least of this crime.

I caught a glimpse of Stan Gibson, looking like all the guests, chatting with the blonde in the strapless black dress near the kitchen doors. I was moving in that direction, planning to get close enough to hear what they were talking about, when a hand touched my elbow. "Come outside for a minute," André said, close to my ear.

I followed his sturdy back out onto the terrace. The stars had come out in the short time I'd been inside, and

113

the wind had turned cold and unfriendly. He shrugged out of his dinner jacket and put it around my shoulders. "I don't like it. There are some pretty sophisticated cops here. Half the people you see could be cops. I think you should leave. Right now."

"Something tells me that it's better to remain visible."

"You are that, my little peacock. Celeste has outdone herself. But something is definitely going down."

"And remember, Stan Gibson can place me on the roof, coming from the tower. So it would look fishy if I disappeared."

He sighed. "You're right. It would look fishy. But look, as long as you didn't leave anything behind, no one can prove you were in that room."

"I didn't. I wore gloves; left no fingerprints."

"And I erased all traces of your entry and exit."

I shrugged. "So, no problem."

"However, I keep asking myself this: Why hasn't your friend Zachary stolen the tapestries himself?"

"He's too big to get into the tower through the archery slits. I almost got stuck."

"And you're willing to believe that he's tried and failed to find an inside access to the alleged secret passage."

I waved my arms at the château. "Look at it. There are four stories, thirty-four bedrooms, twenty-nine bathrooms, a library, a billiards room with animal trophies on the walls, a large and a small dining room, and a ballroom. All of them have portraits large enough to hide a false door, bookshelves, closets, and cupboards of all sorts and sizes. There could be a virtual maze of hidden hallways and stairs."

"Okay. Okay. Maybe he's tried, but it seems to me that someone besides Count Maxime must know where it is."

"I agree." If only André knew what I'd found in the treasure room. "I know how to find it. When the men take the tapestries in the dining room down and put them away—"

"Wait a minute. Why are we even talking about this? You are not going to follow them."

"Not me. You."

He looked at me for a long moment. "The old drunk guest looking for a bathroom routine? And why would I do that?"

"Because something might come up. We might need to know."

He shook his head. "You'd better go in. I'll do it, but I think you should forget the tapestries." He reclaimed his jacket. "I'll come in a couple of minutes."

I ran up to my room and put my tool belt away, along with the earbud. Then, the moment I stepped back into the dining room, Honoré appeared. He showed me to a table where five other people sat, three women and two men who all appeared to know each other. They paused to introduce themselves and then regaled each other with tales of nude sunbathing on the deck of Maxime's yacht the previous summer. I smiled vaguely at my table mates, and they smiled vaguely back.

Out of the corner of my eye, I saw André wandering around the perimeter of the room. He took a seat a couple of tables away, facing me, and sent an impish grin. Regardless of what he said, he enjoyed the intrigue as much as I did.

I couldn't keep my eyes off the tapestries. I had wanted to believe Zachary and Ivanov really would return them to the rightful owners, that they wanted to balance scales of justice. And that if I helped, they would give me the Queen of Persia ring. But with the nighttime delivery of those crates and cops swarming the place and Petar Ivanov dead and stuffed into the trunk, all bets were off.

Once dinner was over, Count Maxime stood. "As you may have noticed before the wedding, one of the groom's uncles, Petar Ivanov, is recovering from an injury. He had to return to the hospital for treatment, but asked me to wish Abigail and Bristol a long and happy life together." He lifted his glass. "To the brand-new Mr. and Mrs. Kozlec."

Interesting. So that's how they were explaining his disappearance.

Amid the following applause and cheers, Zachary marched to my table. "You are a very patient date." He took my hand and led me to the room where the casino had been the night before. It had been transformed into a giant tent worthy of a mighty sheik. A twenty-piece band played waltzes, fox-trots, tangos, and later, some salsa. At some point, I began to feel certain that he did not know about Ivanov's death. I pushed the dead man out of my head and danced to all of it effortlessly, as if I were floating in Zachary's arms.

In fact, I started to think of him as *my* Zachary, and it wasn't just the champagne and dancing and music. He was smart, funny, terribly handsome, and never once stepped on my toes. So, when he escorted me to my door, kissed both cheeks, and bade me sweet dreams, I didn't know whether to be disappointed or not. Okay, that's a lie. I *was* disappointed.

Chapter Sixteen

Ivanov had seemed so cheerful, sporting the Queen of Persia on his finger. Even though it was *my* ring, it didn't seem as if he deserved to be murdered. Actually, no one does. Well, almost no one.

Still, I couldn't feel sorry. As I removed my makeup and brushed my teeth, I tried to be sorry, but the truth was, I wasn't. I wondered if that meant I had a serious flaw in my character.

That's not to say I wasn't shocked. It was plenty shocking to open that trunk and see him stuffed in there like some kid's cast-off rag doll. Gruesome, even, especially with that bandage covering half his head and one eye. And scary if anyone ever figured out that I'd been in that room.

Bottom line: Ivanov was dead. The questions were: who did it, what had happened to the ring, and how the heck was I going to get it back? I hung my skirt and unitard in the armoire and crawled into bed to try to figure it out.

My eyes kept closing, and every time they did, I saw Ivanov, arms folded on his chest and knees drawn up. Green shirt and yellow jacket carefully smoothed. Flowing tie artfully arranged, draped over one shoulder as if the wind were blowing. One blank eye staring at me. I'd seen dead people before; two, in fact, at funerals where the casket was open for viewing. I'd always wondered why anyone would want to look at them. Let alone touch them. Or, for God's sake, kiss them. After the first one, I'd added open-casket funerals to the list of things I was allergic to.

I must have drifted away to sleep because suddenly, I came wide awake again. In faint moonlight, the drapes billowed away from the window. I could feel, rather than see, the shadow that was Honoré as he pushed them aside and tiptoed to the bed. I gripped the long, heavy flashlight I kept under my pillow and held my breath until I caught a whiff of his cinnamon and citrus scent. He slipped under the covers and nuzzled my neck. "You're not sleeping."

"Thanks to you." It felt so good when he snuggled my back against his bare, muscular chest that I let out a great, long sigh. Then I wished I hadn't. I wished I didn't feel that he was always one step ahead of me.

He kissed my ear. "You were missing me."

He didn't need to sound so pleased with himself. I rolled over to face him and pushed him away. "Listen, I need to know who you are."

"You should be worrying about who your date is."

"He's not the one who sneaked into my bed."

"Don't you understand? You need to stay away from him. These guys look great in tuxedos, but that's just staging. They can throw money around as if there were an infinite supply, but the last thing they are is refined, cultured, or whatever you want to call it. They are a bunch of con men and crooks."

"And you are?"

"Let me remind you." His hand cupped my face and he kissed me, long and sweetly. "Remember now?"

His kiss was so sweet, so tender that for a moment,

I felt safe. I opened my mouth to tell him I'd found Ivanov stuffed in a trunk. But just in time, a cold dose of reality swept over me. I'd been burned before—the last time I felt safe.

I pressed my palms against his chest. "Don't try to distract me. You seem to have a list of names a mile long, and you pick and choose which ones to use. You say you're a research scientist. Then you say you're a part-time taxi driver. And then you turn up here, a million miles from civilization, wearing a moustache and serving trays of *gougères* to wedding guests wearing designer gowns."

"That's true." He smoothed my hair off my forehead and tried to kiss me again.

I shoved him away. "Which part of it?"

"All of the above, my lovely little gem. I will explain when it's time."

"I—"

He put one finger on my lips. "Right now, it's late, and even I, Olivier Honoré St. John de Lazarre need some sleep."

"I—"

"Shhh." This time he proceeded to distract me in ways he knew I couldn't resist.

****

A breeze pushed the drapes away from the window and filled the room with clean mountain air. It took several seconds to realize someone was knocking on my bedroom door. Honoré was gone and I was wearing a striped blue nightshirt that must have belonged to him, although I had no memory putting it on.

When I opened the door, Zachary stood there, dressed in jeans and a crisp white shirt with the cuffs rolled back; tassel loafers, no socks. He carried a tall, white mug; steaming and bursting with the aroma of fresh, dark coffee. There was a God, and she had sent me this gift. The coffee, I mean.

He stepped inside and closed the door. "I have news."

The image of Ivanov tucked neatly into the trunk popped into my head, and I sucked in a breath.

He said, "It's not good news. Hop back in bed and I'll tell you."

Glad to have something to do with my hands, I plumped up my pillow, then propped my back against the padded satin headboard and smoothed the blanket over my legs. Zachary handed me the *café au lait*, then climbed up and sat on the bed beside me, right where Honoré had been.

I held my breath. I couldn't look at him.

He took my hand. "My cousin died last night."

"Maxime said he went to the hospital. Did he die from his injuries?"

"No. Unfortunately. And he did not go to the hospital. It looks like homicide."

Heck, yeah. It looked like homicide. Although glad I could finally talk about it, I couldn't look at him. I gazed instead at the opposite wall. "What happened?"

"There's a cold room in the cellar below the kitchen, with a dumb waiter to bring things up. A couple of hours ago, around seven o'clock, a kitchen helper went down to fetch flats of eggs for omelets and started screaming."

Lucky me. Someone moved him. Of course. They had to get him out of the trunk if they were going to put the tapestries back in. "What if he went down there to get something and had a heart attack?"

"I wish. But no, he was tied up in a ball and tucked into a dark corner behind a rack of hanging hams and wheels of cheese."

I turned to gaze at Zachary. Gray lines of grief etched the face that had been so lively the night before. I touched his cheek, then leaned forward and kissed it. "I'm sorry. You will miss him."

He slid off the bed and headed for the door. "There are people who will say it was murder richly deserved, but whatever they might think, whatever he was, we've always had each other."

****

By the time I dressed and came downstairs, a police officer stood at the bottom of the stairway. He directed me to the small dining room where we'd eaten dinner the first night.

Zachary met me at the entrance. In the far corner of the room, a man and a woman in uniform sat at card tables, each talking with one of Abigail's bridesmaids. "Gendarmes from Toulouse are here to interview everyone. No one can leave until they do." He gestured toward the long rectangular dining table, polished and gleaming, reflecting the candelabras spaced every four or five feet along the center. "Will you join me for breakfast while we wait our turns?"

A handful of other guests were there, talking in hushed tones. A server hustled in from the kitchen; plates of food stacked on one arm.

I nodded. "Of course."

But before we reached the table, Stan Gibson, the FBI agent, intercepted us. "Miss Duval, please come this way." He carried a plain brown cardboard box about the size of a shoebox under his arm.

I followed him back out into the hall, then into the larger dining room. There was no one there. It was still full of round, six-place tables. Stripped of their linen covers, they looked scratched and shabby. Without the flowers, the elegant guests, and the bars with their shining glassware and bottles of champagne, the room, which had been so sumptuous the night before, felt dingy and old. It even smelled musty.

Gibson pulled out a chair. "Have a seat." He sat beside me, placed the box on the table in front of us, and removed the lid. "Tell me about this."

For a moment, I couldn't take my eyes off the cable inside the box. The same length as mine. The brand I used. One of my carabiners still attached to one end. It lay there, coiled like a snake ready to strike. Who would have one exactly like it? I willed myself to stay calm. "It's a cable."

His eyes, steady, brown, so much like Honoré's that I wanted to cry, peered at me as if he could see into my soul. "Do you recognize it?"

I shook my head. "No. Yes. I mean, it looks like a rappelling cable."

"Is it yours?"

"No." But I felt the blood drain from my face. My mouth was as dry as the Sahara. I'd gone up to my room before dinner, right after I'd talked to André, and locked it up, along with my tools, in the false bottom of my suitcase.

Gibson's voice came from far away. "Chloe?"

I shook myself. "Sorry. It's not mine."

Someone must have taken it and planted it. Honoré? He'd had the opportunity after I fell asleep. But why would he do that? Tears pressed against my eyelids. I'd almost believed him when he said, "I love you." Last night; only a few hours earlier. I pressed my hands together to keep them from shaking.

"Perhaps you would show me yours."

"Of course." It wasn't mine. I was being silly. It seemed unlikely that someone else had one just like it, but not impossible.

He stood and gestured for me to lead the way. As we went up the broad stairway, he said, "You've heard that a man died last night."

"Yes."

He gazed at me; his face expressionless.

I wanted to grab him by the lapels of his jacket and shake him. I wanted to yell at him and tell him to stop staring at me. But I knew how to look as bland as he. I gave him my blank face. "I get it," I said. "You think he died unnaturally, and that cable is somehow involved, so now I'm a suspect."

"Everyone who was here last night is a suspect."

We entered the room. I saw that a maid had already straightened my bed and folded Honoré's nightshirt at the foot of it. I pulled my suitcase out of the armoire, laid it on the luggage stand, and opened it. "Please turn your back and look out the window," I said.

Gibson did so.

I keyed in the code on my phone, and the bottom popped open. My tool belt lay right where I'd put it, along with my harness, gloves, and climbing shoes. But the cable was gone. My heart began to thump against my ribs. I wiped cold sweat off my forehead. "I must have misplaced it." I closed my case and searched the armoire, the bathroom with its stacks of folded towels, everywhere.

I wished he'd say something, do something. But he just watched, his hands in his pockets, waiting for me to give up.

I peered under the bed, then turned back the blanket, hoping, although I knew it was ridiculous, that I'd find it under the covers.

Finally, I drew a deep breath. "Someone has taken it."

"I see."

Please, not Honoré. Anyone could have come in and stolen it while I was eating dinner or dancing with Zachary. Anyone.

He opened the door and waited for me to leave the room ahead of him.

"Why are you interested in this cable?"

"I am not at liberty to divulge that."

"Look. The gendarmes wouldn't be here unless someone thinks this man was murdered. And obviously, you think I did it. You think I used it as a garrote."

"It doesn't matter what I think."

A garotte would have left a mark on his neck, and undoubtedly, the carabiner had my fingerprints on it. But he had seen me with it after Ivanov died, so this made no sense. "What time did he die?"

"I can't tell you that."

"It doesn't take long to establish the time of death. It's a simple matter of taking his temperature and doing some rudimentary arithmetic."

"That's true."

"They've done that by now, haven't they? In fact, if he had a smart watch, they don't even have to do that. It would tell them when his heart stopped beating."

"I'm sure they have figured it out."

"So why won't you tell me?"

"It's not up to me to divulge that information. The Gendarmerie is responsible for investigations of unexpected death."

I felt cold, then hot, then cold. I wanted to puke. "You mean murder."

We paraded down the stairs and back to the small dining room. So, Ivanov had been found in the cellar, and I'd thought I was off the hook.

Regardless, Gibson could testify that he'd seen me with my cable after the time of death, so what didn't I know? Why were they so interested in it? What wasn't he telling me?

****

I wasn't allowed to leave the small dining room while I waited to be interviewed. They don't like to use the word "interrogation," even though that's what it is. They're just waiting for you to slip up and say something they can twist to fit their preconceived notion of what happened.

About a dozen guests were still there. Nearly all of them were alternately glancing at their watches and scrolling through their phones. The caterers had packed up their equipment and their staff had departed, but Zachary went to the kitchen and returned with a pair of croissants, a pitcher of milk, and a carafe of coffee. "I'm sorry you missed breakfast," he said. He sat down next to me at the long table. It seemed eons since we'd dined there two nights ago. He poured a cup of coffee and set it in front of me. "Who was that man?"

"A cop."

"Obviously." His voice had a sharp edge. "He must have identified himself."

"He did." I watched Zachary's face and saw only the faintest flinch when I said, "He's an American art crimes investigator."

"Art crime is big business, but I don't see that it has anything to do with my cousin's death."

I raised my eyebrows. "Someone must think it does."

"I've been in the art world a long time. Forgeries get passed off as originals. Originals get stolen. There is a huge black market in trafficking. But it's not cutthroat. People don't get killed."

"Then why would he be here?"

"I have the same question. I saw him talking to one of the catering staff last night." He shot me a glance. "The one who couldn't take his eyes off you."

I could feel my cheeks flush. "I have no idea whom that would be." But I did. I held my breath. Why would Honoré talk to Stan Gibson, FBI? I had to hope they merely discussed the *gougères*, but I couldn't dismiss it. I would have to find out.

From where I sat at the long dining table, drinking more coffee than I wanted, I could see that the gendarmes showed photographs to everyone. One of the photos, judging by the furtive glances in my direction, was of me. It became more and more clear to me that they were deferring my interview until they had talked to all the other guests.

For a while, Zachary wandered around, chatting with the other guests, but they were released one after the other. When their number dwindled to five or six, he came to sit beside me.

I said, "They talk to people less likely to be involved first. They attempt to determine who saw what, where, and when. They try to establish who had been seen interacting with the victim or any of the suspects. Then they interview possible suspects."

He raised a quizzical eyebrow. "You think so?"

I'd learned a lot about how detectives build cases while I was in jail, and it was pretty clear that they were gathering evidence that would build a case against me, or trying to.

"Yes. The longer they make us wait, the more likely it is that they think one of us did it." If so, no doubt they would want to search my apartment—and find Ivanov's jacket stuffed in the back of my closet. I excused myself, walked away from the table, and sent a text to Aunt Celeste.

—*I may be late getting home tonight. I hope you can keep Baguette. There is a bag of dog food in my closet. It's in a shopping bag.*—

She must have been at home, because less than ten minutes later, she responded.

—*Baguette is fine. But there was no dog food in your closet. Is there a problem?*—

Bless Aunt Celeste. I didn't want her to worry.

—*No problem.*—

Zachary and I were the last to be interviewed. At three o'clock, after the gendarmes had taken a break and conferred quietly in their corner, they called him to sit down with one of them and me with the other.

As we went to meet them, Zachary, courteous as ever, said, "You'll miss your train, but I will take you home when we're both free to go."

The woman officer, who introduced herself as Constable Hubble, showed no sign of fatigue or ennui. She directed me to sit down across the table from her.

Her navy uniform, tailored to fit her mature figure, remained unwrinkled, and set off the deep blue of her eyes. Her face looked soft and kind, as if she had spent the day baking cookies. She smiled as if inviting me to sit down for a cup of tea.

She opened, as I expected, with questions designed to build rapport; to put me at ease so I would relax and confide my deepest, darkest secrets. First, we chatted about my employment. Yes, I found it interesting and rewarding when my clients' portfolios did well. Yes, living in Paris was a big change from living in Sterling, a small town in Washington State. Yes, I missed my mother and my old friends. And so on, until I was ready to jump out of my skin. I nearly begged her to move on to the next step.

Finally, she did. "Tell me what you know about Petar Ivanov's death."

"I don't know anything about it," I said, "I was awakened by a knock on my door this morning. It was Monsieur Zachary Le Noir. He told me his cousin had died during the night."

"What else do you know about his death?"

"Since you are investigating it, I assume you suspect he was a victim of homicide."

The steal core behind that warm, motherly face showed up at last. She set the cardboard box containing the cable on the table and tapped the lid with a short, blunt, unpolished fingernail. "We believe this belongs to you."

I couldn't resist a smart-ass response. "I don't own a box like that."

She glared at me for several beats.

I raised my eyebrows and waited.

She removed the lid and pushed the box toward me. "The cable."

I pulled it closer and gazed at it. They would find my DNA on it, but that would take a long time. Much more quickly, they would find my fingerprints on the carabiner. But I last handled it with my gloves on, so perhaps they were all smudged. I could hope. "I'm sure you'd like me to tell you it's mine, but all I can say is that I own a rappelling line that looks somewhat similar."

"Perhaps you'd feel better if you told me how you felt about Petar Ivanov."

"I have no feelings at all for him or about him. I didn't know him." I willed my hands to remain open and still, resting on the tabletop.

"A chef identified you as the woman who came into the kitchen from the service stair, which leads to the cellar, near the time of Monsieur Ivanov's death. Another guest told us that you absented yourself from the wedding ceremony just prior to the time the chef saw you in the kitchen."

I gazed at her. I neither blinked nor looked away. "I had nothing to do with him. I had no feelings for or about him. I didn't know him."

"He was bound with this." She tapped the box.

"What do you mean?"

"I mean he was bound with it. That is not hard to understand."

"Tied up?"

She fixed her eyes on mine and waited.

Oh, dear God and all the angels. The time of death was irrelevant. My mouth went dry. I tucked my hands under the table so she couldn't see them shaking. And I stared right back at her.

Finally, she said, "How do you explain this cable?"

"I can't explain it. I own a similar cable. If it were mine, anyone could have taken it from my room. The doors are not locked."

"How well did you know Petar Ivanov?"

"I never met Monsieur Ivanov. I had no feelings for or about him. I had nothing to do with him."

She folded her hands and leaned toward me. "You could help yourself by revealing what you know."

"I don't know what happened. I had nothing to do with Monsieur Ivanov. I had no feelings for or about him. I didn't know him."

She pressed her lips together, then sat back and gazed at me for a long moment. "Look, I know what you're doing. You are saying the same thing over and over again, like a broken record. I applaud your skill at using this technique. You may go for now. But eventually, you will answer our questions."

Chapter Seventeen

Finally, I was allowed to leave. Zachary let me pilot
his red and white helicopter most of the way from Count
Maxime's château to Toulouse. He showed me how to
maintain a constant altitude and how to crab into the
wind so we weren't blown off course.

From the moment I put my hand on the stick and my
feet on the pedals, flying took every ounce of my
concentration. I forgot about Ivanov. I forgot to worry
about my rappelling cable. I didn't once think about
bugging Zachary to tell me what he knew about Ivanov's
murder or for info that would help me find the Queen of
Persia. Later, I wondered if that was why he gave me the
controls.

He took over as we approached Toulouse, and I had
to be quiet as he spoke with the tower and received
landing instructions. He touched the smart little aircraft
down on one side of the airport, near a sleek private jet.
A pilot in a white shirt with four bars on his epaulettes
stood by the stair into the jet's cabin. Zachary wasted no
time handing my bags to the pilot. Then he placed his
hands on my shoulders and kissed both cheeks, and
without saying goodbye, stepped away.

I was the only passenger on the six-seat jet. It was
nearly five o'clock when we lifted off, and in a little
more than an hour, we landed at Orly Airport, Paris. I
sent a text to Aunt Celeste.

—Walkies this evening, say seven-thirty? Then dinner?—

—Oui. Tuileries near the pond. Okay?—

—Okay.—

—Perfect. I'll reserve at Cochon Qui Rit. Oui?—

—Oui, merci.—

As I exited the taxi in front of my building, a woman in black pants and tan trench coat strolled past, studiously avoiding looking at me. I dropped my bags in my apartment and tugged on a pair of running shoes. When I came back down, the woman was across the street in the park, feeding the pigeons.

On my way to the Tuileries Gardens, I jogged a couple of blocks beside the Seine, then crossed the street to peer in the window of a bookstore. The pigeon-feeding woman stopped and peered at the schedule posted at a bus stop only fifty feet behind me. I re-crossed the street, walked a bit, then jogged again.

By the time I got to the Tuileries, the sun had gone down. Wispy red and purple clouds streaked the sky and there was a soft breeze, an unusually warm one for Paris in March. I opened my leopard-print trench coat and let it blow around me. Although I was a couple of minutes late, I did not hurry. I meandered to the big round pond in the center of the main pathway near the Louvre.

Aunt Celeste and Baguette joined me there a minute or two later. I squatted down to pat my dog, who greeted me with cool indifference. No doubt he thought I needed to be punished because I'd been gone. Not that he truly cared. His heart belonged to Aunt Celeste, who greeted me with her wide smile and a kiss on both cheeks. "You have a tail."

"A woman in wide-legged black pants and tan

trench coat."

"Yes. Obvious. She would profit from surveillance training."

"Does she still seem to be alone?"

Aunt Celeste nodded. "So far. Let's bore her to death with a Sunday evening stroll."

We set off down the wide path toward the obelisk in Place de Concorde, arm in arm, in step with the hundreds of Parisians—men, women, and children breathing in soft air, enjoying the first signs of spring, reluctant to return to their apartments, because when they did, the weekend would be over. It would be dark and time to prepare for school and work again.

André fell into step beside me a few minutes later. "What have you gotten yourself into, my little peacock?"

"I think someone is trying to frame me for murder."

There! I'd said it. I couldn't deny it any longer. For a minute my knees felt like they'd buckle, and I grabbed his arm for support.

"Could it be your Zachary?"

"He's not *my* Zachary."

André raised an eyebrow. "It's not nice to lie, Chloe. I saw how you looked at him when you were dancing."

"I did no such thing." I frowned at him. "The gendarmes interviewed him and me last. I think that means they suspect both of us."

"No doubt he deflected suspicion by casting aspersions on you."

Aunt Celeste stepped in between us, handed Baguette's lead to André, and took each of us by the arm. "Let's stick to facts."

I cringed. The problem was, so far, the evidence appeared to be stacked against me.

She said, "I went to your apartment, but someone had been there before me. I could tell they'd snooped around, and whoever it was, they must have taken whatever it was you wanted me to get."

I sucked in a breath. "I bet the Gendarmerie has it."

Aunt Celeste said, "What is it?"

"The jacket Ivanov was wearing when I saw him at the *Cochon* last Monday. When I got home that night, it was in the middle of my bed, and that bottle of champagne you opened was chilling on the coffee table."

André said, "If you'd listened to me, we'd know who put it there. And we'd know who came and got the jacket. I'm upgrading your security system. Tonight. I'm putting in two cameras."

"No. I'll feel like I'm in prison."

"Yes. Or you might *be* in prison."

"André is right." Aunt Celeste squeezed my arm. "The question is, why would anyone put his jacket on your bed?"

"He seemed so flamboyant and jolly. I thought it was just his quirky way of telling me he knew I wanted the Queen of Persia, and that he would bargain for it."

"And maybe it was," André said.

"My rappelling cable is a bigger problem. Constable Hubble said he was bound with it when they found him."

André groaned. "Have they got anything else against you?"

"The kitchen staff found him in the cellar below the kitchen, and a chef saw me come into the kitchen from the service stairway at about the time he died."

Aunt Celeste took my hand. "Purely circumstantial."

"Okay," I said, "I'm going to tell you two. At the

time I was in the kitchen, he wasn't in the cellar. He was in the count's treasure room, all tucked up in the trunk the count stores those tapestries in. And, incidentally, he wasn't wearing the Queen of Persia."

"Aha!" André said. "That's why it took you so long to get out of there."

"But if I tell them that, it'll make it worse."

"I think you're right, sweet pea."

Chapter Eighteen

The interview room lacked charm of any kind.
Neither the furnishings—three wooden chairs, one
facing the other two, bare wood floor, one-way mirror—
nor the two people in it appealed to my aesthetic senses.
No surprise.

I get why they insisted on calling it an interview
room. Clearly, the word "interrogation" had earned a bad
rep—no surprise there, either—and everyone was trying
to distance themselves from it. But if you ask me, being
dragged out of bed before the sun is up and hauled off to
such a dismal place does not portend a friendly chat. It
was an interrogation room, and if they'd been honest,
that's what they'd have called it.

I was a little surprised that the gendarme from the
château, Constable Hubble, with her blue eyes and sweet
face, had dragged her sorry self all the way to Paris. As
if no one else could continue the cozy little conversation
she'd begun. She introduced her partner as Constable
Graham. I'd seen her before, too. It was the woman in
the wide legged pants who had followed me to the
Tuileries so clumsily the evening before.

"Nice to meet you at last," I said. I knew I shouldn't
be snarky, but it felt so good I did it anyway.

Constable Graham's eyebrows went up in surprise.
Did she really think I hadn't known she was following
me? She had a thin, pale face with a nose like a parrot's

beak, narrow eyes, and a pinched mouth that looked as if it never smiled, let alone laughed. No doubt looking at herself in the mirror every morning had soured her for life.

The two of them sat facing me. Hubble put on her motherly look and kindly tone and started off by telling me they'd brought me in for another *interview* simply because they had new information. Ha! The truth was, she hoped to trip me up, pin Ivanov's murder on me, and get a quick, efficient conviction. No doubt she was on a fast track for a promotion to a new level of incompetence at the Gendarmerie.

Smiling as if she were my best friend, she took a jacket out of a box—Ivanov's maroon brocade jacket, the one he'd worn at the *Cochon Qui Rit*, the one someone had placed in my apartment. She shook it out, grasped it by the shoulders, and held it up for inspection. "What can you tell me about this garment?"

I tipped my head to one side and gazed at it for a moment. "It's a beautiful fabric."

"Do you know where we found it?"

I shook my head. "No." Whoever retrieved it from my apartment hadn't done so legally, so she couldn't ask me why it was there. She was just hoping I'd tell her. I sat perfectly still and stared into her eyes.

"Have you seen it before?"

"As I said, it's a lovely fabric."

She gave me one of those looks that I used to get from Mother Joseph in third grade, the kind that said she'd love to slap my face; that she would if she'd been allowed to do so. "Please tell us where and when you've seen this before."

"All I can say is that it's a beautiful fabric." I

yawned. I stood up and stretched. I couldn't help it. I'd missed at least two hours of sleep. "If that is all?"

"Petar Ivanov wore it. Am I correct?"

I shrugged. "I didn't know him. I had nothing to do with Monsieur Ivanov."

Hubble glared. Her sidekick, Constable Graham, looked severe. But most likely, that was the only way she ever looked.

I waited.

"That's all for now," Hubble said.

I strolled right up close to the mirror. You can see through one-way mirrors if you're close enough. Stan Gibson stood there, gazing right back at me. And beside him, Honoré St. Lazarre. I stifled a gasp. I couldn't show any emotion, but my heart raced. I felt my hands start to clench into fists, but made them relax.

Constable Graham grasped my elbow and pulled me away. "This way, please, Mademoiselle Duval."

I declined her offer to provide a ride back to my apartment, got out of the building as fast as I could without appearing to be fleeing, and flagged a taxi.

One thing was exceptionally clear to me. Honoré and I were through. I'd been sucked in by his elegant manners and the fact that he made me laugh. And the rubies and diamonds in his gorgeous cufflinks. And the way I forgot everything else when he climbed into my bed.

But he'd lied to me. He'd told me he wasn't a cop. I swallowed the lump in my throat and pushed him out of my head. It was a darn good thing I'd seen him.

****

It's amazing how much time morning people have before they go to work. I showered, dressed, and took a short walk with Baguette before I escorted him upstairs at nine-forty to keep Aunt Celeste company. I told her about my morning, and she gave me the number for her attorney. I was never going to attend another "interview" alone. And we called a meeting of the *Société* for that evening.

After all that, I hopped on Poppy and sped off to work. I fought my way through throngs of photographers and reporters clustered around the entrance to Rhineland Bankgruppe, all shouting questions. It was difficult, but I managed to open the gate, drive through, and wait for it to close behind me without saying anything rude or casting aspersions on their mothers.

It was a little after ten o'clock. I was only a few minutes late. Way overdue for an espresso, I headed for the common room, but Monsieur Fischer's assistant, a slight, balding man in the required black suit, stepped in front of me. "Monsieur Fischer is waiting for you, Mademoiselle Duval." He led me to the tall mahogany door behind his chrome and glass desk and opened it, then stepped aside to let me pass.

My boss looked like he was about to have a stroke or a heart attack or, more likely, both. His face deep dark red, he stomped back and forth in front of the TV screens on the wall across from his desk. There were three of them. Normally, they displayed real-time stock trades on the major exchanges, but on one, he had frozen a picture of me walking up the steps to the courthouse, escorted on either side by an upright, uniformed police officer. At the bottom of the screen, the news scroll read, *Chloe Duval, Rhineland Bankgruppe Wealth Management Advisor, suspected of murder.*

The second screen looped through the horde of

reporters waiting outside the gate, my arrival on Poppy, the reporters shouting questions, the microphones and cameras thrust in front of my helmet as I waited for the gate open, and my back as I waited for it to close behind me.

I'd heard about people quivering with rage. I'd always thought it was merely a figure of speech, but one look at my boss told me I was wrong. Even his mustache twitched.

I so did not want to have to do CPR. "Monsieur Fischer, you don't look well. Please sit down." I perched on the edge of one of his deep leather chairs and gestured at another. "Would you like a glass of water?"

"Mademoiselle Duval, you have made Rhineland Bankgruppe a *spectacle*. What I would like is for you to leave these premises. *At once*." He opened the door. "You have five minutes to pack your belongings. I shall escort you, personally."

My knees trembled, but I didn't budge. "Regardless of what the news media say, I am not a suspect. I am a witness, and I am helping the police with their investigation."

"That is not what I have been led to believe."

I pulled in a deep breath. "It is the truth."

"Enough!" My boss's voice went up an octave. He bounced up and down on his toes. "This type of publicity will be the ruin of the Rhineland Bankgruppe."

"You can't be sure of that. Think of it this way. Many people have never heard of us. The publicity may generate new business."

That was when he lost it. His face turned purple. He roared, "I said five minutes, and I mean five minutes."

I felt all the blood drain from my face.

"And no one is to see you. You will leave in my personal limousine."

I stood up, but had to hold onto the arm of the chair. "I have my own transportation, thank you."

"You do *not*. Your abominable scooter will be delivered to you."

It was my turn to shake—from the top of my head right down to my bright red toenails. I hadn't expected to be fired, even though it was totally in character for him. I'd thought that I could keep my personal life quiet and separate. I'd thought I'd be able to leave the barely disguised accusations of murder at the office door and be in another world. One where I didn't have to worry about a woman who wanted a speedy conviction.

I'll say this for Monsieur Fischer's driver: He carried my Tuscan funeral urn out to the car and handed it to me carefully after I slid into the back seat, as if he recognized its value as a thousand-year-old antique.

Monsieur Fischer directed him to take me to my apartment, then stepped back and watched to make sure I actually went. I could see him mentally wash his hands of me, as if I'd done great harm to him, personally.

Actually, by sending me out in a car with blacked-out windows, he'd done me a favor. I didn't have to face the reporters. They fell back and let us pass.

So my boss fired me. Who else would desert me? Worse yet, who, besides, Constable Hubble, might decide, based on questionable evidence, that I'd killed Ivanov? Honoré?

Tears crept into my eyes and I stumbled as I hugged my Tuscan funeral urn to my chest and carried it up to my apartment. I loved my job. I was good at it. In the past year, I'd been recruited by two rival companies who offered more perks and bigger salaries, but stayed with Rhineland Bankgruppe because I felt like I belonged. I'd been at home there, debating and sharing financial news with other advisors and managers. And on the bi-annual satisfaction surveys Monsieur Fischer sent out the year before, my clients had ranked me four plus out of five.

I set the urn on my coffee table and went back down to the foyer to pick up the box containing the personal items I'd kept in my desk: lipstick, nail polish, mirror, and Sudoku book. I tried to cheer myself up by reminding myself I had choices, other opportunities that might be better.

But as I stood there holding my box, a panel van pulled up onto the sidewalk. The driver opened the cargo door and there was Poppy, tethered front and back to tiedown rings on the walls. My boss had wasted no time scrubbing all traces of me from his precious company. Seeing her there, all tied up, knocked the last bit of stuffing out of me. I watched the driver unload her and leave her at the curb. She looked as forlorn as I felt.

My phone chimed with a message from Aunt Celeste.

—*Meeting at Robbie's. Tonight. Usual time.*—

I responded with a smiley face, which felt feeble, but the best I could manage at the time.

Chez Gaspard, Robbie Gaspard's restaurant, was closed on Mondays. Robbie always spent the day there, surrounded by the best of in-season fruits and vegetables, perfecting and writing up the recipes for the coming week. For the whole day, the kitchen was his and his alone. No wife-partner-chef to argue with, no sous-chefs to keep in line, no servers hustling back and forth. Just Robbie, tasting and cooking. When the *Société de*

Voleurs de Nuit was invited to meet there, we got to sample his creations. The usual time was 8:30. By then, he was ready to start pouring scotch and hear our praise.

In the meantime, I didn't know what to do with myself. With no meaningful work to do and not a single brilliant idea of how I could prove my innocence, the whole, long, empty afternoon stretched out in front of me.

I took Poppy back to her spot in the garage under my apartment and walked the few blocks to the *Cochon Qui Rit*. Like a magnet, the *Cochon* pulled in all kinds of questionable characters. Maybe someone knew something about Ivanov that could shed light on his murder. And I had eaten nothing so far that day. I scored a stool at the bar in the back of the room and ordered a glass of champagne.

Viane Thibaudet herself set a golden, bubbling glass in front of me. "*Bonjour*, Chloe." She smiled, and for a moment, I could only stare at her. She was so beautiful, with dimpled cheeks, sparkling dark eyes, black hair tucked under her tall white hat. She lived in prison. How could she smile like that?

"*Bonjour*, Viane. I have a question. Petar Ivanov. Did you know him?"

She climbed onto the stool beside me. "I know he appreciated good food. He came here often when he visited Paris." She gazed into my eyes for a minute, as if trying to decide whether to say more. "I saw you on the news this morning. It looks as if you're suspected of murdering him." She toyed with a napkin—watched it as she turned it around and around on the polished wood counter. Finally, she lifted her head. Her eyes met mine in the burnished old mirror behind the bar. "So." She paused. "I assume you'd like to know who killed him."

"I would."

She leaned in and spoke very softly. "Désirée Bellepont, one of my staff, may know something useful."

"Did she know Ivanov?"

"She knew who he was. More importantly, she knows Count Maxime de Charpentier. She used to work for him, and she claims she is in prison now because he and his favorite fixer framed her."

"Do you believe her?"

A shadow fell across Viane's face. "As much as I believe anyone. We all have our own reality, you know."

"True."

"They'll frame you, too, if they can." Viane sent me a wry smile. "But she has some information that might help you. Last week, when Petar Ivanov dined here with his cousin—I'm sure you saw him. He was too flamboyant to miss—according to Désirée, one of Count Maxime's thugs ate here too. He followed them out and got into a car that pulled up behind Ivanov's."

My mind flashed back to that night. I'd been across the street, focused on snapping photographs of Zachary, so I hadn't noticed anyone else. But since the street was too narrow to allow other cars to pass the big luxury sedan, at least two other cars had stopped behind it. It would have been easy for someone to slide into one of them without my noticing them. And a couple of vehicles had stayed between Ivanov's car and Honoré's taxi as we raced toward the Arc de Triomphe. "He was attacked in the Metro that night."

"Correct. And Désirée says Maxime's enforcers always work in pairs. If you see one, there is another nearby, maybe more. She's betting Count Maxime's favorite was the one who actually attacked him."

"Not the one who followed him from here?"

"Correct. His job would have been to track Ivanov and let her know when to expect him to show up, and maybe set up a distraction." Viane slid off the stool. "In any case, the count would not have been pleased that she didn't succeed in killing him. Therefore, she would have had to try again."

"She? This fixer is a woman?"

Viane rolled her eyes. "What, you think women don't commit murder?"

Chapter Nineteen

Viane Thibaudet's cynical retort hit me like a cudgel. Women do commit murder. And they do get sent to jail.

And if the server Viane told me about was telling the truth, Count Maxime had framed her and sent her to jail. And that could happen to me. A hard, hot band squeezed my chest so tight I could barely breathe. Being behind bars for something I'd done was bad enough. Being convicted of murder on the basis of false testimony would make me completely crazy.

And if the server was right, Count Maxime was probably the one who killed Petar Ivanov. Essentially. As father of the bride, he had been in plain sight all evening, so he clearly hadn't done it himself. But that's what men like him have fixers for.

And what about my client Zachary Le Noir? Did he have a hand in it? I believed his grief. But still.

I hustled back to my apartment. I needed information. The more I could gather before meeting with the *Société* in the evening, the better. I booted up my laptop and typed in "Count Maxime de Charpentier."

The gossip mongers loved photos of celebrities, and in their circus, Maxime was the brass ring. A ton of links came up, so I narrowed my search to the last five years. Then, because pictures tell more than words, I leaned close to the screen in order to search for familiar faces, then scrutinize their expressions. Every time I saw Petar Ivanov or Zachary Le Noir as well as Count Maxime, I saved the page.

Soon, I'd saved a dozen photos that included all three of them. Half had been taken at racetracks near Paris. They stood together with horses and jockeys, holding trophies, shaking hands, laughing—full of camaraderie. The odd thing was that all of these were taken between three and five years ago.

I retyped my search and looked at photos of Maxime taken at the same tracks in the last two years. In each, he was alone with his horse and jockey. When I searched the races held at the same tracks on the same dates, Ivanov's and Zachary's horses had also competed. Zachary's had even won one race, but in the winner's circle, he stood alone. The three of them were not hanging out together.

I looked at other types of events: black tie charity balls, weddings, and gallery openings. Same thing. Up until two years before, the three men were often together and seemed to enjoy each other's company. Since then, they showed up at the same event sometimes, but without the earlier signs of camaraderie. Generally, in these photos, Zachary stood or sat between the other two. While Ivanov looked jovial, Maxime pouted like a sullen child.

I surmised about two years ago, something happened to cause a rift. Could it have been enough to make Count Maxime kill Petar Ivanov?

Next, I scanned for other people who showed up repeatedly at the same events and found the tall, athletic blonde who'd worn the strapless black dress at the wedding in several pictures. Even when her image was blurred by distance from the camera lens, her Nordic looks and statuesque shoulders could not be mistaken. A couple of times, she was hanging on Maxime's arm. In a photo taken only two months ago, he was pointing at something behind the camera, and they were leaning together and laughing. The caption read, "*Lili Jensen, Maxime's Main Squeeze.*" I saved a copy.

Question: Did "main squeeze" translate into "favorite fixer?"

I wanted to rush right over to the *Cochon Qui Rit* and show it to Désirée Bellepont. But even though I viewed Désirée as an ally, she was not a friend. She was in prison, and in prison, information was a special kind of currency. If she helped me, she'd want something in return. I needed to think about what that might be.

Time to go for a long run and let my subconscious mull everything over. I laced on my shoes and set out in lightly falling rain, past André's apartment and the Eiffel Tower, then right onto the broad walkway beside the Seine with its slowly moving barges and hop-on-hop-off tourist boats.

When I came to Pont Neuf, I slowed to a walk, turned right, and headed toward Aunt Celeste's shop. I needed her advice.

When I stepped inside, Baguette ran to greet me, prancing and wagging his whole body. Aunt Celeste's assistant, a tall, thin, red-headed Irishman wearing a cream-colored leather jacket trimmed with chocolate brown, finished ringing up a sale for an elderly woman. "*Bonjour*, Chloe. I'll be with you in a minute."

I headed for the fitting booth with the panel that opened into my aunt's workroom. "I just dropped by to see Aunt Celeste."

He handed the woman a large bag, then stepped in front of me to block my way. "She asked that she not be disturbed."

That meant she was showing a special selection of jewelry to a carefully vetted, cash-paying customer. Someone who was allergic to dogs. Her assistant, of course, knew nothing about that side of her business. "Will she be long?"

He turned his back and began to rearrange the handbag shelf. "I don't know. Shall I give her a message?"

I couldn't put my finger on it, but something didn't feel right. "I'll run a little farther, then come back."

I jogged toward Boulevard Saint-Germaine. Half a minute later, Aunt Celeste was coming toward me, walking arm in arm with a man twice her size, a tall, square-shouldered, square-jawed man with thick black hair. It was the same man who'd greeted André Dubillard at the Darwin Centre the day he'd posed as a building inspector and checked to see if Honoré actually worked there. Raphael Aragon, Darwin Centre manager, part-owner, and security expert.

He and Aunt Celeste looked like a pair right out of an old black and white movie. Holding a large umbrella to protect her from the rain, he bent toward her and said something that made her gaze up at him and laugh.

WTF? Short of breath, slightly dizzy, I pivoted and pretended to peer into the window of a beauty salon. I didn't think they'd seen me, but my aunt stopped beside me, rested a hand on my arm, and said, "Hello, darling. May I present Raphael Aragon?"

I turned and tried to smile, but couldn't. "*Enchantée.*" I couldn't speak another word. I could barely get that one out.

He bowed. "*Enchanté,* Chloe Duval."

I glared at my aunt. "Your assistant said you were busy." Rude, but I couldn't help it.

She restrained her smile, but her dark eyes sparkled. "And so I am."

I felt betrayed. What was she hiding from me? I blurted out a curt "see you later" and ran until my clothes were drenched inside and out. She had never given me any reason to mistrust her, and sooner or later, she would tell me about her relationship with Aragon. Of course she would. At her own time. But no matter how hard I tried, no matter what I told myself, that awful sick feeling stuck with me.

By the time I returned to my apartment building, I had pushed Aunt Celeste and Raphael Aragon out of my mind. I had work to do and I needed to get on with it. I rummaged in the recycle bin in the room at the back of the foyer and found a copy of Sunday's *Paris Today*. It had exactly what I'd hoped for—a whole page of photos of Count Maxime's daughter's wedding.

Back in my apartment, I scanned for photo credits and found them in the tiniest imaginable font at the bottom of one taken the moment Maxime draped the bride's veil over her face. The helicopter stood by in the background as the four flower girls adjusted her train. The address was www.WeDoWeddings.com.

I copied the website address and sent it via text to André. He sent a note back:

—*Shall I assume you want to see all the photos of the wedding?*—

—*You shall.*—

I thought maybe "shall" was bad grammar, but I

couldn't figure out what would be better, so I left it. I pored over the write-up and photos in the magazine until five o'clock. By that time, the grey, gloomy clouds that hung around the top of the Eiffel Tower had sucked up all the daylight and I had found nothing helpful. Maybe I was crazy to think I could prove I wasn't guilty of Ivanov's death. I needed help. I needed to be with my friends.

I turned on every light in my apartment and put on some 1930's and 40's jazz. Then I showered, plaited my still-damp hair in a single French braid, and pulled on my new wide-legged pants and matching black-pinstripe-on-copper jacket with wide lapels and a nipped-in waist. The hope was that donning the latest fashion would give me the illusion that I had some control over my life.

Chapter Twenty

Half a second after I walked in the back door at *Chez Gaspard*, I was sorry I'd arrived early. The ever-passionate-about-bagpipes Robbie Gaspard had three students, two girls and a boy, aged eleven to thirteen. He marched around the restaurant, up the aisle between booths upholstered in elegant black and gold striped fabric, down between the wood-paneled bar and a row of tables, then up the aisle again. He piped heartily and banged his feet down rhythmically on the scratched and scraped but polished wood floor, keeping the beat: one, two, three, four. As if he were the Pied Piper, his pupils followed, their instruments screeching, bleating, and occasionally hitting the same note at the same time, and once in a while putting a foot where it belonged when it belonged there. I shut my ears with my fingers.

Robbie grinned and waved a hand toward the bar. He didn't have to do it twice. I fixed a kir royal, and by the time I'd consumed half a glass, the noise sounded sort of musical, so I leaned on the bar and watched. The kids, still in their white school shirts and plaid skirts and pants, were so deadly serious that I couldn't help tapping the bar in time and thinking it would be nice to be a kid again.

They left via the front door amid Robbie's admonishments to protect their instruments from the pelting rain outside. Seconds later, André and Aunt

Celeste entered through the back door and traipsed down the hall past the restrooms. Baguette peeked out of Aunt Celeste's red cape. She bent over to set him on the floor. André took her cape and shook the rain off. Baguette begged to be picked up, but as soon as I complied, he wanted to get down and check out the treat Robbie had put beside a bowl of water. I sent Aunt Celeste my "we-must-talk" look.

She kissed my cheeks, then stepped back and held both of my hands. "Darling, you must not worry."

That was about as reassuring as one of those Bible tracts that people used to hand out when the biggest church in Sterling, Washington held revival meetings and invited everyone to attend. The message was simple: believe and you will be fine.

I hung back behind the others as they migrated to the kitchen. I needed a moment. I didn't know why. I just did.

In the kitchen, Robbie's eight-burner range gave off a pleasant warmth. He dragged barstools to the gleaming stainless-steel work counter that stood in the middle of the room, then opened the giant refrigerator. "Okay," he said, "bring me up to speed. What do we need to do to get this Constable Hubble off Chloe's back? Do I need to woo her with my Gallic charm?"

"As if." As Aunt Celeste helped him set out platters and dishes, she swatted him with a stalk of celery. "We need to figure out who killed Petar Ivanov, you idiot."

Robbie threw an arm around my shoulders and pulled me in for a hug. "And so we shall, lass. Rest assured. We shall."

Together, they added a filet of poached salmon and a tray of pastries to the array of spring vegetables already on the counter while I found plates, napkins, and utensils, and André connected his laptop to a large screen. We filled our plates and pulled our bar stools close beside him.

André tapped on his keyboard. "I should have been able to get into the coroner's report, but I've been blocked. So, I haven't been able to find out what killed him or the exact time of death. But Chloe saw Ivanov at the pre-wedding cocktail party, so we know he was alive then."

Aunt Celeste raised her eyebrows at me.

I said, "And he was dead before the wedding was over."

Robbie gazed at the others for a moment. "Huh. It appears I'm the last to know. But okay."

André tapped some more. "I got into the wedding photographer's database and copied all his photos. So, let's figure out the last time Ivanov showed up in a picture and note what time it was, who was nearby, and what was going on around him."

"But first—" I held up the photo of the woman in the strapless black dress, then handed it around—"take a good look. Her name is Lili Jensen. According to one of the servers at *Cochon Qui Rit*, Count Maxime de Charpentier has a couple of fixers. I think she may be his favorite so let's especially watch for her. Also, I believe Count Maxime and Ivanov were close in the past, but something happened about two years ago that created a rift. We should watch for interactions between them.

"Okay," André said. "Let's do this. Everything from the photographer's database is time-stamped and in chronological order. Before the ceremony began, the camera was on a boom above the crowd, so you can see most of what's going on. During the ceremony, the focus is pretty tight on the wedding party, so we won't find much there."

"One more thing," I said. "Honoré St. Lazarre was there, dressed as a waiter, and I saw him this morning with Stan Gibson, the guy from the FBI, watching my interrogation."

Aunt Celeste raised her eyebrows, as if genuinely surprised.

"Are you worried about that, lass?" Robbie said.

"Yes. No. I'm done with him. I really don't want to talk about it. Just watch for him. Gibson, too."

André began to scroll through the photos, then paused. "There are five hundred and fifty-seven of them. At this rate, it will take forever to see them all. So, if they're not relevant, say 'skip,' and when you see anything that looks important, say 'save.'"

For nearly an hour, we all stared at the screen, calling out "skip" or "save." I wondered what the expressions on Honoré's and Gibson's faces might tell me, but the photographer had never captured them in the same frame.

By the time we finished, André had saved thirty-six photos and I thought my eyes were going to cross permanently. We all stood up and stretched.

Robbie handed out espresso, then we sat back down and looked at those we'd saved. The most interesting one focused on Count Maxime. He was pointing up at the helicopter bringing the bride, but the interesting part was that in the background, Lili Jensen, possibly one of his fixers, pushed Ivanov's wheelchair toward the door of the château. The time stamp read 6:54 P.M.

"This is it," I said. "The last photo containing

Ivanov; look who he's with."

The next one we'd saved was taken five minutes later, at 6:59 when Maxime lifted his daughter from the helicopter to the ground. Neither Lili Jensen nor Ivanov were there, but she showed up again two minutes later, at 7:01, coming out of the château alone as the other guests filed into the rows of white chairs festooned with bows and Maxime escorted the bride up the path from the helicopter.

"As far as we can tell, she was off-stage for seven minutes," Aunt Celeste said, "between the time she pushed Ivanov in and when she came out alone. Time enough to kill him, but a little tight for disposing of the body. So, if she's our murderer, she must have had help, which means they planned it. It was not a crime of passion."

I shuddered. It must have been about 7:20 when I saw him, less than half an hour after she pushed his wheelchair into the château and possibly killed him. If I had touched him, he would still have been warm.

"You think this Lili Jensen's the murderer?" Robbie sounded skeptical. "A woman?"

Aunt Celeste's eyebrows went up. "Why not? Think black widow."

André said, "Your Zachary's friends are not nice people, sweet pea."

I cringed. "He's not *my* Zachary." Even though, if I'd been honest with myself, while floating around the dance floor, I'd been tempted. I leaned my head on my hands and closed my eyes. "I need to take a break."

I had to get away. They were doing their best to help me, but seriously, we couldn't prove anything. It had stopped raining, so I fastened a lead to Baguette's collar and, wine glass in hand, took him out into the fresh breeze to a tiny patch of grass and weeds beside Robbie's service entrance.

When I came back, André had opened a second file. "I've saved the best for last," he said. "It's grainy and a little dim, but good stuff. A video I downloaded from the Metro's security company's database. Apparently, Ivanov's attacker hit him in a CCTV blind spot, so we can't see who did it, but here goes."

On the screen, Ivanov's head and torso tumbled into view, and landed upside down on the steps, just the way I'd seen him. The camera caught my back as I approached the bottom of the stairway. An officer, the one who prevented me from approaching, rushed down the stairs toward me, holding up both hands. His face was obscured by his uniform cap, but he was tall and blonde, and in my gut, I knew.

"That isn't a man. It's Lili Jensen." Then we saw the top of my head as I turned and hustled away, my leopard print coat streaming out behind me. André backed the video up and froze it on the officer.

We all leaned in close and squinted at the screen. Aunt Celeste and André agreed with me. It looked like Lili. Robbie wasn't sure, although he conceded, "It does look like her." He patted my shoulder. "Along with the photo of her pushing the wheelchair, it could be good evidence. I think you should take it to your constable."

"I don't think so. That's clearly me in the next frame. I could be running away. Besides, undoubtedly, Constable Hubble has already seen it." No wonder she thought she could pin the murder on me. I'd had big hopes for this meeting with our *Société* but things were getting worse.

I wanted to stick my head under a pillow and shut everything out, but we pored over the video André's drone had taken at the Saint Francis Hotel, especially the party on the terrace of the penthouse suites. Zachary Le Noir and Petar Ivanov were both there, Ivanov bundled in a wheelchair, his leg elevated. Count Maxime, Lili Jensen, and about twenty other people milled about. André froze a frame of Ivanov talking to Maxime. Ivanov had raised his good hand in the unmistakable gesture of contempt. Maxime, arms crossed on chest, sneered back at him.

It proved nothing, but this was my only hope. That I could dig into their past and find a motive for murder.

Chapter Twenty-One

I should have been a big enough person to respect the fact that Aunt Celeste had a life of her own. But the minute I saw her walking arm in arm with Raphael Aragon, I knew they weren't just friends. One does not look at "just an old friend" the way they looked at each other. Why had she lied?

I could understand her not wanting to share everything with me. But I'd told her André Dubillard was going to go to the Darwin Centre posing as a city building inspector, and later found out that her just-an-old-friend Raphael partly owned it. Why hadn't she told me she knew him? And that he was part owner?

I tried to believe she had a good reason. Maybe she didn't know he was part owner. But what if she did? What if she told Raphael about our ploy? And what if Honoré St. Lazarre's claim that he worked at Darwin Centre was an alibi—a lie? All they had to do was put Honoré's name on an office door and a mailbox. And I, thinking how clever I was, had taken the name plates as proof that Honoré did indeed work there.

I was an idiot. Not that it mattered, since I'd broken up with him. I sighed. No matter what I told myself, seeing Aunt Celeste beaming away at Raphael Aragon as if she were a mouse and he were a giant wedge of gorgonzola made me no ordinary idiot. I had turned into an angry, resentful, suspicious idiot.

I wanted her to tell me I was wrong, that she hadn't told him André would come, posing as a building inspector. I wanted her to reassure me, as she always did. But on the way home from Robbie Gaspard's restaurant, when we were alone in the taxi, when she could have told me, she said not a word, and I couldn't bring myself to ask her. On top of everything else, it was just too much.

****

Perhaps if I believed in praying, I could have fallen asleep. The lights on the Eiffel Tower had gone out hours earlier, and my eyes were still open. I couldn't stand to see the tower so dark and quiet, so I got up and for the first time ever, drew the drapes across the window and shut it out. Baguette snuffled around in his bed, as if he, too, was having a hard time sleeping.

I climbed back in, rolled onto my side, and reached across for Honoré's pillow. I hugged it to me and inhaled his cinnamon-citrus scent. Honoré St. Lazarre. I tried to shut them out, but his name still rolled around in my brain; six short syllables with their own sweet rhythm.

****

Baguette's toenails pattering across the parquet floor as he pranced back and forth from his bed to mine woke me up. My room was so dark I thought it was the middle of the night, but my clock read 10:00 A.M. Poor Baguette. His bladder had to be ready to burst.

I pulled on a pair of tights and a big sweater. Normally, by ten o'clock, he would have been upstairs with Aunt Celeste, and I'd have been driving Poppy into her tiny garage at Rhineland Bankgruppe. My boss's face, purple with anger, his jowls quivering, popped into my mind, and I shoved it back out. I didn't need that memory. I didn't need him. Or his lousy investment group. I'd had offers of other jobs. Jobs that paid better.

I snapped a lead onto Baguette's collar, opened the door, and stumbled over a huge red and white bouquet that sat right outside. I reached for the card, but Baguette tugged, so I left it there and hustled to the elevator.

When I returned fifteen minutes later, the bouquet was gone and my door stood open. Aunt Celeste was in the kitchen. She'd filled Baguette's dish, made coffee in the French press, and was adding water to the vase of flowers. "You left your door unlocked, darling." She handed me a cup of coffee, then lifted the vase out of the sink and set it on the drainboard. "Who's it from?"

I sipped my coffee. "First, I have a question. Why didn't you tell me?"

"Tell you—?" Her eyebrows went up. "Ahh! Raphael Aragon." Her smile could have melted a Greenland iceberg.

Even the cold block of fear in my chest thawed a bit. I couldn't help smiling back. "I've never seen you blush before." Seriously, she looked like a schoolgirl with her first crush.

She grabbed the vase of red roses, baby's breath, and white chrysanthemums and thrust it at me. "For now, just know that he helped me trace my grandparents and find out what happened to them in WW II. That was years ago, and we've been friends ever since."

I sucked in a breath.

She held up a hand. "Another time, darling, I'll tell you the whole story." She stood on tiptoes and kissed my cheek. "Now, these posies are quite stunning, and I'm dying to know who sent them."

Feeling like a kid who'd been patted on the head, I bit my tongue and carried the flowers to the coffee table.

I was still pretty miffed, but we perched side by side on the edge of the sofa, and I pulled the little white card out of the holder. It read, "Meet me at your office at noon today. Zachary Le Noir."

My phone vibrated with an incoming text from my boss's assistant: "Please telephone at your earliest convenience." He'd sent two identical messages earlier, and when I checked my call log, he'd been phoning every fifteen minutes for the last two hours. Fortunately, my phone was in silent mode.

I handed it to Aunt Celeste, who read the text. She lifted her coffee cup. "Don't cut your nose off to spite your face, darling." She winked at me over the rim of her cup, then gave my phone back to me.

I rolled my eyes but dialed the office. Two rings. Then a couple of clicks. The call had transferred automatically to my boss. "Ah, Mademoiselle Duval. Thank you for calling in." Monsieur Fischer sounded as smooth as if he were schmoozing a prospective client. "Your client, Zachary Le Noir, insists that I bring you back to manage his portfolio. I shall send my car for you at 11:30. Please be prepared."

My hand was shaking. "Prepared?" I struggled to catch my breath. "What, exactly, should I be prepared for?" 11:30 was a little more than an hour away, and I wasn't going to be prepared for anything by then.

"Hem. Ah. My driver will bring you here. I shall escort you to your office. You will have access to Monsieur Le Noir's account. Hem. You will perform whatever service he requires. Hem. Ah. I shall escort you back to my car, and my driver will deliver you home."

"I'm sorry, Monsieur Fischer. That does not work for me." As soon as I said that, I felt calm. I had regained control of my life. Not all of it. But part.

"Monsieur Le Noir's account is important to Rhineland Bankgruppe. I shall make it worth your while."

"I'm sorry, Monsieur Fischer. I understand that you want to retain his account, but I can't agree to those terms. Have a pleasant day." I pressed the red button, tossed the phone onto the coffee table, and grabbed my coffee cup. "Aunt Celeste, I need to shower. I'll be fast. Then let's go to the *Cochon Qui Rit*."

****

At the *Cochon*, we sat up at the bar, and Désirée Bellepont, the server who once worked for Count Maxime de Charpentier, brought our croissants and coffee, along with freshly squeezed orange juice. I showed her the photo of Lili Jensen. "Do you recognize her?"

Désirée glared. "She's the one." She stabbed a finger at it. "She's as cold as your tits at the North Pole. No one has ever proved anything, but I know for a fact she's the count's enforcer—one of them—his favorite. If she has a single grain of good in her, it's lonely."

"What has she done?"

Désirée shivered. "Even in here, it's not safe to tell you." She turned and hurried toward the kitchen.

I left a generous tip. Outside again, in the spring sunlight, Aunt Celeste and Baguette headed off to her shop.

I pulled my phone out of my pocket and called the number Constable Hubble had given me. It went straight to voice mail, so I hung up. Then I noticed two calls from her, so I hailed a cab and went to her office. For once, I wasn't shunted off to the interrogation room, but sent down a long, shadowy hall to her office, which was small, dark, and cluttered.

She had two cardboard boxes on her desk and was busy putting pencils, pens, and notepads in one. "I'm leaving. I phoned to tell you today is my last day." Her lips curved in a wide smile. "From now on, you will be speaking to Constable Graham. She is taking over the case."

For a moment, I didn't know what to say, so I just stood there, gaping at her. She glanced up from her task. "I'm not cut out for this work. I'm no good at it, and luckily, I've inherited a tea shoppe on the coast near Bordeaux."

I could see her in a little shop crowded with lace-covered tables and full of flowery tea pots, delicate cups and saucers, shortbread cookies, blueberry muffins, and chocolate opera cakes. She looked so motherly. I plopped into the chair beside her desk. "May I talk to you then?"

She cleared a pile of clean, folded uniforms off her chair and perched on the edge of it. "Of course. You must know that I can't tell you anything, but you can talk to me."

I told her Désirée Bellepont had recognized one of Count Maxime de Charpentier's thugs and that he followed Petar Ivanov out of the *Cochon Qui Rit* the night he was attacked in the Metro station. I showed her the photograph of Lili Jensen and told her I felt certain I'd seen Lili posing as a Metro police officer on the Metro CCTV the same night, and that Désirée had identified her as the count's favorite fixer. I said I had photographic evidence that Lili had pushed Petar Ivanov's wheelchair into the château just before the wedding and returned alone several minutes later.

She leaned back in her chair and gazed at me in silence for a full minute, then reached for Lili Jensen's photo. "If I may, I'll make a copy and pass it on to Constable Graham. And send me the other photo, too."

"Of course." I handed it to her. She tapped it on the desk, turned it over in her hands, tapped it again, then got up and closed the door. "Don't expect too much."

I felt the blood drain from my face. "What do you mean?"

"Murder is serious, of course, and the job of the Gendarmerie is to investigate the death of Petar Ivanov. But there is another investigation going on, with much more at stake, at least in the point of view of some people, and that takes precedence over everything else." She sighed and rubbed a hand over her eyes. "I have to agree that it's big. It's important. Interpol and several other international agencies are involved." She leaned toward me and spoke very softly. "If you mention this to anyone outside this room, I shall deny telling you, but this investigation has hindered me; made it difficult for me to do my job."

"Do you believe I killed him?"

"I can't say."

"Where does that leave me?"

She gazed at me as if weighing her response. "You haven't been charged." She picked up the stack of uniforms and started toward the door, then smiled and motioned for me to go ahead of her. "My advice is this, Mademoiselle Duval: get on with your life. Perhaps you will visit my tearoom when you are in Bordeaux."

Chapter Twenty-Two

I returned to my apartment, but didn't feel like going in. My feet wandered across the street and into the broad, green Champs de Mars while my mind wandered to the Queen of Persia ring. I'd been totally distracted by the murder and my terror over being treated as a suspect.

I plopped down on a bench in the sun and watched the steady stream of ant-sized figures, tourists with not a care in the world, climb up and down the stairs of the Eiffel Tower. Ants don't let obstacles in their path stop them. They find a way around and keep on, at their steady pace, heading toward their goal.

So why was I sitting in the park in the middle of the day? I needed to stop looking over my shoulder. I needed to stop worrying that a meaty hand would clamp onto me and drag me off to jail. Constable Hubble was right. I needed to get on with my life.

I needed figure out what had happened to the Queen of Persia. When Petar Ivanov died, someone had taken it. Who? And where was it now? I'd go for a long run, let my subconscious mull everything over. I started toward my apartment.

The gleaming English antique car with the mile-long hood, stood on the sidewalk in front of the building, a uniformed chauffeur at the wheel. Beside it, Zachary Le Noir paced back and forth. He turned and strode toward me, his steps long and purposeful. I met him in the middle of the street.

He took my arm and tried to hustle me toward the car. "It's way past noon. Let's go."

I stopped, pushed his hand off my arm, and took a step back. "It's nice to see you again, too."

"Look." He scowled at me. "You should be thanking me. I spoke with Monsieur Fischer and insisted on having you manage my portfolio. He finally agreed to allow you to do that, and he is waiting to see us."

"How utterly wonderful of you."

The chauffeur pulled the car up beside us and stopped. Zachary opened the door and motioned for me to climb into the back seat. "This is important. I need to transfer some funds as soon as possible."

I shook my head and crossed my arms on my chest. My phone vibrated in my pocket. I pulled it out and looked at it. Monsieur Fischer. He had to be desperate to hang onto Zachary. I pressed the green button.

"Hem. Ah. Hem. Mademoiselle Duval, please come to the office. We must talk."

Not only did I have two other standing job offers, but I had a fat bank account, thanks to the emerald pendant set in platinum I found on my Christmas trip to the Saint Francis Hotel. "*Désolée*, Monsieur Fischer. We have nothing to talk about. I'm not going to return, not for even one minute, unless you apologize for treating me the way you did *and* reinstate me with all the privileges I had, including my corner office, *and* raise my salary to meet the one I've been offered at Bancraft's." I pressed the red button and tucked the phone in my pocket.

I missed my job—the stimulation, the excitement of the living, breathing entity that was the stock market, the challenge of buying and selling at the right moment, the gratification of seeing my clients' steadily increasing account balances. And my biggest client ever was standing in front of me frowning, unhappy with me for not jumping to meet his wishes just because he snapped his fingers. But I didn't care.

I turned my palms up and shrugged. "*Désolée*, Monsieur Le Noir. I can't go back unless Monsieur Fischer agrees to my terms."

Zachary turned to his chauffeur, who stood, holding the rear door open. "Go." He waved a hand, as if to shoo him away. "I will be in touch."

"Now, Mademoiselle Duval." He offered his arm. "If you won't help me, would you be willing to walk with me?" His smile looked strained, and I felt a small pang of sympathy for him. He and his cousin had been close. No matter what Petar Ivanov had done or what sort of person he was, he didn't deserve to be murdered—no one did.

I tucked my hand into the warmth in the crook of his arm and we started away from the street toward the cool, green Champs de Mars. "At the wedding, you called me Chloe."

He smiled and suddenly looked his elegant, charming self again. He put his hand on top of mine and squeezed it gently. "And you called me Zachary."

I sighed.

"And I danced with the most beautiful woman at the ball."

I'd loved every second of it. Even if I shouldn't have.

We walked without speaking for several minutes, until we came to a crowd milling around a pair of jugglers riding unicycles and tossing flaming torches. He said, "Too many people here. Let's turn back." When it was quieter again, he said, "I made it clear to Monsieur Fischer that you have not been charged with a crime, that the Gendarmerie is simply investigating. He has no reason not to reinstate you."

"Except his pride."

"I have friends who could make him very uncomfortable."

"I would prefer that he bring me back on my own terms."

"I appreciate that, and I'm willing to wait, but only for a day, maybe two. However, if he does not come around, I shall make sure he regrets it."

I let go of his arm and crossed my arms on my chest. "If that is what causes him to reinstate me, I will not go back. I shall resign."

He stuffed his hands in his pockets and glared at me. "We shall see."

"We shall." I took his arm again and nudged him to continue walking. "In the meantime, tell me about your cousin. He seemed to be a friendly, fun-loving man."

"He *was* a friendly, fun-loving man. He loved practical jokes, riddles, and puzzles. And he inherited a huge estate with a lot of money, so he lived a big life. He collected thoroughbreds, cars, planes, art, and all kinds of friends."

"And you both were friends with Count Maxime, I believe."

"True."

"He must have collected at least one enemy as well."

"Obviously."

"Who?"

"It wasn't me."

"Look, I'm still being investigated. If you know something that would help convince the gendarmes I didn't do it, I'd appreciate your telling me."

He laughed. "I'm being investigated myself, and I was in plain sight all evening. I saw you sneak out of the ceremony, however, and you didn't come back until the end."

"You told the gendarmes that."

"No. Not yet."

"Is that a threat?"

"I could be persuaded to forget I saw what you did."

I knew a threat when I heard one.

Chapter Twenty-Three

So, if I didn't cave in, go to the office by the next afternoon, and do what he wanted, Zachary Le Noir would tell the gendarmes I'd skipped out of the wedding, which would imply that I could have been the one who killed his cousin. Sweet. And if I did cave in, I'd be nothing but his toady. There was no good way out. I put on my running gear and ran long and hard. And when I finished, tired and dripping with sweat, I still could see no good way out.

In fact, the only good thing was that I had an appointment to get my nails done. I showered, hopped on Poppy, and buzzed over to the *Salon de Beauté*.

I was sitting there, next to the window, with warm water swirling around my feet and a cup of ginger tea at my elbow, when a man driving a sporty little car with the top down stopped at the curb, hopped out, and breezed into the salon on a gust of cool afternoon air.

He wore a tawny knee-length coat over a black cashmere turtleneck, fine black slacks, and tasseled loafers without socks. Removing a Greek fisherman's hat, he glanced around the salon, then headed straight for me. He carried a plain cardboard box, and I knew. My heart beat faster. It wasn't just any old box.

He balanced it on the arm of my chair, but kept his hand on it. "Chloe Duval?"

I could barely breathe. "Yes. Who are you?"

"I am a messenger sent by someone you know, who instructed me to impress upon you the fact that he obtained the contents of this package while acting, not in any official capacity, but as a private person." His teal-blue eyes twinkled, and he grinned, showing even white teeth. "Do you understand?"

I gripped my hands together to keep from ripping it away from him. "May I see what's inside?"

"I take that as a yes." He placed it in my lap and walked away.

I lifted the lid and peered in. A large paper tag with an alpha-numeric code scrawled in bold black characters stared back at me. Under the tag and wired to it, neatly coiled, lay my rappelling cable.

Outside, the man was watching me through the window, one hand on the open door of the sports car, ignoring the line of traffic piling up behind him.

I blew him a kiss.

He hopped in, gave a little two-finger wave, and zoomed away. His taillights streaked around the corner.

I wanted to take the cable out and run my hands along the length of it. I wanted to hug it. I wanted to jump up and dance around the salon with it, but my aesthetician approached, warm towels in hand and curiosity all over her pretty heart-shaped face. So I put the lid on the box, smiled blandly, and sipped my tea. But I could hardly sit still. It seemed forever until my toenails were bright red again and dry.

The cable was the only significant piece of evidence Constable Hubble had been able to dredge up against me. Assuming the gendarmes found both Petar Ivanov's and my DNA on the cable, they might have been able to pin the murder on me, but without it, they didn't have a case.

The word of the chef who'd seen me come into the kitchen from the service stairway and the fact that someone had found Petar Ivanov's jacket in my apartment might have been used to further incriminate me, but alone, they were merely circumstantial.

So, who was the "someone acting as a private person, not in any official capacity?" After the morning's conversation with Constable Hubble, I suspected her, but something told me it wasn't like her to bend the rules that far.

No matter. I sent a group text to Aunt Celeste, André Dubillard, and Robbie Gaspard.

—*I have my cable back! Celebration's on me! Dinner at Robbie's!*"—

And Zachary Le Noir could just go eat worms.

Chapter Twenty-Four

Back beside Poppy, I tucked the box containing my cable into the compartment behind the seat, buckled my helmet, hopped on, and almost ran over Stan Gibson, the FBI art crime agent. Dressed in jeans and a leather bomber jacket, he stood in front of my scooter, feet planted on either side of the front tire, both hands in the air.

He was up to something, probably something I wouldn't like. Instead of paying attention to my surroundings, I'd been jabbering on my phone to Aunt Celeste about getting my cable back, so it was my own fault he'd cornered me so neatly. That made me even less happy to see him.

But what if he'd been the one who sent me my cable? I put one foot on the ground, slid my phone into my pocket, and scrubbed the scowl off my face.

"So," he said, "the grapevine has it that the cable which allegedly belonged to you has disappeared from the evidence locker."

I folded my arms on my chest. "How could that have happened?"

"It's a mystery." He grinned and came to stand beside me. "How about we go for a walk somewhere?"

Feeling certain I was making a deal with the devil, but too curious to refuse, I tipped my head toward the back of my scooter. "Hop on." I had to find out what he knew. And, sure, he was a cop, but if he'd been the one who retrieved my cable, he couldn't be all bad.

He wrapped an arm around my waist and tensed up only a couple of times as Poppy flew between lines of cars. I parked near a little botanical garden in the Marais. Just inside the gate, we came to a pond and started off on the path that ran around it. A fat white duck came to check us out and wobbled along beside us, keeping pace. I waited for Stan to speak, but he kept wandering to the edge of the path to read the names on the signs at the base of the trees and plants.

"This is lovely," he said. "Steps away from a busy street, yet peaceful and quiet."

"It is." I frowned at him. "The cable disappeared how?"

He took my hand and gave it a little squeeze. "As I said, mysteriously."

"Thanks to someone acting as a private person."

He laughed. "Exactly."

"I'd like to thank whomever it was."

"I expect that person prefers to remain anonymous."

Exasperating man!

"By the way, I could get used to holding your hand, and that is not a good idea." He lifted it to his lips and kissed my fingertips without actually touching them, then let go. "Please put it somewhere else, in your pocket, for instance."

I hoped he didn't see my smile.

We rambled on in silence and, to my surprise, I didn't mind being there beside him at all. In fact, after the tension and worry of the last few days, when our elbows bumped together, it felt good.

Farther on, we came to a couple of chess tables beside the path, one of them occupied by a white-haired man eating a sandwich and reading a newspaper. I nudged Stan. "You said you had more news."

"I do. The victim, Ivanov, wore a smart watch. It shows that his heart stopped beating at 6:57, the very moment the helicopter landed bringing the bride. One of the guests took a photo of you watching the landing with Zachary Le Noir. He handed it over yesterday when he heard you were a suspect. It's pretty clear proof that you were not the killer."

"Why didn't someone tell me?"

"I just did."

"Stan Gibson, you could have told me right away."

"I thought you liked suspense."

I held my breath until the desire to punch him in the nose passed. "What I don't get is how he came to be bound with a cable that allegedly belonged to me."

Stan shrugged. "When they found him in the cellar, he was lying on his side, but his blood had pooled in his back. That means he lay on his back for at least two hours, possibly longer, after he died."

A vision of Ivanov staring up out of the trunk in the treasure room flashed into my mind.

"Where he was during that interval remains a mystery. But it makes sense. The caterer's staff was all over the kitchen and cellar when he died. They would have noticed if someone had dragged in a dead body, so he had to be stashed somewhere else and transferred to the cold room after they closed the kitchen for the night. And for my money, the only reason to truss him up with your cable was to frame you for murder."

A chill crept over me. "I think you're right."

"I believe I am. Therefore, I think it's only fair and just that it was returned to you."

Tears crept into my eyes. "Thank you."

He leaned toward me and dropped his voice. "If it were me and I wanted to hide a body temporarily, I'd lock it up somewhere, say, in a well-protected, secure room, until I was ready to move it." He raised his eyebrows and wagged his head back and forth a couple of times. "I wonder if you might have any ideas about that."

My heart rate kicked up. Even if he had been the one to retrieve my cable, I couldn't let my guard down. "The château is huge." We'd reached a children's play area, and I stopped as if to watch a handful of kids jumping on and off the swings and slide while I decided what to say. "I imagine there are a number of places the body could have been hidden."

He stood beside me, hands in the pockets of his jacket, his tone casual. "Just between you and me, several facts lead me to believe you know more than you pretend. I have not shared them with anyone else, nor will I."

"What! There's something you didn't tell Constable Hubble? An upright lawman withholding evidence?"

"Not."

I was dying to ask what facts he was talking about. But that was probably a bad idea, so I resumed walking, faster this time, toward a gazebo waiting for a string quartet or a flock of oboes to set up and start playing.

He fell in beside me. "If I thought it would help solve the murder, I would tell the gendarmes, but I think they're irrelevant to that case, and if the word gets out, it will hinder my own investigation."

I couldn't stand it any longer. "You can tell me. My lips are sealed."

"I thought so. My team found clothing fibers, the

same blue as the unitard you were wearing when I met you on the roof, on one of the archers' slits in the château's east tower. They had not been exposed to the elements very long, so I think it's safe to say you left them there, which leads me to believe you got inside the tower. Secondly, although none of us were small enough to squeeze through those narrow slits, we put a camera through a couple of them and photographed footprints in the dust."

"Why would you go to all that trouble if it has nothing to do with the murder?"

"Murder is not my problem. My job is to track down perpetrators of international cultural art trafficking. Rumor has it Count Maxime de Charpentier has a secret room containing many stolen items, all extremely valuable, in that tower."

I stared straight ahead. "I wouldn't know. As I keep telling you, I was merely practicing rappelling."

"I believe you do know."

"How? How would I know? If he does have a treasure room there, you can be sure it has a darn good alarm system, one that would be difficult to circumvent."

"There's one more fact I find interesting: Exactly fourteen minutes before I found you on the roof, someone switched the château's security cameras off and looped all the surveillance video feeds to make it look as if it was working."

I gave him the big eyes and shrugged. "I have no idea how anyone would do that."

"You know someone who does, and I have to say, my hat is off to him. He figured out we were onto him and backed out of the system, covering his tracks as he went, and remained undetected. If Raphael Greenbank

Aragon couldn't catch him, then he's good."

Raphael Aragon! Aunt Celeste's old friend. I couldn't repress a little gasp.

"There are only two or three people in Europe who could have recognized and avoided Aragon's search. I'm guessing it's your friend André Dubillard." He gazed at me for a long moment.

I shrugged again. "You suspect everyone. It's an occupational hazard."

Stan grinned and his eyes sparkled. He was playing cat and mouse and enjoying it. "For my money, you had just enough time to get in, grab a couple of trinkets, and get out."

"My unitard fits like my skin. You saw it. It's impossible to hide anything."

"So you got in but didn't take anything."

Damn! I should have kept quiet.

Grinning, he wandered to side of the path to read the label at the base of a bush before continuing on. "This is a lovely park, but, look, we've walked all the way through, and I've worked up a powerful thirst." He gestured toward the street. "How about we find a place to sit? I'll buy you a glass of wine."

Now what? He was up to something. "Make it champagne and I'll agree."

"Done." He opened the gate, then followed me out of the fresh, green oasis onto the asphalt; into the noise and bustle. "I have a story to tell you." He gazed at the cars backed up into the intersection and pedestrians snaking between them, then pointed at a café on the other side of the street and raised his eyebrows.

I nodded, blew a kiss at the driver who stopped and waited for us, and jogged across, keeping pace with his long strides. We settled in a patch of spring sunshine, side by side at a little round table with our backs to the windowed wall of the bistro. I unfastened the buttons on my coat and loosened my scarf.

After he'd taken a sip of his Bordeaux and I'd tasted my champagne, I prompted him. "You have a story to tell."

He nodded. "Once upon a time, an ancient ring featuring the Queen of Persia diamond resided in Alexander's Museum of Antiquities in Istanbul." I could feel him looking at me. "A clever thief stole it and replaced it with a replica, a very fine replica," he murmured. "So fine, the museum didn't realize the original had been stolen until your friend Zachary Le Noir and his cousin sued them, claiming it was among a group of family heirlooms stolen from their ancestors during the Turkish occupation of Bulgaria in the 1800's. The museum offered a significant reward for the return of the ring, and a recovery agent retrieved it from a wine cellar in the little town of Sterling, Washington."

My hands tightened into fists. *Damn you all the way to hell, Stan Gibson!*

"For a time, based on surveillance videos, Celeste Bertrand seemed the most likely thief, although it didn't fit her profile, but now we have reason to believe it was you."

Cat and mouse. I could hardly breathe. The cat was about to pounce. "I think you have an overactive imagination." I stifled the urge to run to Poppy and ride as fast and as far as I could.

He laughed, took a sip of wine, then threw his head back and laughed some more. "The agent took it to the museum but was intercepted by a thug posing as an employee and knocked senseless. The ring disappeared again and only recently turned up."

I forced myself to sit still and keep my hands open on the table. "How intriguing."

"There's more. The evening of the wedding, Petar Ivanov wore that ring, but when they found him the next morning, it had been replaced by a different replica, a cheaper one this time." He squinted his eyes and wagged his head back and forth, and kind of raised his eyebrows at the same time.

There was nothing I could say. If I'd spoken, I'd have lost.

He said, "It would have fit nicely in that tool belt you wore."

"I don't know whether you're implying I found him and took it from his finger or that I would exchange the ring he was wearing for a cheap replica, but I assure you, neither of those things is true." Unfortunately, because I was going to have to find it again.

"I knew you were going to be good." He tapped the back of my hand with one finger a couple of times. "I have a job I'd like you to consider."

"I don't need a job, and I'm getting tired of telling you—I was merely practicing rappelling."

"Then let me give you some advice. You're flirting with danger. These guys, your friend Zachary Le Noir, Count Maxime de Charpentier, and the now deceased Petar Ivanov, play or played in a tough, cut-throat league with enormous stakes. Namely, they traffic in stolen art and cultural treasures. Priceless, irreplaceable one-of-a-kind pieces of art. It's no big surprise that one of them is dead."

"Zachary Le Noir is not my friend. He is my client

at Rhineland Bankgruppe, and he invited me to the wedding as his guest. Period. I'm neither working with them nor playing with them."

"You may not think they're cultivating you, but they are."

I shrugged. "You may think whatever you like."

"Why do you think Petar Ivanov was at the *Cochon Qui Rit*, flaunting the Queen of Persia in your face? Why were you invited to attend the wedding as the guest of his cousin, the charming Le Noir?"

I pulled in a breath. "My client needed a date."

He held up a hand. "Spare me your lies, Chloe Eugenie Duval. You played along. I'm guessing it was your intention to get your hands on the Queen of Persia ring. That's why you jumped up and followed them from the *Cochon Qui Rit*."

"Who told you I followed them?"

"I have sources."

Honoré St. Lazarre. Of course. My taxi driver. Stan's sidekick. Hah! Honoré was probably following them, and I'd blundered right into his cab.

Stan said, "And, sure, the wedding was a spectacular social event that anyone would want to attend, but it was a way to suck you in. That's how they operate." He gazed at me for a moment. "I'm willing to bet Ivanov wanted you to do just one little thing for them."

I held out my wrists. "So you're going to arrest me?"

"Nope. My jurisdiction begins and ends with transportation of stolen goods in or out of the United States. I assume that at some point, you did transport the ring in question across the US border, but I don't have the resources to prove that, nor do I want to. The fact is, I don't care about it. Lovely as she is, she's relatively small potatoes, and so far, you don't present much of a threat."

I sat up straight. "That's kind of insulting." I frowned at him. "What's your point?"

"First of all, I don't want you to get hurt, so I'm warning you to steer clear. Thugs, thieves, and ruthless killers come in all shapes and sizes. Both Count Maxime de Charpentier and Zachary Le Noir have plenty of them to do their dirty work, and they'd all rather scoff at the law than eat breakfast."

He was trying to scare me onto the straight and narrow. "Well, whoop-dee-freakin'-do."

"Listen." He pursed his lips and gazed at me for a long moment. "Illicit trafficking of cultural treasures is a huge business. The grim reality is that it's not just a game. Not only is it a lucrative trade for relatively civilized collectors, but it finances a lot of terrorist activities. Many, too many, innocent people get killed."

"And?"

"I'm part of a work force that is far too small and underpaid to be able to stop them or recover even a fraction of stolen goods. That's why no one can afford to spend their time on the Queen of Persia ring, for instance, however much you value it. We have bigger fish to fry. By default, we must stick to things that are big enough to merit the time and energy."

"You're telling me this because?"

"I'm hoping I can convince you to play on my team. I was this close—" he held up his thumb and forefinger, half an inch apart "—to getting my hands on a statue worth more than ten million dollars and thereby exposing a ring of criminals of the worst sort." He got out his phone, pulled up a photo, and handed it to me.

It was a picture I'd seen on one of my news feeds several months earlier. "This was stolen from that museum in New Orleans."

"Correct."

"It's lovely." A tiny model of a trebuchet, a medieval war machine capable of hurling large rocks long distances, it had been beautifully crafted in gold and decorated with sapphires and diamonds. "Does it work?"

"It does. See the little balls in the trough at the bottom? Six more or less round, absolutely priceless Burmese rubies. That's the ammunition. If he hadn't been killed, I would have been able to prove Ivanov had it in his possession, and I and my European colleagues could have rounded up the lot of them."

"And somebody figured out you were onto him. And that's why he got bumped off."

"I suspect so."

I repressed a shiver. "I should care because?"

"This is just one problem among many. You have abilities I lack, and the good guys could use your help. We need your skillset." He did that thing where he squinted his eyes and wagged his head back and forth, and kind of raised his eyebrows at the same time, which was really pretty cute—for a cop. Then he stood up and placed a twenty-euro bill on the table. "Think about it."

Chapter Twenty-Five

I watched Stan Gibson stroll away. That bomber jacket showed off his buns in their tight jeans, and they weren't bad—for a cop. Huh! Who knew?

He hadn't finished his wine or held my hand again or anything. Huh! "Don't play in that league," he says. Then, "Help the good guys," he says. So his goal was to entice me to steal some priceless cultural artifact that could land me in jail for a very long time. Like, snatch an ancient ten-million-dollar war machine replica from the very same gang of cut-throats he warns me not to play with.

My phone vibrated in my pocket. Again. I pulled it out. Rhineland Bankgruppe's number blinked at me, and before I could think about it, I pressed the green button. I heard a couple of clicks, and my boss, himself, answered. "Hem. Good afternoon, Mademoiselle Duval." No warmth in his tone. But polite as ever.

"Monsieur Fischer."

"Mademoiselle, would you be willing to come to the office and, hem, ah, talk about reinstatement here at Rhineland Bankgruppe?" The man didn't know how to be impolite. Even when he was cutting you off at the shins, he was polite.

I wanted my job back. Absolutely. But he'd insulted me. He'd cast doubt on my integrity. He'd dismissed me without listening to my side of the story. He hadn't cared what firing me did to my equanimity and self-esteem. I stifled the childish urge to mimic his hems and ahs. "I could do that, monsieur."

"Very soon, then. Right away, if possible. If you would be so good." He sounded almost humble.

Amazing! The old dear was practically apologizing. "I can be there in about an hour."

I caught the waiter's eye as he hurried past, his long white apron flapping about his knees, and ordered *crème brulée* to go with the rest of my champagne. For once, I didn't care that it packed too many calories for the food value it contained. I just wanted to taste it and savor the silky, creamy custard on my tongue. Of course, by the time it came, I had to order another glass of champagne to go with it.

Not my normal happy hour, but this was not a normal day. I needed to talk to the boss who'd fired me without considering the facts, and I needed to be mellow enough to do it without saying something snotty and sarcastic.

I drove Poppy up to the gate to the Rhineland Bankgruppe building and pressed the button on Poppy's handlebar, betting it wouldn't work, but the gate swung open. So, he'd reinstated my access code. Or his assistant had forgotten to revoke it. Whatever. Thanks to two glasses of champagne, it wasn't important. I idled in and waited for the gate to close behind me. Poppy's little garage was still there, at the far end of the parking area, but, with a certain sense of triumph, I took the space closest to the door, one reserved for the company's well-heeled customers' luxury sedans. I would have taken it if it had been the middle of the day.

It was a little after five o'clock when I strode into

the reception area, removed my helmet, and tucked it under my arm. The place was dead silent. Everyone had gone home except my boss, who stood at the entrance to his office. He motioned me to step inside, then followed me in and closed the door.

Perhaps I shouldn't have been surprised to see Zachary lounging in one of the deep leather armchairs facing the desk, one ankle resting on the opposite knee. I nodded. "Monsieur Le Noir. How nice to see you." Not.

He gazed at me with a self-satisfied smirk, as if to say, "You may thank me."

His promise to make my boss regret firing me had come across loud and clear. "If this is your doing, I'm leaving right now." I glared at him.

Monsieur Fischer stood behind his desk and crossed his arms on his chest, looking as if it pained him, but he was determined to rise above our quarrel. "I, and I alone, have made this choice."

Zachary grinned. "Don't misunderstand. I merely cleared the air."

I wanted desperately to roll my eyes.

My boss leaned forward and put his hands on the desktop. "Mademoiselle Duval, I would like to, ah, hem, put this event behind us as soon as possible." He opened, then closed a file folder with my name on it. "It was unfortunate that you were accused—"

"Monsieur, I was not accused." I sat down on the edge of the chair that matched Zachary's, so I could watch both of them at once.

Zachary lifted one eyebrow.

"Hem. It was unfortunate that you were suspected—"

"Monsieur, I was not suspected. I was merely

assisting with the investigation."

Zachary grinned.

My boss scowled. He drew himself up tall and puffed out his chest. "Regardless, Mademoiselle Duval, you brought unwarranted and unwanted attention to Rhineland Bankgruppe."

"Through no fault of my own."

His face flushed and he pressed his lips together. "Hem, ah, I concede that may be true. Monsieur Le Noir has assured me that you were never blamed for the unfortunate and untimely demise of his cousin." He glared at me for a several beats, then took a deep breath. "Nonetheless, in the media, there was the appearance of complicity, and it is my duty, above all, to protect the reputation of this firm."

I tried my best to look prim. "Of course."

"I cannot allow our image to become tarnished."

I folded my hands and bowed my head in submission. "I understand."

"Well, then. We are agreed." His shoulders relaxed and his mouth tried to smile. "Therefore, you may return to your work." He looked me up and down, took in the helmet on my lap and my jeans and sweater. "Except for today, I expect you to be properly attired."

I couldn't help it. I did roll my eyes. "Of course."

The color rose in his face as he stared at me.

"But I have not agreed." I stood up, lifted my hands, palms up, and smiled. "I have been offered another job with ten percent higher pay." I took a step closer. "I am considering accepting it."

Beside me, Zachary cleared his throat and shifted in his chair.

Monsieur Fischer removed his glasses, pinched the

bridge of his nose between his thumb and forefinger, and looked pained. "I will match that offer."

I nodded. "There's one more thing. I assume you've reassigned my office and my clients. Do you intend to return them to me?"

"I have not reassigned your clients." He gestured toward Zachary le Noir. "As you can see." His tone was as dry as old shoe leather.

"And my office?"

"Hem. Ah. It is being painted and recarpeted."

I raised my eyebrows. "For someone else, I assume."

His face flushed again.

I waited. My boss deserved every bit of discomfort he might be feeling.

He pulled himself up tall. "Your office will be ready for you tomorrow."

Someone, probably the senior of the two silver-haired men who took care of the wealthy widows, was going to be unhappy about that. "Then I agree. I will return tomorrow."

"For today, you may assist Monsieur Le Noir in the guest office."

I raised my eyebrows at Zachary. "We have agreed on tomorrow, Monsieur Le Noir. Perhaps you would prefer to schedule an appointment then."

My boss winced. Zachary sat up straight and put both feet on the floor. "I would not."

"*Désolée*, but I am not prepared."

He stood. "Mademoiselle Duval, I think we can begin without difficulty."

The guest office, which was kept ready at all times for visiting personnel from the head office in Munich, matched Monsieur Fischer's in size and opulence. A computer specialist waited there to help me sign on to the system and select a new password, then left me alone with Zachary, who was circling the room, peering at paintings of old sailing ships and leaving a trail of footprints in the thick navy-blue carpet. He ran his fingertips around the edge of one frame, then tipped his head to peer at the back.

It was the obvious place to stick a camera. I arched my eyebrows at him. "Satisfied?"

Grinning, he came to the desk and pulled up a chair facing me.

I opened his portfolio, studied it for a couple of minutes, then turned the computer screen so we could both see it. I pointed the cursor at the box that compared the current total with the total on the day we opened the account. Even though it had only been two weeks, a couple of stocks had split, and it looked good. Better than good. "Overall, you're doing well, Monsieur Le Noir." I'd chosen some great vehicles. "I think you should leave it alone, but is there something you want to change?"

He reached into his briefcase and pulled out an envelope of heavy, cream-colored stationery. He opened it and handed three sheets of matching paper to me. "This is a summary of my cousin's investments."

I raised my eyebrows. "And?"

"As his executor and heir, I want to transfer everything to Rhineland Bankgruppe as soon as possible. And I want you to manage it."

"You are his sole heir?"

"I am."

I sank back in my chair and started reading. Two and a half pages, double spaced, with a dozen accounts per page, many in different banks or brokerages, some with huge amounts and some with relatively small sums of money—only five or six million.

When I came to the end, I looked up. Zachary was watching me with a smirk on his face, as if he'd done something clever and wanted me to be impressed.

I kept my expression neutral. "Have you totaled it?"

"Only the first half of the first page—approximately three-hundred-seventy-three million euros."

"Keeping track of this many accounts would be a pain. Any idea why he spread it around like that?" As if I didn't have a pretty good idea.

He grinned. "He didn't have you, and he didn't know how to manage his money, so it's a mess."

"Actually, it's worse than a mess." Except for diamonds, nothing is more interesting than money and what people do with it. I was willing to bet Ivanov had been playing a shell game. Laundering buckets of money. I'd know as soon as I dug through the account histories. And if I was right, wouldn't Stan Gibson love to get his hands on the records? I tapped the sheaf of papers. "It's somewhere between a nightmare and a catastrophe. It will take me at least a week just to contact each entity. And before I begin, I'll need proof that your cousin truly did bequeath all this to you."

He handed me another document. Ivanov's will.

I glanced at it, rifled through the pages, then waved it at him. "Our attorneys will have to certify this. I'll get it to them first thing in the morning."

"Thanks." Zachary rose to his feet. "I'm hungry, and dinner's on me."

****

It was not quite seven o'clock and at Chez Gaspard,

only two seats at the bar were occupied. The occupants were sipping wine and talking in hushed tones.

Robbie Gaspard popped out of the kitchen and kissed both of my cheeks. "We're not ready to open for dinner, but for you, I shall find something." He brushed crumbs off the gold and black upholstered seat in the booth nearest the kitchen and laid a starched white tablecloth on the table. "Please, sit here."

Zachary waited until Robbie set a pair of martinis in front of us, bowed, and disappeared again. "As my cousin's heir, I feel bound to honor and complete his obligations, just as he would have done." He gazed at me for a moment. "That means I still need you to get the tapestries. Soon. Before Maxime concludes a deal to sell them. Returning them to the family from which they were stolen is at the top of my list of priorities."

"Oh, sure." I snapped my fingers. "Easy. Cops are swarming the chateau, trying to figure out who killed your cousin. You think they won't notice if I try to sneak out with a pair of bulky, heavy tapestries?"

"The police have wrapped up their investigation. Maxime closed the place up and went to his yacht. It's deserted except for the caretaker."

"Impossible. Even if I were to get them, they're big and they're fragile. The only way to get them out of the château without damaging them is to carry them out the front door." I glared at him. "Under the nose of the caretaker, who is much bigger and stronger than I. And his rottweiler."

"It's a Doberman. And there is another way. The Cathars who first built the castle made an escape route via a ladder that can be dropped down from the dungeons. When we were there, I looked at it. The ladder is not in good condition, and the old footpath is overgrown but you could lower the tapestries from the trap door."

Except for the fact that I had no desire at all to go back to the château, that sounded like a great solution. I shook my head. "*Désolée*. I can't help you."

"Look. We have a deal."

"Excuse me. We do not have a deal. I never agreed to it. Besides, you promised to give me the Queen of Persia ring, and I bet you don't even know where it is."

He put his hand inside his jacket, withdrew it, and held his closed fist over the table. I could hardly breathe as I put out my hand. He dropped the warm, heavy ring into it. I slid it onto my third finger, where it belonged, and gazed at it, turning it to catch tiny, rainbow-hued shards of light as they danced out of the depths of the diamond.

Robbie appeared bearing a charcuterie tray. "I have prepared for you a fig and pear chutney to accompany the foie gras, a warm Brie with honey and black pepper, spring Comte cheese, the finest prosciutto, the best of jamon Iberica, and, as you can see, gorgonzola and almonds." Yum! No wonder Robbie was kind of round.

As he set it on the table, I draped my other hand over the ring, but not until he had a chance to see it. One eyebrow twitched ever so slightly as he stepped back.

Zachary laid a slice of prosciutto on a piece of toasted rye bread. "*Merci*, monsieur."

I blew Robbie a kiss. He winked and headed back to the kitchen. I helped myself to some of the Brie, balanced it on a hunk of baguette, and took a big bite. Just in time, a server appeared with a couple of glasses of white Sancerre.

Zachary watched me, looking annoyed. "You do everything with such gusto. Rappelling down from the dungeons would be a piece of cake for you. So why won't you get the tapestries?"

"You have plenty of money. Why don't you just outbid whoever is buying them?"

He tipped his head back and laughed. "Maxime would rather die than sell them to me."

"Why?"

"Spite. Pure spite. Maxime is not disposed to give me anything I want."

"But you seem to be friends."

"We were. Once upon a time."

I spread a thick slice of foie gras on a piece of baguette.

"As I told you, Maxime's mother was the old Baron Ivanov's mistress. The baron acknowledged him as his son and promised everything would be his.

"Things changed when the baron adopted my cousin, but the three of us still got along okay until the baron died and left his estate to my cousin instead. Maxime put on a big show of pretending not to mind. He claimed he had so much money of his own that the inheritance would have been small potatoes. But he's had a chip on his shoulder ever since.

"My cousin tried to make amends by naming Maxime and me joint heirs in his will, and for a while, that appeased Maxime. But as time went on, he became more and more resentful."

"So what happened?"

"Maxime is an accomplished backstabber. He cut my cousin out of some very sweet deals. He opposed and undermined him every way he could, all while pretending not to."

"So your cousin, Petar Ivanov, rewrote his will and gave everything to you."

"Correct."

"When did Maxime learn of this?"

"A couple of years ago, right after Petar had it drawn up."

"And now your cousin is dead, and Maxime resents you, too, so he's selling the tapestries."

"And I am honor-bound to return them to the family that rightfully owns them."

"Or maybe you just want to even up the score."

"Look. Keep the ring. Get the tapestries. And if you happen to find a miniature gold trebuchet decorated with diamonds and emeralds"—I covered my mouth with my napkin and faked a cough—"bring it along and I'll throw in a nice bonus."

It nearly killed me to pull the Queen of Persia off my finger. I gave it one last look and handed it back to him. "No. No. And more no."

He stood, tossed the ring in the air, caught it, and tucked it back in his pocket. As he started toward the door, he looked back over his shoulder. "You make a charming opponent, my dear."

Chapter Twenty-Six

It was my first day back at work, and I stayed an extra half hour to get started on transferring the accounts Zachary Le Noir was due to inherit to his account at Rhineland Bankgruppe.

Baguette was going to be one unhappy puppy if I didn't get to Posh Paws, his grooming salon, before it closed. I blazed through rush-hour traffic on my bright red scooter. If I didn't make it in time, I'd have to ring the bell and wait for the owner to come. It would take Baguette's favorite doggie treat to soothe him, and I hadn't thought to bring one with me when I left for the office. When I couldn't find a parking spot within three blocks of the salon, I drove Poppy up onto the sidewalk and left her right beside the Posh Paws door.

Chérie, Baguette's groomer, was trimming the nails on a miniature Australian shepherd. She looked up and puffed a wisp of auburn hair that had escaped her ponytail out of her eyes. Her lips curved into a can-I-help-you sort of smile.

"Baguette," I said, thinking she must have forgotten which dog belonged to me, although that would have been strange, since he'd had regular appointments for the last two years.

Her summer-sky eyes filled with concern. "Where is Baguette?" She put down the clippers and began to undo the harness holding the Aussie in place on the table.

My mouth gaped open, literally, for a moment. "He's not here?"

"Your aunt, she was going to bring him?"

"Yes, like always."

Chérie gave the mini shepherd a treat and tucked him into his carry case. "She has never forgotten before."

Aunt Celeste never forgot anything. I pulled my phone out of my pocket and dialed her number. It rang five times, then went to voice mail. "Baguette isn't with Chérie. Where are you? What's wrong?" I sent the same message via text.

Chérie laid a plump, dimpled hand on my arm. "Don't worry. I'm sure she's okay."

I ran to the door. "*Merci*, Chérie. I'll let you know."

Let her know what? That someone gotten into my aunt's workroom, cleaned out her supply of diamonds and other sparkly stones, and left her dead on the floor beside the big round coffee table?

I zoomed over to Chez Celeste. Thierry, who manned the shop, looked up from folding a shirt and putting it a bag for a tall man in a long, black cashmere coat. "*Bonjour*, Chloe."

"Aunt Celeste?"

He looked a little concerned, but nowhere near as worried as I felt. "I haven't seen your aunt today, or Baguette."

It was almost six o'clock in the evening. He would have opened the shop at ten. Normally, Aunt Celeste arrived around eleven. Together, they decided what articles needed to be restocked, reviewed special orders, and blocked out time on her schedule to design, cut, and sew them. Then she went to work in her workroom at the back of the store.

I dashed into the fitting room, slid my hand behind the gold shantung panel on the back wall, flattened my palm against the cool, smooth security pad, and waited for it to read my fingerprints. The panel swung open, and I stepped into the kind of stillness that tells you at once that no one is there. I turned on the lights and glanced at the coffee table and red velvet chairs in the little sitting area. Everything looked normal. "Aunt Celeste! Baguette!" My voice bounced off the ceiling and walls. I marched past the shoji screens that separated the sitting area from the workspace. What could have happened to her? She'd been fine when I took Baguette up to her at quarter to ten. I searched under the cutting and sewing tables and behind stacked bolts of fabric.

As I hustled back out through the shop, Thierry said, "If she arrives, I shall telephone for you."

I zoomed to our apartment building, raced up six flights of stairs rather than wait for the elevator, turned my key in the lock on Aunt Celeste's front door, pushed it open, and stopped. Omigod! What if she and Raphael Aragon…? And I came bursting in on them?

My cheeks started to burn. What an idiot! I started to close the door again. But no. Baguette would have been there to greet me. I peeked in. The bedroom door stood open. I could see the bed, all tidy, with the covers straightened and the pillows leaning against the headboard. The apartment held the same hush as her workroom.

I rushed through the bedroom and checked the bathroom and found nothing out of place. Until I came back to the door. Her phone lay on the shelf between the door and the peg that still held Baguette's lead.

With all my heart, I wished I'd burst in on her and

Raphael in a moment of torrid passion. I could have forgiven myself for that. I could have tolerated the embarrassment. But something had happened to her. Something not good. If she'd suddenly become ill and needed to go to the hospital, she would have told me. If she had called for emergency assistance, the apartment wouldn't have been so tidy and clean. There would have been some sign. Something would have been out of place. I pulled my phone out of my pocket and pressed André's number.

"Wait right there," he said after I explained what was—or was not—going on.

I telephoned the pharmacy around the corner, where the staff was especially fond of Celeste and Baguette, but she had not been there. They would have remembered. I telephoned the two nearest hospitals, but she was not there.

A ray of sunlight broke through the clouds and sent bright rainbow shards of light dancing across the walls and ceiling, splashing little bits of rainbows across my arms and hands. *Merde*! In my haste, I'd missed the diamond cuff link lying next to the bouquet of red and white tulips on the antique table beside the sofa. One of the pair that I'd admired the first day I met Zachary Le Noir, the pair I'd vowed to make my own.

As if I needed to confirm what I already knew, I picked it up, turned it over, and read the name of the maker.

"A clue?"

It took a minute to realize André had arrived and stepped up beside me. He took it, gazed at it for a moment, gave a low whistle, and put it back in my shaking hand.

"Le Noir. It's his." I couldn't call him Zachary anymore. Traitor, yes. Con man, grifter, kidnapper, yes. Zachary, no. It wasn't fun anymore. "What could he want with my aunt?"

"He wants to get your attention, obviously." André marched through the apartment, pausing every few steps to scrutinize the carpet, the furniture, and even the drapes. "That's it? Have you seen anything else?"

I pointed toward the front door. "Her phone. And she always put Baguette on the lead."

"So she didn't leave of her own accord. When did you last see her?"

"This morning, just before ten, when I left Baguette here before I went into the office."

André had picked up her phone. "What's her password?"

"I don't know."

"Let's guess." He tapped on the screen. "Not Baguette." He tapped some more. "Not Chloe either."

"Try Raphael. Or Aragon."

"Bingo. Raphael." He scrolled through her messages, then checked her phone calls. "No help here. There's nothing except your messages since last evening. But let's take it with us." He zipped open a pocket on his black leather jacket and dropped it in. "Did she make it to the store this morning?"

I shook my head.

André gazed at me for a long minute. "So she's probably been gone seven or eight hours already."

"She could be anywhere." I bit my lip. I'd shrugged off Stan Gibson's warning, not wanting to believe. I'd been stupid. And now, what had I done? What would I ever do without Aunt Celeste?

André said. "He could have forced her into the secret room at Chez Celeste."

"But Thierry was there all day. He would have seen them."

"It's possible that your Zachary was able to find a way in through the back—through that old loading dock door."

"It hasn't been opened in years."

"Doesn't mean it won't open."

"But it's impossible to lock her in the secret room. Her handprint controls the lock. She would have been able to get out."

"Not if he cut the electricity."

I gasped. "If he did"—I ran out into the hall—"they'd have run out of fresh air by now."

We raced down the stairs. André had left his big black bike parked by the door. He leaped on. I climbed on behind him, wrapped my arms around his solid waist, and laid my head against his shoulder. While we flew to Chez Celeste, I prayed.

Thierry looked up from the cash desk as we barged into the shop. "Any news?"

André said, "None."

In the fitting booth, I pressed my hand on the security plate and the panel swung open. André followed me in. I crossed the sitting area to the long counter that held the bar sink, the little refrigerator, and the espresso machine. I leaned over the sink and pounded on the wall that hid her secret room. "Aunt Celeste, Baguette." I banged with both fists. I listened with all my might. Nothing.

André rummaged around in the drawers at one end of the bar and pulled out a pair of earbuds. "Excellent. I

can use this to bridge the plate that reads her handprint."
He popped a piece of gum in his mouth and tossed the
packet at me. "Here, chew a big wad of gum."

Grabbing a pair of scissors from another drawer, he
cut a length of wire from the earbuds and stripped the
coating from it. Next, he opened a side panel on the
espresso machine, exposing a keypad and a circuit board
the size of a cell phone. He unfastened a pair of wires
from the circuit board and replaced them with a length of
the earbud wire, twisting the ends around the contact
posts. He tucked his ball of gum around one, then held
out his hand for mine. "Insulation."

"Earbuds and chewing gum?"

"Have faith." He tapped a bunch of numbers into the
keypad, tugged on the espresso machine, and the wall
pivoted, swinging toward us. Immediately, the lights in
the hidden room came on and the air conditioner started
to hum. Le Noir might have tied Aunt Celeste up and
gagged her, but he had not cut off the electricity. Aunt
Celeste and Baguette were not lying on the floor, gasping
their last breaths. I blinked the tears back.

Under the spotlights designed to show them off in
all their glory, Aunt Celeste's treasures winked and
gleamed at me, just as they always did. But where was
she?

Chapter Twenty-Seven

André dropped me off at my apartment, then went home to put his ear to the tracks—whatever that means in the cyberspace world he inhabits.

I dialed Zachary Le Noir's number, the one he'd given my office. The detached, metallic voice of an electronic assistant shunted me to that bottomless black hole known as voice mail. I telephoned the Saint Francis Hotel, and a human, but equally impersonal operator put me through to his penthouse suite, with the same result. I tried his art gallery on Île Saint-Louis. The phone rang and rang and rang.

The streetlights had come on when I hopped on Poppy and zoomed over to the gallery. The wind, birthed by an iceberg in the North Atlantic, blew right through me and left my stomach churning with fear for Aunt Celeste and Baguette. It was my fault they faced the night, probably shackled, maybe without warmth or comfort of any kind. I had to find them.

The sign in Le Noir's art gallery window read "Closed," but I saw a light shining under a door in the back. I banged on the showroom door, counted to ten, then banged and pounded some more. I kept on until a woman in a smart cream-colored pantsuit flung the door in the back of the gallery open and strode across the floor in five-inch heels. "The gallery is closed." She scowled at me through the glass.

"I am going to hammer on this door until you open

it."

She glared at me for a long moment.

I lifted my fist, and she reached for the lock. It scraped and clicked, and the door opened a crack. I gave it a shove. She took a couple of steps back. I pushed it open and marched in. "Thank you. I must speak to Zachary Le Noir."

"I will be happy to take a message for Monsieur Le Noir." Looking anything but happy, she strolled to a Louis XV desk that sat in the middle of the floor. Only a single red rose in a crystal vase stood on the surface.

"I already left a message. You need to tell me how I can reach him. Now."

"He left half an hour ago, and he does not tell me his plans." She sat down, opened a shallow drawer, and picked up a pen. Then, as if she'd decided to be helpful, she put the pen down and stretched her raspberry-red lips in a phony smile. "If this is something to do with the auction next Tuesday, I can help you. I manage this store, and he leaves the details to me."

I wanted to punch her in the nose. With every cell in my body. Instead, I drew a deep breath. "If you won't tell me how to reach him, please phone him yourself and tell him Chloe Duval needs to speak to him."

"Oh, you're Chloe Duval." She rolled her eyes. "You should have said so. He left you a message." She opened the drawer, pulled out an envelope, and handed it to me.

I ripped the thick, cream-colored envelope open. It contained a single sheet of matching paper and a handwritten note: *Did you know people survive only three days without water?* My hand shook so hard I could barely read the rest. *You know what I want. The clock is ticking.*

My knees felt as if they were made of limp noodles. I stumbled over my own feet as I headed toward the door. The woman smirked. "I hope it's not bad news."

It would have felt really good to smack her.

Outside, a downpour had begun, and the icy wind flung it at my face. For a change, I felt grateful. The stinging drops cleared my brain. I phoned André as I steered Poppy one-handed between rows of cars racing along beside the Seine. "I have to go to the château and get the tapestries."

"Not without me."

"Now," I said. "Tonight."

"I expected this. I'm on it. Pack your cold weather gear. A bizarre late snowstorm is hitting the Pyrenees. It's already dumping down and will get worse."

The minute I got home, I double checked my tool belt and stuffed it into my bag along with ski bibs and jacket, then added an extra cable, my ascent gear, and a granola bar. André was at the taxi stand by the time I got there, holding a cab. "We'll fly to Toulouse and drive from there."

At Orly Airport, we ran to the gate and had barely buckled in before the airplane backed away. At ten minutes after ten, we dove down through thick clouds and spied the lights of Toulouse. At ten-thirty, we picked up the all-wheel-drive SUV André had rented and headed south-east out of the city. Large, fluffy white flakes danced in the headlights. For a while, although snow clung to the early spring grasses and weeds accumulated along the edges, the road remained bare and wet. Mile by mile, as flat land gave way to foothills, then mountains, it fell harder. Gradually, it crept up onto the road, then inch by inch toward the center until it covered everything.

Like a giant's hand, gusts of wind shook the car. André turned the windshield wipers on high. The defroster blasted hot air, but only the half-circles in front of our faces remained clear. Tracks ran ahead of us through two inches, then four, then six, then eight inches of snow. I could hear the undercarriage scraping the icy tops of drifts, and where other cars had turned, our tires caught in frozen ruts and lurched, skidding to one side or the other.

Occasionally, a single light shone vaguely through the blizzard from somewhere on the mountain beside us. But we were the only idiots out there driving in the swirling white nothingness. At last, a large truck pulled out from a side road. André backed off to let it go ahead, then hung tight behind those big red taillights. We weren't alone, and I could breathe again.

The truck abandoned us in the tiny medieval village of Rénard, where, on the day before the wedding, Zachary had picked me up at the train station. André and I headed up the mountain toward the château. There were no more tracks. The edges of the road had been obliterated long before. Snow spiraled in the headlights. Both of us sat forward in our seats and peered ahead. Our eyes strained to see.

André managed to keep us on the road, and true to its advertised worth, the sturdy vehicle carried us slowly upward between tall trees. The wind diminished. As it got colder, fluffy flakes changed to tiny round pellets that fell straight down, then gradually tapered off and stopped. The trees grew sparse. The moon shone sporadically through gaps in the clouds.

We were alone in the vast, still, white night. Andre's shoulders drooped and he rubbed his hand across his eyes repeatedly before we spotted glimmers of light here and there through the trees. When we reached the inn at the bottom of the trail to the château, it seemed like we'd been driving forever; we'd been on the road for more than three hours.

A man wearing a plaid jacket and a knitted hat paused in his task of shoveling a path from the parking lot to the entrance and came to greet us. He slapped André on the shoulder. "Welcome back, monsieur. What the hell are you doing out here this time of night?"

André shook his hand. "Hoping to see a little snow."

He chuckled. "You and a bunch of other folks." He gestured toward a row of snowshoes and skis standing on end in the snowbank under the windows. "A pack of hikers and skiers came in ahead of the storm. Lucky for you and the missus, we have one room left."

"The missus and I will take it." André grinned at me for the first time since we'd started our epic journey.

I jabbed him in the ribs.

We stomped the snow off our boots and left them on a mat in the foyer. Music, laughter, and hearty voices poured out of a brightly lit room on our left.

Our host waved a hand at the clock above the doorway. The big hand pointed at twelve and the small hand pointed at two. "It's closing time, but there's no point. No one's going anywhere, so you might as well enjoy it." He pulled a key from a cubby hole on the wall and handed it to André. "Leave your bags here for now. Come on in and get a drink. You can register in the morning."

André led the way to the bar and ordered coffee for

both of us. We'd taken a sip or two before I recognized the man who sat on the other side of André—Count Maxime de Charpentier's caretaker, the stocky, fortyish guy who had run up the steep little path to the château with my suitcase the night before the wedding as if he were a gazelle. A large, mean-looking dog—the Doberman, I assumed—crouched between his legs and stared at me as if he'd like to bite my leg off.

The back of my neck prickled. The caretaker could have lifted Ivanov into the trunk as easily as if he'd been a baby. I shivered. Fortunately, Mr. Musclebound didn't even glance in my direction. He was drunk or well on his way and doing his best to make eye contact, or lip contact if luck smiled on him, with the woman at his other elbow.

The lights blinked, came back on, blinked a couple more times, then went out. "Hold tight, everyone," the bartender shouted. "The generator will come on in a minute."

The caretaker yelled, "Hell, where would we go? If the power's off here, it's off everywhere." He guffawed. "All this snow? I barely made it down here."

I tugged André's sleeve and slipped out of the room. A few seconds later, he followed. We were halfway up the stairs when the generator roared to life. Pale lights blinked on and gleamed softly on varnished wooden handrails and worn wood stairs.

I whispered, "How long will it take you to shut down the château's security system?"

"No can do," he whispered back as he unlocked the door to our room. "As long as the power's off and the internet's down, I can't hack in."

I felt the blood drain from my face. "You have to figure out a way."

"Can't."

I tossed my bag onto the bed, which took up most of the room. "But Aunt Celeste may have been without water for a day already, and it could be hours, maybe days before it's up again."

"Not arguing. Think about it. The château's security cameras probably have generator or battery backup, but the guy who's supposed to be watching the video feed and guarding Maxime's treasures is down there in the bar, drunk and determined to get laid. If he admitted that to his boss, he'd be dead. So, no worries. If there's a video, he'll erase it."

"You're brilliant."

"I'm André."

Whether he was brilliant or not, I had to get the tapestries. I'd deal with the consequences later. "I have to go."

"You are not going up there by yourself." He shook out his ski bibs and pulled them on. "Remember how narrow that trail is? And how it drops off to nothingness? If you slip off, nobody will find you until the snow melts."

Chapter Twenty-Eight

We zipped our bibs and jackets on. I checked my equipment twice, then donned my harness and tool belt. André gave me his code scanner, and I tucked it in with my tools.

Downstairs, the crowd in the bar was noisier than ever. We had no trouble sneaking past the open door and into the porch. We pulled our boots on and crunched out into knee-deep snow. From the row of snowshoes standing on end beside the entrance, I selected a short, wide pair and strapped them on. André chose a longer, narrower style. After starting off in the wrong direction a couple of times, we found a slight depression in the snow, judged them to be the caretaker's tracks, and followed them to the trail, then upward between scrub brush and stunted trees.

I'd always thought snowshoeing was just walking, but it was hard work. We had to climb the steep slope, and the steps were hidden under the snow. I kept tangling my feet and falling. Hot and sweating, I paused to open my jacket and stepped too close to the edge. The bank under one foot broke away. It slid out from under me and I landed on my stomach at the edge of the abyss. André grabbed my arm and flung himself down flat. "Don't move. If more snow breaks off, we'll both go down." He inched upward, pulling me with him, until I was back on the trail.

We both lay there panting; me wishing I could get my hands on Zachary Le Noir's neck. Then André got to his feet, gave me a hand up, and started off ahead of me. "I've got the hang of these things now." Slowly, carefully, he planted each foot. I swallowed my desire to be the one to blaze our way through the snow, to save Baguette and Aunt Celeste all by myself. Instead, I accepted my dose of humility and followed, and thanked all the good in the universe for his help.

One minute, we were struggling upward, and the next, the ground flattened out and we stood on the little plateau. The moon broke through the clouds, and with all the snow, it was as bright as day. I dropped to my knees and pulled André down beside me. "If anyone's here, they'll surely see us."

For several minutes, we didn't move. Clouds covered the moon again, and not a single light shone anywhere. The black bulk of the château towered over us, dark and silent as a dead man. "I think we're alone," André said.

In the shadows at the base of the tower where it butted up to the castle, he put on a headset, then handed one to me. His voice came clearly through the earphones. "Ancient technology, and super easy to use. The mic is voice activated. All you have to do is talk."

My rappelling cable wasn't long enough to reach the top of the tower, so I shot it to the roof of the château, which was slick as spit with ice and snow. Slowly, moving one limb at a time, I crawled on hands and knees to the dormer window I'd climbed out of while the bride and groom pledged their troth. I stood up and braced myself against it as I shot the second cable to the crenellated top of the tower. I gave it a good tug to make sure it was anchored, checked that my hand ascenders were gripping well, and then swung out.

For a moment, I was airborne, and in that moment, I forgot everything—Aunt Celeste, our struggle to get there, the deadly importance of my mission—in the joy of feeling the air rushing past my face and the thrill of being up there all by myself, flying free, like a bird.

I slid my feet and legs through the same slit I'd used before and was thinking it was all too easy when I got stuck. What an idiot! I hadn't reckoned on the extra bulk of my ski gear. If I'd had half a brain, I'd have put my tool belt and harness on underneath the jacket so I could take the jacket off, but there I was, half in and half out; unable to get either all the way in or back out.

If I unfastened the harness, I might fall, so I wriggled and swore until I managed to get my arms out of the sleeves. "Arrgh!"

"What's going on? You okay up there, Chloe?"

"I'm too fat."

With a last frantic yank, my jacket flew off over my head, taking my headset with it. I grabbed the headset, but when I tried to catch the coat, all I got was air. Cold air. "Yikes! My jacket!" And I was still stuck, sixty feet off the ground, hanging by a titanium thread in the brittle white light of the moon.

"Got your coat. You going to be okay?"

"I'm sweating." The fabric of my bibs caught on the edges of the slit and held. I shoved at the rough stone with both hands and all my might. I blew out all the air in my lungs and flailed and kicked. Finally, only my head and shoulders remained outside. I was as hot as if I'd run a marathon. "I'm in." It was freezing inside the tower and by the time I came to the fourth landing, the one with doors to the treasure room and what I assumed was the secret passage, my teeth were chattering. Facing the treasure room, I pressed in the code I remembered, and on the keypad, a red light flashed. "Rats! They changed the code."

"Take your time. I'm keeping your jacket warm for you."

I placed André's scanner over the keypad.

"Hold the scanner steady and let it do its job," he said.

How did he know my hands were shaking? I pressed it against the pad and watched the numbers, then the letters scroll by. It stopped first at G, then 0, 2, H, E, L, L. "Go to hell instead of Gate to hell," I said it aloud to help burn it into my brain, then put the scanner away and entered the code. The door clicked open.

A fan purred somewhere in the ceiling. I couldn't hear a generator running, so apparently the climate control system and lights had battery backup. The temperature, a tropical fifty-nine degrees Fahrenheit, according to the display on the wall, was the same as it had been the night of the wedding. Soft lights shone down on the same row of ancient gold collars and tall pointed gold hats embossed with rings of curious symbols—an ancient script?

Between two tall hats stood a miniature golden trebuchet. It hadn't been there before, but I recognized it immediately, and it took my breath away. I would have recognized it even if Stan Gibson hadn't showed me photos when he told me he'd purchased it from Petar Ivanov. It's theft from the French Heritage Museum in New Orleans four years earlier had been broadcast worldwide, but no trace of it had ever turned up. Until now.

Almost a foot high, it was so beautiful I could hardly breathe. No wonder Zachary Le Noir wanted it. I picked it up and turned it slowly in my hands. It had been crafted entirely of gold, including the chain that attached the sling designed to hold the payload to the crossbeam. Seventeen diamonds, at least a carat each, alternated with sixteen emeralds on each of its four legs. Smaller emeralds circled each of four wheels like tiny tires. Sapphires crusted the upright and horizontal beams. Six loose, round rubies the size of small peas lay in a trough at the bottom, ready to shoot. The bucket that formed the counterweight held irregularly shaped semiprecious stones: garnets, amethyst, lapis, and one large tiger eye. I placed a ruby in the sling, released the sling from its tether, and turned the wheel to crank the counterweight up.

I was about to shoot my payload when André said, "Awfully quiet up there, sweet pea."

The clock was ticking. How could I have forgotten Baguette and Aunt Celeste, even for a moment? I put the ruby back in the little trough and refastened the sling.

"You're supposed to be getting the tapestries, remember?"

"On it." I set the trebuchet down and turned to the trunk.

I touched the lid, and in my mind, I saw Ivanov lying there in his yellow jacket and bright floral tie with his knees tucked up to his chest.

The trebuchet! Count Maxime de Charpentier must have discovered he'd sold it to an art crimes detective. That was why he died.

"Help the good guys," Stan had said. But how could

I tell him what I'd found and where I'd found it?

Holding my breath, I lifted the lid of the trunk. The embroidered linen wall-hangings lay side by side, rolled around wooden dowels and wrapped in linen covers that fastened with leather straps. I struggled to lift one of them out. I could barely get my arms around it, and it weighed forty or fifty pounds. "I'm going to have to carry these one at a time."

"Try pushing the trunk."

I nudged it. To my surprise, it rolled easily. "Great idea." I put the tapestry back in. "And lucky me, there's room for something else."

"Is that a good idea?"

"Better than good. It's a great idea. A fabulous idea."

Stan Gibson would give anything—well, a lot, anyway—to get his hands on the little gold war machine. I set it in the depression between the two rolls and closed the lid. If I needed a get out of jail free card, I'd make a deal with him. And if it turned out that I didn't have to give it to him, it would look lovely on my coffee table. On the nights I was home alone, of course.

Back on the landing, I reset the alarm code and opened the door into the secret passageway in the château using the same numbers and letters: G, then 0, 2, H, E, L, L.

My headlamp showed that the passage sloped downward, steeply at first, then leveled off. It smelled of mold, dust, and mouse droppings. I tried not to breathe deeply. It was claustrophobically narrow, and the ceiling was bare inches above my head. In fact, at times, I bumped it. Fortunately, small spaces didn't bother me. "I wonder what floor I'll end up on. Any clue?"

"When I followed the caretaker the night of the wedding," André said, "he put the trunk on a dumb waiter in the laundry room behind the kitchen on the main floor. Then he walked up to the third floor and went into a linen closet near the top of the stairs. He didn't come out, and when I went in and looked, the dumbwaiter was empty, so I expect the tunnel starts there. I'd have searched for it, but Maxime's toadies were lurking about."

I came to the end of the passage and faced another keypad. "I think I'm there."

When I tapped in G, 0, 2, H, E, L, L, a section of the wall slid open like a barn door, exposing a wooden panel. I pushed and shoved until part of it trundled away from me, creating an opening at either end. I rolled the trunk in. From the inside, the section I'd moved looked like a huge bookcase with shelves full of neatly folded towels and sheets. "You were right, André. I'm in a linen closet. And there's a dumbwaiter."

"If the power weren't out, you could put the trunk in and bring it down to the main floor."

"Give me a minute." I shone my light in the window on the front of the lift. I could see ropes and pulleys, but the darn thing wouldn't budge.

I couldn't hear a generator in the main building, either, and when I opened the door into the corridor, no lights were on. But the alarm system would surely be running on batteries. I fashioned a hood out of a pillowcase and draped it around my head and shoulders, hiding my face, before I stepped out of the closet. If André was right, the caretaker would erase the camera feed, but I'd already taken too many chances.

"I know where I am," I whispered. Several doors

away was the room I'd slept in. "I'll go out onto the roof the way I did at the wedding." I lugged one tapestry, then the other, down the hall. It took only a couple of seconds to disable the deadbolt on the door to the servants' staircase and a few more minutes to carry them up to the fourth floor. I put them on the single bed in the tiny room where I'd left my peacock blue skirt and fascinator hat.

I went back down to the linen closet, wrapped the trebuchet in a fluffy white towel to protect it, then bundled it into a pillowcase, so I could carry it like Santa's sack. I set it aside with a couple of blankets while I pushed the trunk back to the treasure room.

I would have loved to take one of the gold collars, but didn't give myself even a minute to think about it. Instead, I pulled my compact out of my toolbelt and snapped close-up photos of them and the tall gold hats. They should have been in a museum, along with most of the paintings and sculptures that ringed the walls. I made a video, turning slowly in a circle, capturing Count Maxime de Charpentier's entire collection. Stan Gibson might not be interested in all of it, but he'd certainly know someone who was.

"What's up, sweet pea?"

"Locking up."

With deep regret for leaving all those treasures behind, I reset the alarm, went back to the linen closet, re-armed the secret passage, and pushed the shelves back into place. Then I picked up the trebuchet and blankets and climbed to the fourth floor, relocking the stairway door behind me.

I wrapped a blanket around each tapestry and lifted them out the attic window one at a time. On hands and knees to keep from slipping on the ice, I dragged them to the edge of the roof and rappelled down with them, first one and then the other, clutching them to my chest with one arm and praying not to fall. Then, with the pillowcase containing the trebuchet over one shoulder, I closed the window and descended for the last time.

André took the pillowcase and handed me my jacket. "Helping Santa, I presume."

"That might be my get out of jail free card." I grinned as I shrugged my coat back on. "Wait 'til you see it."

He'd found a pair of skis on a bench beside the back entrance. We wove one of my cables back and forth between them, forming a stretcher, and used the other cable to lash the tapestries and trebuchet to it. We each took one end and started back down the trail.

By the time we got back to the inn, the wind had picked up and it was snowing hard again, almost blinding us, and covering our footprints almost as quickly as we made them. We locked the tapestries in the back of the rented SUV, climbed the stairs to the attic room, tugged off our outerwear, and tumbled into bed. It was four o'clock. I didn't even have the energy to show him the trebuchet. I was asleep before my head hit the pillow.

An hour and a half later, André nudged me awake. "Time to go, sleepyhead."

Chapter Twenty-Nine

We returned the car and were back in the terminal in Toulouse at eight-thirty. On the TV screen, a woman in a skin-tight red dress stood in front of a weather map and chirped happily about the storm, as if it was so much fun! As if people's lives weren't threatened and farmers weren't worried to death that their cows might perish. As if it didn't matter a bit that the tarmac was a sheet of ice and our flight, along with dozens of others, had been canceled.

André and I took turns guarding the tapestries and standing in a long line of complaining customers hoping to get seats on another airplane. I tried again and again to reach Zachary Le Noir, to tell him we were on our way, to beg him to let Aunt Celeste go.

Eventually, a little after two-thirty, we took off. We arrived at Orly Airport in Paris at four, and at last, as we stood in line for a taxi, I reached Le Noir and agreed to bring the tapestries to his art gallery.

André possessed a lot more patience than I, but we were both dead tired, grubby, and cranky. In the taxi, he finally snapped. He glared at me across the two tapestries propped on the seat between us. "I don't care if Zachary Le Noir told you to come alone. I don't care if he told you to bring both of them. And I don't care what you say. I'm going to hold onto one."

I scowled. "You will not."

"Look. It's the only leverage you've got."

"You could ruin everything."

"You have to be firm. Tell him he can have the second one when we see Celeste."

I sucked in a breath to yell at him but he reached across and squeezed my hand. "I care about Celeste, too, Chloe."

What would I do without André? If I'd looked at him, I wouldn't have been able to hold back the tears that pressed against my eyelids. "I have to do this my way."

He said, "Okay. You can go in alone if you insist, but I'm keeping one of the tapestries. And I'm going follow you to his gallery. And if you don't come out in three minutes and tell me that bastard is releasing her, I'm coming in."

"Give me five minutes."

"Okay, five. I will not wait longer than that."

"Fine." I clamped my jaw shut and stared straight ahead.

With more grace than I could have mustered, he took my bag, the trebuchet, and one of the wall hangings up to his apartment for safekeeping. "It'll be okay," he said.

I had the driver wait until André came back outside and climbed onto his motorcycle. He shadowed the taxi to the gallery on Île Saint-Louis, then disappeared around the corner.

Zachary Le Noir himself sat at the desk with the single rose in the gallery. Alone. I came in, hugging a tapestry to my chest and, without speaking, laid it in front of him.

He unfastened the straps, removed the blanket I'd wrapped around it, and started to unroll it. He bent over and peered at the linen backing, then ran a finger along it, near the bottom.

I leaned in. Someone had embroidered a list of names into the backing, in the hem, where it wouldn't show through on the face, in blue thread. Names of people and cities with symbols in between: Shoemacher 2Lv Munich, Milner 17Y Dresden, Schiff 5A3 Vienna, and so on. I caught my breath. "What is that?"

He unrolled a little more. The names went on. "This is what gives it enormous value." He followed the list with his finger.

I touched the blue stitching. "It's names of people the Nazis stole from, isn't it?"

He smiled, his indigo blue eyes dancing with excitement, like a kid with a mouth full of cookies and a hand in the cookie jar. "Clever girl."

I memorized the first three while he went to the door, opened it, and stepped outside. He peered around for a minute, then came back in, locked the door, and turned the sign that read "open" around, so it read "closed."

"And the symbols are clues to where they hid it. Where it might still be hidden. Am I right?"

"You catch on fast."

I glared at him. "You never meant to give this to the owners, did you?"

"What owners?"

Even though I'd expected it, a shockwave vibrated through me. I took a step back. Zachary Le Noir was a charming companion, a heart stealer in fact. I'd wanted to believe his motives were pure. But he didn't have a heart. He was a heart breaker. A con man, a grifter and worse—the devil incarnate. I felt chilled to the core.

"Where is my aunt?"

Please, God, don't let him be a murderer, too.

"Where's the other tapestry?"

I stiffened my back. "You will see it when I see my aunt and Baguette."

He strode back to the desk. "You will see her when I decide you will see her. But since you've brought it up, I need you to do one more thing for me first." He sat on the edge of the desk and crossed his arms on his chest.

He'd lured me into a trap and was about to slam it shut. If I did one more thing, I'd be his gopher forever. I'd never get free of him. I gripped my hands together to keep them from shaking. "You promised. You said you'd release my aunt."

His violet eyes held no warmth. "*Tant pis*. Too bad. Something has come up."

I stood as tall as I could. "I don't work for you."

"You got the tapestries. Therefore, you do work for me."

"Tell me where my aunt is, or I'm going to the cops."

He put his hand under my chin. "Your type of people doesn't go to the cops."

I shoved his hand away.

He chuckled. "My cousin owned a miniature golden trebuchet."

I stifled a gasp.

"You Americans call them catapults, although that name is incorrect."

"And?"

"As his heir, it now belongs to me."

"And?"

"It disappeared the night my cousin died. I'm certain

Maxime has it in his treasure room."

Wrong. It's in André's apartment, hanging out with the African masks he and Suzanne bought on their honeymoon.

He pulled his phone out of his pocket and tapped the screen. "Here's a photo."

I glanced at the photo and shrugged.

"Don't be coy. You must have seen it."

"Everyone has seen it. It was all over the news when someone stole it from a museum in New Orleans."

André knocked, then shook the door.

I started toward it, but Zachary got there first and stood with his back to it. "Look. Don't be tiresome. You give me what I want, and I'll give you what you want. Meet me at your office at ten tomorrow morning. Bring the other tapestry, and I'll fly you down to the château in the helicopter."

André knocked loud and long.

Zachary leaned against the door, crossed one foot over the other, and put his hands in his pockets, relaxed and at ease.

I clenched my fists and gritted my teeth. "And Aunt Celeste?"

"Up to you. Her fate is in your hands."

Chapter Thirty

I climbed onto the back of André's spookily silent black bike. "I need to find Aunt Celeste. Now. Tonight." If I didn't, I'd be Zachary Le Noir's toady forever.

My phone quacked with an incoming text. My heart beat wildly as I grabbed it, but it was only Robbie Gaspard.

—*I'm worried about you. Are you okay?*—

—*I'm with André.*—

—*Good. Come to the restaurant. Both of you. I need to see you with my own two eyes.*—

André said, "Put your helmet on. Let's go. We need to eat. And Robbie can help us come up with a plan."

At Chez Gaspard, André and I sat in the back booth, the one nearest the kitchen, and I told them Le Noir wanted to meet me at the office in the morning; that he expected me to bring the tapestry, then go get the trebuchet.

"Not good," André said. "You could give him everything right now. But I don't like it."

"Definitely not good." Robbie scowled and shook his head. He disappeared into the kitchen and came back carrying a tray with two bowls of fragrant onion soup, my favorite. Gruyère cheese, melted and browned, floated on top of savory croutons. "Eat. You can't think on an empty stomach."

It might as well have been blackboard chalk. I put

my spoon down. "Le Noir could have taken Aunt Celeste and Baguette anywhere in his helicopter. How could anyone know where?"

Robbie handed me my spoon. "It won't help to starve." He poured two glasses of red wine and set the bottle on the table.

I said, "Le Noir has friends who could make my boss regret firing me. His goons could be anywhere, doing anything to her."

He crossed his arms on his white chef's jacket. "Now, lass, what good does it do to ruminate on that?"

"He wouldn't even have to dirty his own—"

"Chloe. Stop." Robbie held up a hand. "Why would Zachary Le Noir harm Celeste? What good would it do him? Listen to me. You guys are dead on your feet. You're not thinking straight. You both need to get some sleep. In the meantime, I'll ask around. Meet me here first thing in the morning, and we'll decide what to do." He strode back into the kitchen.

André reached across the table and took my hand. "He's right, sweet pea. Robbie has more connections than the Pope. He'll put out some feelers. Le Noir is not going to hurt her. And by morning, we may know where she is."

"I'm afraid we'll just spin our wheels."

André's brow wrinkled. "I understand. I do. Totally." He leaned across the table and grabbed my hand. "But listen, if you give in and hand over the stuff, will that be the end?"

"I have no illusions about that. He will have me where he wants me—at his disposal."

André nodded and sank back in his chair. "That's what I'm worried about."

"If I give in to him, there will always be one more thing he wants. I get that. And I hate it. The thought of being sucked into his orbit scares me to death. But I hate myself right now, too, because, bottom line, with every minute that passes, Aunt Celeste is suffering, and it's because of me. What if we don't find her in time? What if she dies?"

"She won't. I promise."

I couldn't imagine getting up every morning and going about my day without her being there to share it. Ever since I moved to Paris, she'd been there for me. She'd helped me get my apartment. I saw her almost every morning and most nights. She was the fabric of my days. *Please, God, keep her safe, and I'll find the Queen of Persia and take it back to the museum.*

André sighed. "Look." He picked up his spoon. "Except for an hour or two, we were both up all night. Robbie's right. We'll be smarter after we get some sleep."

We ate our soup and he took me home—walked me all the way up to my door and looked around inside—then went home to his wife, Suzanne.

He phoned a few minutes later to tell me Suzanne thought I should stay with them that night. I said thanks but no. Instead, I took a twenty-minute nap, then showered and dressed in black leggings and hoodie and slipped my feet into my running shoes. I added my lock picks to one pocket, along with a pair of thin plastic gloves. In another, I put a headband with a variable intensity light.

If I stood at one side of my bedroom window and peered out, I could see the man who had been sitting on a bench in the park across the street when André brought me home. He wore a newsboy's cap, a hip-length pea coat, and jeans. He was still there, but now he was smoking a cigarette and pacing back and forth, just outside the circle of light cast by the streetlamp. I took the stairs to the ground floor, and rather than walk out the lobby door, went into the storage room where the garbage and recycle bins stood. I climbed on top of one, and when the man across the street turned his back to pace in the other direction, I slipped out the window, dropped down to the sidewalk, and strolled away. Around the corner and out of sight, I broke into a jog and headed for Île Saint-Louis.

It was nine-thirty by the time I crossed the bridge onto the island, and although light spilled out of shop windows and made bright yellow squares on the street that ran down the center of the island, it was deserted except for a woman walking her dog and a couple sauntering along ahead of her, pausing to gaze at displays of handbags, hats, jewelry, and clothing. A cold wind sent a piece of paper, postcard sized, aimlessly flipping and scudding along the street. I shook myself. I didn't have time for aimless drifting. I didn't have time to feel tired. I didn't have time to wish I'd eaten more dinner. I needed to be on my toes.

I turned a corner and walked past Le Noir's art gallery. It appeared to be all closed up. I went on and circled the whole block. Nearly all the doors and windows were shuttered, quiet, and dark. Thanks to the city's attempts to conserve electricity, widely spaced streetlights shone only dimly.

Back-to-back with the gallery, an old hotel stood empty and shrouded in plastic and scaffolding. A bare bulb hanging from the scaffold illuminated a temporary fence that ran along the sidewalk, preventing pedestrians from falling into a long trench that exposed pipes and cables. Water dripped slowly but steadily from a leak somewhere, making mud in the bottom of the trench.

A man blazed by on a bicycle, balancing a pizza box on one arm. Then all was still again. I circled back around to the front of the gallery and pulled my lock picks out of my pocket. Perhaps I could find a reference to properties Le Noir owned, to people he knew, something that would lead me to my aunt.

To my surprise, although the door had an expensive and effective lock, it wasn't engaged. Only the doorknob was locked. It took me less than a minute to defeat it. Inside, a single glance at the panel beside the door told me the alarm had not been turned on. I waited and listened, but heard nothing. A streak of light leaked under a door in the back.

I tiptoed around a couple of shoulder-high, metal-sculpture beasts that looked vaguely like water buffalo. I put my ear against the door and hearing nothing, tried the latch. Locked. But it, too, had only a common lock on the knob. Something was wrong. This was way too easy. Was I walking into a trap? Holding my breath, I picked it open and peered into a storage room lit by fluorescent fixtures on the high ceiling.

Wooden shipping crates with blue and white labels took up most of the space, small stacked on top of large. Along one wall, a microwave and coffee maker sat on a narrow counter beside a bar sink. On the opposite side, a row of gym lockers lined the wall, except for a gap in the middle where a door opened to the outside. The door swung spookily back and forth—out into the darkness and back toward the light. It led to a small, disused courtyard. On the other side, the old hotel, shrouded and scaffolded, towered over me. Directly across the courtyard, the plastic sheathing had been cut from the ground up to head height. It flapped and snapped in the breeze. My heart began to pound. What better place to hide Aunt Celeste?

I hurried across the courtyard and ducked through the opening; stopped, listened, and waited for my eyes to adjust to almost complete blackness. The air smelled of drywall dust and paint with underlying mustiness and mold. Somewhere above me, a door opened and closed. Footsteps clicked across a floor, the distinctive sound of high heels.

A hand clamped over my mouth and an arm came around my waist. I took a long step back and placed one foot between my captor's legs. I started to duck, ready to hit him behind the knee and spin out of his grasp as his knee buckled.

Honoré St. Lazarre's citrus and cinnamon scent washed over me. "Shhh."

I paused. His breath puffed in my ear. "We need to hide."

The footsteps clumped down bare wooden stairs.

I relaxed and he took his hand off my mouth, grabbed my hand, and tugged me away from the entrance. "Watch your step." As my eyes grew accustomed to the darkness, he pulled me to a row of five-gallon paint cans. We crouched behind them.

The footsteps came closer. A beam of light bobbed up and down on the dusty plastic sheathing. The gallery manager emerged from the gloom. She minced across the litter in her stilettos, pushed aside the plastic, and left the way I'd come. Seconds later, a door slammed.

Thank God she hadn't set the gallery's alarm. If she had, I'd have cut the wires, and she'd have known something was wrong. As it was, she'd have no clue I'd been there. It was pure luck that she'd been so careless. I pressed both hands against my mouth to stifle a hysterical giggle.

"Come. She should lock up and go home now." Honoré started across the floor, which was littered with debris and crisscrossed with large electrical cords. I followed, treading quietly and carefully.

We groped our way up a wide stairway to the first floor and stopped on the landing. He turned toward me. "I think we can talk. Quietly. What are you doing here?"

"You lied to me. You're not a research scientist."

"I am, actually."

"Ha!"

"Truth. But that's not all I do. I paid my college and Oxford University fees by recovering stolen property for museums. And I'm good at it. But your friend Zachary Le Noir's thugs stole something from me."

"So you want it back."

"Correct. I want it. And I will get it."

"And it's here?"

"No, but I think he's holding Celeste Bertrand captive in here, and I thought you'd cut me a little slack if I rescued her—maybe even speak to me again."

"I might."

I blew out a long breath. "Why do you think she's here?"

"I listened in on a conversation with his gallery manager, and I heard a dog barking in the background. Sounded like your dog." He took a step away. "Look, this could be dangerous. Why do I have a feeling it would be useless to tell you to go away?"

"You'd be right."

His voice softened. "Partners, then?"

"For now."

He aimed a dim light down at the floor. We were in a narrow corridor with three doors on each side and one at the end. They were all closed. He took one side and I took the other. As we came to each one, we put an ear to it, then turned the knob and opened it. They were all empty. The three rooms on my side appeared to be freshly painted. The smell of paint hung in the air, and windows on the exterior walls had been left slightly open. On his side, the windows were covered with paper and painters' tape masked the woodwork. A five-gallon bucket and a paint sprayer sat in the middle of one. That left only the door at the end. Honoré opened it, and we found it crammed with a jumble of furniture from the other rooms: Beds, chests, chairs, lamps, writing desks, and rolled up carpets had been piled in until it was stuffed from floor to ceiling.

On the next floor, the rooms were bare except for the one at the end, which was stuffed the same way. We went on up the stairs and repeated our search on the third and fourth floors, with the same results. If she was there, she had to be on the top floor, the fifth. But when we repeated our search, the rooms were all the same as the ones on the lower floors. The last room was crammed to the ceiling with stuff. No Aunt Celeste.

I slumped against the doorpost and tears started to pour down my face. Then Baguette gave one short, sharp bark. His toenails scrabbled on the bare wood floor and a second later, my black and tan dachshund leapt from a tall armoire into Honoré's arms.

"Aunt Celeste!" I yelled.

"Hello, darling."

I grabbed a stack of chairs and dragged it into the hall. "You're here!"

Honoré pulled out a fat, overstuffed armchair, and we found a narrow path that wound between the heaps of furniture.

"I am indeed." I could hear a smile in her voice. "Thank you for dropping in."

Shining his light over my shoulder, Honoré pushed in right behind me.

Aunt Celeste sat with her back against the headboard of a single bed jammed against the far wall. Her hands were cuffed together and fastened by a length of chain to the bedframe. She hugged a comforter to her chest. Except for a faint glow from the drape-covered window, the room was dark, but a small electric heater on a shelf beside the window was keeping it warm.

I flew at her and wrapped my arms around her. "You're okay."

"I wouldn't be any use to them if I were dead, darling." She kissed my cheek. "I see you've brought a friend."

I pulled out my lock picks and went to work on unlocking her handcuffs. "People die without water in three days. Did they bring you water?"

"Of course, darling. What a strange idea!"

"Are you starving?"

"I've been fed rather well."

Honoré knelt and unlocked the second cuff just as I got the first one off.

"Ahhh. Thank you." Aunt Celeste scooted to the edge of the bed and dangled her legs over the side. She

233

was pretending to be okay, but tears trickled down her soft, wrinkled cheeks.

I sat beside her. She slumped against me, and we hugged each other and cried.

I wiped my face with the back of my hand. "I've never been so scared."

"Huh," Honoré said, gruff and angry. He lifted a corner of the drape and peered out the window. "You could have asked for my help."

Baguette raced around the bed, jumping up on me, then my aunt, bestowing kisses and ignoring Honoré.

He said, "Okay. Quiet! All of you. We're not out of here yet." He pulled his phone out of his pocket and held it to his ear. "We've got her. Yes… There are two of us. Yes… Chloe Duval… Okay… Okay… Ten minutes." He put the phone away. "Celeste, where are your shoes?"

"They took them."

I yanked my runners off and tried to give them to her.

She whispered, "No, darling. I'm fine."

"You are not fine." I thrust them at Honoré. They were too big for her, but he knelt and tied them on my aunt's bare feet. "Okay," he said softly, standing up again. "Let's go."

As we descended the stairs, he led, my aunt followed, and I came last with Baguette in my arms. I clamped my hand around Baguette's nose like a muzzle. At the landing above the ground floor, Honoré said, "I'm turning off the light now. So be extra careful."

We crept the rest of the way down, then crossed the ground floor to the street side of the building, where a dusky light filtered in. "Here's the plan," Honoré said. "Celeste, you will go first. A black car will pull up and stop. Just get in and go. Chloe and I will follow in a few minutes."

He peered out through the plastic draped over the scaffold. "Shhh. People walking by."

Several minutes passed. Then a boxy black sedan pulled up to the curb. Honoré patted my aunt on the back. "Go now." A man in a fedora and black overcoat got out of the front, opened the back door, helped her in, and they were gone.

Five minutes later, Honoré said, "It's time." A second black car drove up. He scooped me up, Baguette and all, and carried me across the muddy trench between the building and the sidewalk, then set me down. Only a driver sat in the front street. Honoré opened the rear door. I got in and he slid in after me.

Chapter Thirty-One

I sank into the back seat of the big black sedan, too tired and full of gratitude for Aunt Celeste's and Baguette's safety to be able to speak. I let out a long sigh.

Thanks to all the good in the universe, I didn't have to bow to Zachary Le Noir's demand that I meet him at the office in the morning. I would have done whatever he wanted. And then he'd have owned me. I'd have become one of his minions. I could see how he'd planned and orchestrated that from the beginning. And he'd almost succeeded.

As it was, the only thing I'd given him was one section of the tapestry. Yay for me. Things had gone well that evening. I tallied the score this way: Zachary Le Noir, one. Chloe Eugenie Duval, two. No, three. Not only had I not caved to Le Noir, but I'd found Aunt Celeste and Baguette. Or I would have, even without Honoré. "Who sent the cars?"

He smiled. "You'll see him soon." He put his arm around me. "You look pooped."

I laid my head on his shoulder. The moment I'd recognized his cinnamon and citrus scent, I'd felt a huge relief. It didn't matter who he was. He'd helped rescue Aunt Celeste. Therefore, he was one of the good guys. He snuggled me close and in the quiet comfort of the back seat, I fell fast asleep.

We bumped into a courtyard paved with blocks of

pale limestone and I woke up with a start. A U-shaped building three stories high surrounded us. Large pots overflowing with bright, multicolored spring flowers stood under each white-shuttered window. The sign above the door nearest the street read *Hôtel Chez Nous.*

We got out. The driver nodded at Honoré, touched a finger to his chauffeur's hat, and backed away.

Baguette and I followed Honoré into a small, rectangular lobby. A fiftyish man perched on a high stool behind a tall desk. His hair was cut military short and his navy and white striped tee shirt did nothing to conceal the fact that he had muscles everywhere. He smiled but said nothing as we walked past him and started up a curving flight of stairs with heavy wooden handrails.

A thick carpet muffled our footsteps as we walked the length of the first-floor corridor. At the far end, Honoré used a keycard to open a door, and we stepped into a small apartment. On the left, a sofa faced a fireplace with a flickering gas flame. On the right, through double glass doors, I spied a pair of beds with fluffy white duvets and many pillows. Straight ahead, in an all-white Pullman kitchen, a medium-sized man with brown hair turned around from the refrigerator holding a bottle of my favorite champagne. He lifted both arms in welcome.

"Stan Gibson! It was you in the other car. Where is Aunt Celeste?"

"Your aunt went straight to the shower, and who can blame her?"

I looked from Honoré to him and back to Honoré. "Please explain."

Stan turned to pick up a glass from the counter. He held it in one hand and the bottle in the other. "There are more thieves than cops, and cultural artifacts are stolen every day. We can't keep up. We don't have the manpower or the budget, so we have to focus on big ticket items. When it comes to smaller pieces, both private individuals and museums know that if they wait for the police, hell will freeze over before they get their stuff back. So, when they discover a theft, they contract with recovery agents like Honoré to find it."

Honoré nodded, looking pleased with himself.

I tapped my toes on the floor. "So you steal stuff, and the cops turn a blind eye."

Honoré smiled, and a heart-stopping sparkle appeared in his molten chocolate eyes. "Blind eye? Not exactly. But as long as I don't tread on his patch; that is, as long as I don't transport stolen cultural artifacts across the US border, he has no reason to challenge me, and we both benefit from exchanging information."

"I get it. You're not a scientist who drives taxi part time. You're a burglar who drives taxi part time."

"Au contraire. I am all three."

"And you have two identities."

"More or less. When I publish in a scientific journal, I use my full name. But otherwise, I'm just Honoré St. Lazarre."

Stan handed us each a glass, then lifted his. "To a successful rescue. And a fine example of collaboration. Drink up. We have plenty. And I need you, Chloe, to tell me what you know about Zachary Le Noir."

Before I took even a tiny sip, I said, "I want to see him behind bars."

Stan said, "That's my goal also."

I took a deep breath. Better to throw myself on his mercy than become Le Noir's toady. "I think I can help

238

you."

Stan started grinning.

Knowing I risked incriminating myself, I told him about the tapestries and trebuchet.

Stan's eyebrows almost disappeared under his hair. "You've got the trebuchet? Hot pastrami mommy! Petar Ivanov was going to hand it over the night of the wedding, for a bundle of money, of course. I was all set to arrest both of them and the count, and then everything went tango uniform." He raised his glass. "To Chloe." His eyes sparkled like a kid's on Christmas morning. "This is perfect. I'm not even going to ask where you found it."

"He expects me to bring him the second tapestry in the morning, then go get the trebuchet."

"Excellent. We can work with that."

Honoré said, "Count me in. We have to act fast, before he realizes Celeste is free."

Stan pulled out his phone. "We are going to need some help."

Aunt Celeste came through the bedroom with a towel wrapped around her head and wearing a terrycloth robe and slippers. She looked herself again. I grabbed her and hugged her hard until she pushed me gently away. "Darling, I do need to breathe."

I let go a little. "Are you totally okay? Are you going to have nightmares? They brought you water, didn't they?"

She patted my cheek. "You asked me that before. Of course they brought water. I'm fine. I was warm enough. They brought food from a different restaurant for every meal, and it wasn't all that bad."

"It couldn't have been good. I was so worried."

"Thinking about what Le Noir might demand from you was the worst part. After that, the boredom. But I had Baguette, and he did his best to amuse me."

Hearing his name, Baguette pranced around her in happy circles.

Stan and Honoré were huddled in a corner, planning, so we sat in front of the fire, drank champagne, and hugged each other while we told our stories. The corner of the sofa felt welcoming and warm and soft, and at some point, my eyes closed. I drifted away to the sound of my aunt's voice.

A buzzer woke me up.

Aunt Celeste said, "I bet it's André. I phoned him as soon as I got here."

It was a little after eleven o'clock. I hadn't been asleep long, but I felt refreshed. And hungry.

Stan slipped out into the corridor and returned a few minutes later, followed by Robbie Gaspard and André Dubillard. André carried a market basket. "Suzanne sent a selection of clothes for Celeste to choose from," he said, putting it down beside my aunt, "and Robbie brought chicken cacciatore." Robbie set a heavy pot on a table in the corner of the living room. It smelled divine. I decided I was starving.

Stan and Honoré took their plates to the kitchen and asked André to join them. I dug in and ate elbow to elbow on the sofa between Aunt Celeste and Robbie, my plate on my knees. Baguette snoozed, his nose on his paws beside her feet and his back half beside mine. As Robbie served tarte tatin, Stan came back. He said, "Celeste, when do you think they'll discover you're gone? What time will someone go up to check on you?"

"This morning, the manager of the gallery came up

at nine."

"So, by eight, then, preferably before, we want to get to Zachary Le Noir. We have a plan, and I need to bring Chloe up to speed." He winked at me. "If she can manage to stay awake, that is. Then, Celeste and Chloe, I want you to sleep here. I have an agent coming to make sure no one bothers you." He stretched his arms overhead and yawned. "The rest of us have work to do and it's already midnight, so we'd better get on it."

Chapter Thirty-Two

In the morning, as daylight arrived in Paris and folks stumbled out of their apartments to search for croissants, Stan Gibson sat beside me in the back seat of a black sedan and we talked through the plan one more time.

There was this weird disconnect between my expectations of him and the gleeful way he talked about the trap we'd laid for Zachary Le Noir. I can't explain it, except that Stan seemed like the kind of guy who would go around reciting the Boy Scout pledge and promising to always tell the truth. But entrapment, by definition, was deceitful—dishonest, and he was loving it. Why that bothered me, I have no idea. But I felt disappointed in him. It was like discovering that George Washington lied about cutting down his dad's cherry tree.

The car stopped and I got out at the Metro station closest to the Saint Francis Hotel. I walked down the hill toward it, my hand in my pocket, fingers wrapped around the security badge André had fabricated. He lounged on a bench about half a block away in the middle of the park, looking as if he was reading a magazine. "André?"

His voice came through my earbud, quiet and reassuring, as if he sensed my misgivings about going in wearing a wire. "*Oui.*"

"Is everything okay?"

"Yup. You're on, sweet pea."

"I wish it were dark. Doing this in daylight scares

the shit out of me."

"That's only because you're a night owl."

"What's happening? Where's the drone?"

"I've pulled it back into the treetops. I can see everything, but it's unlikely anyone will spot it."

I couldn't see it through the trees. Just then, somewhere ahead of me, a chainsaw sputtered to life. It roared for a few seconds, then stopped.

André said, "The tree service guys have set up the scissor lift and chipper next to the hotel, and they've cut the lower boughs off one of the trees. Right now, they're strapping on safety harnesses, getting ready to go up and trim the higher branches."

"Any sign of Zachary Le Noir?"

"He showed up on his terrace less than a minute ago. According to the maids' duty roster, he's right on schedule. He's alone, in pajamas and robe, and he's turning on one of the firepits and pulling up a chair. Looks like he's going to sit down with a newspaper and a glass of orange juice and wait for the maid to show up and bring him his coffee. That would be you, petunia. Drapes in his apartment are open. Lights on in the living room and kitchen. No sign of anyone else."

"How about his cousin's suite on the other side?"

"It's dark and the curtains are all drawn. The drone didn't pick up any movement, sound, or heat signals, so I think it's safe to say Le Noir is the only one on that floor."

I followed the narrow sidewalk that ran along the side of the hotel to the service entrance at the rear. For several moments, I closed my eyes, slowed my breath, and focused on the task ahead; as I did when I stood on a rooftop or prepared to scale a wall. I could not allow stray thoughts into my mind. I had one task. Only one. Get into Zachary Le Noir's apartment, set the trap, and get him to incriminate himself. A bell in a distant church tower chimed seven times. Time to go in.

I swiped my card, entered, and strode down the hall to the maids' locker room. André had hacked into the maids' scheduling system and given the penthouse maids the day off, and the men and women who served the lower six floors were already at work, having started an hour earlier. So far, so good. I was alone and on familiar territory.

It took a minute to locate the locker that contained the beaded black flapper dresses, shoes, and headdresses the penthouse staff wore. I slipped one of the dresses on over my head and found a pair of T-strap shoes that were only a shade too big. After I stuffed tissue into the toes and tightened the straps, they felt like they would stay on my feet. Finally, I pinned my hair in a loose knot at the back of my head, made sure it hid my earbud, and fastened one of the beaded black headdresses on. When I checked the mirror, *voila!* I'd been transformed into a 1920's flapper girl, a proper seventh-floor-penthouse-suite maid. Fortunately, there was a tiny pocket in each side seam, just big enough for a lacy hanky. I put my compact in one and my smallest set of lock picks in the other.

In the cavernous linen room next to the locker room, I chose a cart with a set of cleaning supplies in a pouch hanging off one end. I laid a pair of sheets and half a dozen towels on the shelf. "Ready to go." I pushed the cart down the hall toward the lobby.

"Good luck." André said.

"Right on time." Stan Gibson's voice.

When I'd visited the lower floors at the Saint Francis, dressed in the uniform of the maids who worked on those levels, I'd carried towels over my arm and bustled along the way they did. This time, I reminded myself the flapper costumes were part of the spectacle that made Saint Francis a place to go and be seen; that I should relax, slouch a bit, look around, and smile.

I turned into the lobby, passed the bank of elevators, and strolled toward the reception desk. At the same moment, a man with a *Paris Delivery* logo splashed across the front of his brown jacket stalked in from outside, pushing a handcart with a small wooden box stacked on top of a larger one. It was the guy who had returned my cable to me in the nail salon. He cut in front of me as if he hadn't seen me, as if his time was more valuable than mine, and spoke to the woman at the concierge desk. "I have a delivery for, ah, let me see—" he held up a clipboard and frowned at it —"Monsieur Zachary Le Noir."

Her smile never faltered, but her eyes flicked over him. She stood and peered over her computer screen at the dingy old handcart. Most likely, she regarded it as an affront to her polished marble floors and pots of subtropical plants.

I raised my eyebrows and sent her a sympathetic smile, then stepped up beside him. "*Bonjour*, monsieur. Monsieur Le Noir is anxious to receive this. I will take it to him."

He turned. His eyes ran from my headdress down to my shoes and back. "Ooh-la-la." He grinned at me, then produced a pen from his shirt pocket with a flourish. "Sign right here, mademoiselle, and I'll be on my way."

I exchanged glances with the concierge, as if I

shared her disdain.

He rubbed his hands together. "Got a busy day ahead."

I scribbled a line at the bottom of his clipboard and handed it back to him. He lifted the crates onto my cart, gave a little two-fingered salute, and strolled back toward the entrance, his step jaunty, pushing his despicable trolley as if it were a thing of beauty.

In the elevator, I swiped my badge. "Show time," I whispered as it rose.

"You've got this," André answered.

I got out on the sixth floor, which was as far as that elevator would go, turned around a corner, and stopped in front of the door that gave access to the two penthouse suites. For the required fifteen seconds, I stared at the retina scanner on the doorframe and held my breath. Would it work?

I needn't have worried. André had conquered the security system, and the door swung silently open. I marched into a brightly lit room with a very high ceiling and a round glass elevator in the middle. A staircase, enclosed in glass, spiraled around it. I smiled for the cameras suspended near the ceiling in all four corners. The elevator lifted me smoothly to the seventh floor and let me out in a handsome marble and wood foyer with two doors; a retina scanner beside each. Behind the door on my left, I would find Zachary Le Noir's apartment; on my right, his deceased cousin's.

André's voice in my ear: "You're golden. Le Noir is reading his paper and he's facing the fire. He can't see what's going on inside."

I left my cart beside the coat closet in Le Noir's entry, opened the smaller box, and lifted out the trebuchet. Loving the weight of all that gold and gemstones in my hands, I carried it into the living room and set it on a low glass table in front of one of the sofas.

Thick off-white carpet muffled my footsteps as I did a quick look around. In the bedroom, closet doors opened to reveal a safe. It was four feet tall and two feet wide and had an old-fashioned combination lock any street kid could have defeated. Still, it took me seven minutes, and I was starting to worry when the last tumbler fell into place. I sent a prayer of thanks to the universe and opened the door. Yes! The Queen of Persia ring gleamed at me from the top shelf. The mate to the cufflink Zachary had left in Aunt Celeste's apartment lay there, too. I put the ring on my finger and tucked the cufflink into my pocket.

On the shelf below, a filigreed gold crown and gold and silver chalice stood side by side. I pulled my compact out of my pocket and snapped a couple of photos.

"Chloe."

"André?"

"Le Noir is getting up. Walking over to the balustrade. The tree cutters are at his level, making a lot of noise, and he's looking annoyed."

I could hear the chainsaw and Le Noir's voice, loud and angry. The saw stopped. A couple of other men were shouting. This was good. As long as the voices continued, I had time. At the top of the safe, there was a set of shallow drawers. I opened them one at a time. A lovely diamond tennis bracelet. A pearl and ruby ring with an old-fashioned gold setting. Eighteenth century Austria, no doubt. And a couple of gold Celtic torcs. Each exquisite and priceless. I snapped shots of all. In another drawer, I found a stack of papers and a photo of the trebuchet, with the amount of twelve million dollars scrawled on the back. I took the photo and folded it along with the papers so they were long and narrow and tucked them into the top of one stocking.

André said, "Incoming."

I ran to my cart, grabbed a feather duster, and headed for the living room.

Without a glance in my direction, Zachary strode through the wide doors from the terrace.

Halfway to the espresso machine on the kitchen counter, he stopped and whirled to look at me. "You!"

"Good morning to you, too, Monsieur Le Noir." Now that the game had begun, my nervousness evaporated. It was deadly serious, and I had to play to win. I sank onto the sofa and flicked my duster over the coffee table.

"I brought you the other tapestry." I pointed at the crate on the laundry cart.

He turned and stared at it, then strode toward me.

I flicked the duster at the trebuchet.

"What the hell are you doing?"

I looked up and smiled. "Dusting." I got down on my knees beside the coffee table. "This looks like it works." The six round rubies lay in a trough on one side of the miniature war machine. I picked one up.

"Don't touch that." He knelt, grabbed my hand, and glared at me. Then he shook his head, as if coming to an agreement with himself. "I guess I shouldn't be surprised. It goes like this." He released the little golden sling from its tether. I tucked the ruby into the sling, and he turned the wheel to wind the counterweight up. "Now it's ready to fire." For a moment, we might have been a pair of kids playing with a new toy. Then he put the ruby back in the trough and tethered the sling.

I said, "When I saw it, I had to take it. It's a lovely little bauble."

He got to his feet. Hands on hips, he stared down at me. "This lovely little bauble, my lovely little friend, is the cause of my cousin's death." Bitterness laced his words.

I jumped up. "Why? How could that be?"

"He sold it to an undercover cop."

"So it belonged to him?"

"It belonged to us."

"It didn't belong to either of you. It was stolen from a museum in New Orleans."

"I have the bill of sale. It cost my cousin and me a shade under twelve million."

"Euros?"

"US dollars. That's too much to leave on the table for Maxime de Charpentier."

"So you bought it in an alley in Las Vegas." I shrugged. "Makes no difference to me. And he sold it to a flic. And someone found out and killed him. Who would do that?"

"Since you're working for me, I'm going to give you some advice. Never turn your back on Count Maxime de Charpentier."

"Or Lili Jensen?"

His eyebrows went up in surprise. He gazed at me for a long moment. "Or Lili Jensen."

"Have the gendarmes arrested them yet?"

He snorted. Outside, the tree service guys started their chainsaw again. Scowling, he closed the sliding glass doors to the terrace. "Don't be naïve. Hell will freeze before they find enough evidence to arrest anybody."

"Well, *tant pis* for your cousin." I pulled the cuff link out of my pocket and held it up. "Now, where is my aunt?"

He put his hands on my shoulders and edged me backward until my knees bumped into a chair and I sat down. He placed a hand on either arm and leaned down, pinning me in. "I need you to move some money to an account in the Caribbean for me. Pronto."

"I told you I don't work for anyone else."

He laughed. "But you do. You manage my investments. You got me the tapestries, assuming the second one is in that crate." He tipped his head toward the linen cart in the foyer. "And you brought me my trebuchet."

I shoved his hands away and jumped to my feet. We stood nose to nose. "If I worked for you, I would expect you to keep your word. But you have not done that."

"*Tant pis* for you." He leered at me. "As for your aunt, the clock is ticking."

I elbowed past him to the center of the room. As I'd hoped, he turned to face me, his back to the sliding glass doors.

Outside, the chainsaw noise continued. Over Le Noir's shoulder, I saw Stan Gibson climb out of the scissor lift onto the terrace, followed by a second man.

Le Noir chuckled. "Since you're here, you can join me for breakfast. Then we can go to your office. You can take care of business for me, and we can be done by noon."

"And then you'll release Aunt Celeste?"

"Of course."

"Guaranteed?"

"Absolutely."

His phone rang. He yanked it out of his pocket, glanced at the screen, frowned, and accepted the call. He listened for several seconds. His face turned red, then purple, and he gripped the phone so hard his knuckles turned white. He shouted, "When did you last see her?" He stomped back and forth, listening, his handsome face a picture of rage. He bellowed, "I will deal with you later" and pitched his phone across the room so hard it bounced off the wall.

He glared at me. "Your aunt escaped."

I crossed my arms on my chest. "Yes, she did." I smiled, and it felt really good.

He lunged toward me.

I stood my ground. "I was there. I helped her." I couldn't resist taunting him.

He grabbed my shoulders. "You've switched teams. You will pay for this. You—you—you—"

"I was never on your team." I stomped on his foot, right on the instep.

He flinched and wrenched his foot away but didn't let go.

Stan Gibson pushed open the sliding glass door to the terrace.

Le Noir gripped my shoulders so hard they hurt and shook me. "You fucking bitch," he yelled.

Stan stood beside me. "Zachary Le Noir. Let her go. You're under arrest for the transportation of stolen cultural goods across the US border."

Le Noir spun me around and jerked me back against his chest. He dragged me a few steps backward into the kitchen, snatched a long, sharp knife off a magnetic strip on the wall, and held it to my throat.

Stan froze. Two other men came in from the terrace and stopped where they were.

Le Noir shouted, "Get out." He waved the knife at them.

I swung my foot out to the side, hooked it behind Le Noir's, and planted it as I threw my entire body weight backward and toward that side, knocking him off balance. His knee buckled. As he toppled to the floor, I twisted out of his grasp.

For a moment, he lay there, looking dazed.

"Well done, Chloe." Stan grasped his arm and yanked him up. "As I said, Zachary Le Noir, you're under arrest, not only for trafficking but, as my colleagues here will be happy to tell you, also for theft and kidnapping."

Chapter Thirty-Three

It was noon before I got to the office. I'd been in the common room approximately thirty seconds, just long enough to—at last—grab a cup of decent coffee when my boss's assistant showed up and told me Monsieur Fischer wanted to see me. At once.

Monsieur Fischer stomped back and forth in front of his desk, his face red and the veins in his neck threatening to burst. "What is the meaning of this, Mademoiselle Duval?" He waved a remote control at the three TV screens on the opposite wall.

A camera had caught me that morning, still wearing the flapper costume, as I walked out of the elevator at the Saint Francis Hotel between Stan Gibson and his counterpart in the French art crime team, followed by two plain-clothes cops. And now the photo was all over the news.

My boss stopped pacing and glared. "Explain, please, mademoiselle, if you would be so kind."

I crossed my arms on my chest to shield myself from the heat of his anger. Then I reminded myself not to do that and fastened a button on my black suit jacket instead. "You will recall that my client, Zachary Le Noir, demanded that you bring me back. He claimed that he inherited a number of bank and investment accounts from his cousin, and he wanted me to transfer everything to Rhineland Bankgruppe immediately."

"You are not answering my question."

"I began to wonder why there were so many accounts and why he was so insistent that I do this at once. And I remembered a movie I saw once, in which a thief set up a variety of accounts, just like the ones Monsieur Le Noir's deceased cousin owned. It was part of a scheme to hide money he'd extorted from wealthy victims. I woke up in the night worrying that Le Noir might be putting Rhineland Bankgruppe at risk for participating, unknowingly, of course, in a money laundering scheme."

"You saw this in a movie."

"Yes." The sweat in my armpits started to trickle down. I took a deep breath. Lying to my boss was harder than I would have imagined. "So I contacted the financial crimes police and asked some discreet questions. It turned out that they were happy to hear from me. They had been investigating both Monsieur Le Noir and his cousin, and that is all I can tell you until they finish their investigation."

He marched back and forth for a full minute before he spoke. "Hem, ah, I assume these police will corroborate your story. Until then, please remain in the common room." His face was still red, though not purple, and he actually raised a finger as if to shake it at me. "Do not go to your office. Do not touch a computer."

I left a voice mail for Stan Gibson, appealing for help. I drank espresso and ate a chocolate croissant before I sank into a grey leather armchair, kicked off my shoes, and tucked my feet up. All my colleagues were at their desks, so the common room was quiet. I fell asleep and neither heard nor saw anything until Monsieur Fischer's assistant tapped me on the shoulder. I checked my watch and discovered I'd slept all afternoon. It was almost five o'clock.

I tried to brush the wrinkles out of my skirt while he escorted me back to my boss's office. On one of the screens, a reporter promised an interview with "top art crimes police" in a few minutes. A couple of seconds later, flanked by his French counterpart and an agent from Interpol, Stan Gibson faced the camera and spun it this way: "Today, with the help of Chloe Duval, an up-and-coming financial wizard at Rhineland Bankgruppe, we have broken the back of a notorious ring of criminals, thieves who have thumbed their noses at international law authorities, cleverly avoiding capture, for seventeen years."

A photo of me, standing beside my desk with my hair up, dressed in my sober work suit and gazing earnestly into the camera, hovered at one side of the screen.

When the newscast resumed, my boss said, "Mademoiselle, ah, hem, ah, I congratulate you. Your good work has not gone unnoticed. I have received a request from Interpol for detailed information regarding Zachary Le Noir's financial transactions and investment histories. Also, any information you have regarding his cousin, Petar Ivanov. How soon can you prepare a comprehensive report?"

****

It took a full week of ten-hour days to trace the investments Le Noir claimed to have inherited. When I stitched what I learned, together with what Stan Gibson, Interpol, and the French art crimes teams knew, we produced a clear trail, proving that they, along with Count Maxime de Charpentier, bought, sold, and trafficked stolen cultural artifacts.

It became clear that the three of them played different roles and that they kept each of their functions relatively separate. Compartmentalizing their activities—a clever ploy—had made it difficult to pin them down.

Petar Ivanov negotiated purchases and sales and sent and received the money. Count Maxime de Charpentier handled shipping, often transporting treasures from one country to another on his yacht, which carried a helicopter on its rear deck. Zachary Le Noir laundered the money. For a long time, buying and selling gold had been a great way to do that. But when Ivanov died, the price of gold was relatively stable whereas the stock market was relatively volatile. I assumed that was why he'd wanted me to run their caches through Rhineland Bankgruppe instead.

I suspected that Ivanov had siphoned off some of the funds for himself. I couldn't prove it. But it may have given the other two a motive for murder.

Chapter Thirty-Four

Since he helped me rescue Aunt Celeste, Honoré, who published in scientific journals as Olivier Honoré St. John de Lazarre, had taken to running with me a couple of evenings a week, preparing a delectable dinner with ingredients from a wonderful deli near my apartment, and then staying over. I wasn't about to turn that kind of attention down. But I planned to keep a certain distance.

In spite of myself, his name, Honoré St. Lazarre, started to tumble around in my head with its own sweet rhythm. Not good. I mean, what kind of a long-term relationship would we have? A cat burglar—*moi*—hooking up with a recovery agent—Olivier Honoré etc., etc.—who returned stolen property to lawful owners. It sounded like something out of a goofy comedy movie in which the heroine is bound for disaster. Okay, as long as he didn't feel the need to return one of *my* treasures, it could work, but I wasn't jumping into it.

That wasn't all. He traded information with Stan Gibson, FBI agent extraordinaire, who had held my hand once. On the surface, they each benefitted from this arrangement because Stan's jurisdiction began and ended with transportation of stolen cultural artifacts across the US border. So, technically, as long as neither he nor I transported anything in or out of the USA, and as long as no other cops got involved, everything would be fine. Maybe.

I thought of my mother giving up burglary, marrying my stepdad, and living quietly in quaint little Sterling, Washington. I definitely was not ready for that. I knew that for sure. The whole thing was making me crazy.

Honoré brushed his fingertips down my arm. "You are not sleeping."

"No."

He smoothed my hair back off my face and his breath whispered across my cheek. "A problem, perhaps?"

"Honoré, you are fishing."

"Ahh. Yes. Fishing. I am fishing." He snuggled me closer. "I am wondering what this beautiful, enchanting, mysterious woman with her head on my shoulder is thinking."

The big problem at the moment was my promise to God, made at the height of my anxiety, that if I found Aunt Celeste unharmed, I'd give up the Queen of Persia. "What makes you think I'm thinking?"

"I can feel the synapses in your brain buzzing."

I couldn't forget that I'd promised to return it to Alexander's Museum of Antiquities in Istanbul. "If a person makes a promise under extraordinarily stressful circumstances, must that promise be upheld?"

"Ahh. I see. You are wrestling with an ethical dilemma."

"Exactly." Actually, I had Baguette to thank for finding Aunt Celeste. Maybe the universal good had played a part, but Baguette—

"You can tell me."

I sighed and rolled onto my other side, my back toward him.

"You wound me, Chloe Eugenie Duval."

At that moment, thousands of lights, glittering like diamonds, began to dance up and down the Eiffel Tower, filling my window. I pointed. "Look."

He nestled his long, firm chest against my back and pulled me close. "I know. You tell me every time. You never get tired of watching."

I laced my fingers through his. All that sparkle breathed life into my soul. It made me want to stay on top of my game. Whatever else happened, I would not give it up.

He kissed the back of my neck.

And the Queen of Persia was mine. I wouldn't part with it again. God would understand. The dancing lights subsided. Honoré rolled me over on top of him. Every inch of my body pressed against his well-muscled, not-quite-six-foot body. Did he know how irresistible he looked, his hair all tousled, his deep chocolate eyes unfathomable in the soft light from the lamp on the nightstand?

"I have had a miraculous recovery of my strength."

I put a finger on his lips. "Impossible."

He nibbled my finger. "Perhaps I shall surprise you."

And he did.

****

When he fell asleep, I got out of bed, slipped my arms into my robe, and went to the cupboard in the kitchen. I looked in the sugar bowl, then dumped the sugar out. My heart raced and my knees quivered. Barely able to breathe, I pawed through the heap on the counter.

I took every bowl, then every cup out of the cupboard. The Queen of Persia wasn't in any of them. I stood on tiptoes and felt the shelves. I reached into the dark corners at the back. I pulled open the drawers under the counter, tossed kitchen towels and cutlery into the sink. Finally, I knelt and ran my hand under the toe space.

Dressed in shirt and pants, Honoré came out of the bedroom. He lifted his jacket off the peg beside the door and shrugged into it. He slid a hand into the inside breast pocket. "I suspect you're looking for this." He held my ring between his thumb and forefinger.

I sat back on my heels and stared, unable to speak.

"Are you surprised? I told you what I do. My job is to return it to the museum you stole it from." He tucked it back into his pocket.

"So that's why you've been so eager to cook dinner." Slowly, as if I were old and tired, I got to my feet and leaned against the counter. He'd been playing me. I crossed my arms on my chest.

"My reputation is at stake," he said. "When Alexander's Museum of Antiquities discovered it had been stolen, they offered a reward for getting it back. I signed a contract with them. I promised to bring it back, and then I lost it."

I'd been such a fool. "You were the one who stole it from me the first time."

"Correct."

His hair was still tousled, and he still looked adorable, so I turned my back and started putting cups and bowls back in the cupboard. "How did you know where to find it?"

"It wasn't difficult. Except for the main floor, where there are cameras, the museum's alarm system only covers the doors and windows, so when I discovered a ventilation shaft that was big enough to accommodate a slender person, I figured that was how the thief got in.

"Next, I searched for records of thieves who might be small enough to fit in that shaft and found three, including your mother, whose name came up in records from Montreal."

My eyebrows went up and I whirled to face him. "My mother was never tried for anything."

"True." He nodded. "Then I spent days watching old security tapes from the main floor to see if any of the three thieves I'd identified showed up. When I saw Celeste Bertrand standing behind a table in front of the same ventilation duct two floors below, apparently representing early French fabric and lace design, I figured she was also small enough to fit. Although she had no record, I came to Paris to meet her, and when I bought my cufflinks from her, I saw a photo of your mother in her back room."

"Brilliant."

"I found the ring in your mother's wine cellar and returned it to the museum, but before I could hand it over, a thug posing as an employee mugged me and made off with it."

I put a stack of plates in the cupboard and glanced at him over my shoulder. "How sad."

The irony was lost on him. He went on as if I'd said nothing. "I tracked the thug. He turned out to be a mercenary who did odd jobs for Petar Ivanov. So I kept watch, and when the ring turned up on Ivanov's finger, I followed him back to Paris. I thought he might fence it, and there are only a couple of people who could handle it, so I was keeping an eye on your friend Robbie Gaspard and Celeste, too."

"And you 'happened' to meet me in baguette class—"

"I saw you walking with Celeste and Baguette and I realized it was you, not your mother, in the photo in your aunt's back room. You were the one who stole it from the museum."

I put the knives and forks back in the drawer and finally turned to face him.

He reached out, as if to take my hand. "I hoped to get to it before you did."

I crossed my arms on my chest and hugged myself hard. "But you didn't. And then we broke up. That's why you helped find Aunt Celeste, so I'd take you back and you could search my apartment."

"No." Frowning, he shook his head. "Rescuing her had nothing to do with the ring. I care about her."

"And Stan Gibson? Why did he help? Does he care, too?"

"Gibson wanted Zachary Le Noir."

They'd both been using me. I didn't want to believe that, but it was pretty plain. I held out my hand. "Give me the ring, please."

He laid it on the counter, his eyes on my face.

I should have grabbed it, but I didn't. Which proved either I was stupid or my brain was addled by good—no great—no stupendous—sex. I said, "When Le Noir kidnapped Aunt Celeste, I promised I'd take it back to the museum if she was safe and unharmed."

"Ah, the ethical dilemma you were worrying about."

"Yes."

"Then take it," he said.

I stared at it for a long moment—too long a moment.

"Let me solve that dilemma for you." He picked it

up and put it back in his inside pocket, dropped a kiss on my forehead, opened the door, and stepped out into the hall. I watched his back all the way to the stairway.

He'd sucked my soul out of my body. And then he'd gone on about how clever he'd been to do it. And he still looked achingly irresistible.

He didn't look back. Not even once.

Chapter Thirty-Five

I began to believe Zachary Le Noir was right about the likelihood of his cousin's killer being brought to justice. It wasn't going to happen. Count Maxime de Charpentier, who undoubtedly was responsible, regardless of who actually did the deed, seemed to be above suspicion of murder.

The Gendarmerie brought his tall, blonde fixer, Lili Jensen, in for questioning. She implicated the château's caretaker, the guy who had carried my bag up the steep pathway the night before the wedding. The guy who had been looking to get laid in the inn the night of the snowstorm. He, in turn, implicated her. And in May, two months to the day after Ivanov died, both of them were arrested, but the cops couldn't find enough hard evidence, so they had to let them go.

The way the universe rolls, the homicide business never stops booming. Detectives everywhere have plenty of other cases to work on, some of them actually solvable. So Ivanov's file got tossed onto a towering pile of cold cases.

Zachary himself faced trial for kidnapping, cultural artifact trafficking, and money laundering. If the news media could be believed, he posted a large bail as guarantee that he wouldn't leave the country. In my opinion, once his crimes had been revealed, he'd have had a hard time finding a country that would support his lifestyle and wouldn't extradite him. And his wife, from whom he had been separated but remained friendly, initiated divorce, so there was no point going back to Brazil.

The fickle public latched onto other scoundrels who had committed more recent crimes, and the media went right along with them. Which was fine with me. Petar Ivanov, his suspected murderers, and Zachary Le Noir disappeared from the news; reporters stopped following me around sneaking unbecoming photos and asking for comments.

****

Stan Gibson took to eating at *Chez Gaspard*. I bumped into him there at lunchtime almost every Tuesday, and we fell into the habit of sitting together. He had a quirky sense of humor and a way of looking at me that made me feel I could have fallen in love with him if he hadn't been a cop. Occasionally, he reiterated his suggestion that I commit to helping the good guys. I'd tell him once was enough and he'd laugh and pat my hand. But he never held it again. I liked him, and there were moments when, although it was a bad idea, I would have welcomed his warm hand holding mine.

Robbie Gaspard frequently came out of the kitchen, sat down beside me, and glowered at him like a stern papa keen on dampening potential sparks. When Robbie leveled his fierce highland stare at someone, you could see why the Scots were so feared in battle in ancient times. That plus the wild skirling of their bagpipes, of course.

"Stan Gibson's a good man, lass, as cops go," he said one day when I sat there alone, "but you must be canny."

Robbie thought it necessary to remind me, too, of Honoré St. Lazarre. As if he needed to. I'd blocked his phone, texts, and sent e-mails straight to the trash bin. But I couldn't forget him. Even though I hadn't known him all that long, he'd left a big hole in my life.

I was as bad as a kid picking at a scab until it bleeds. Every morning, before I went to the office, I checked the website for Alexander's Museum of Antiquities to see if they reported the return of the Queen of Persia. I scanned the local news for tidbits about the Darwin Centre, hoping he would be mentioned. From time to time, I hung out at the bouquiniste stall where, allegedly, informants mingled with cops. I examined every single book and eavesdropped like mad. But his name never came up.

In the evening, when I ran beside the Seine, occasionally, my heart would lurch at the sight of a not-quite-six-foot-tall man, diamonds glinting under a smartly tailored cuff, brown hair ruffled by the breeze. He might be walking or leaning against the balustrade, gazing down at the river. But it always turned out to be someone else.

Honoré St. Lazarre. I no longer allowed his name to tumble around in my head, but I missed the lovely rhythm of those six syllables. I missed turning the corner and seeing him waiting for me at the entrance to my apartment building. I missed finding a red rose at my door with a ribbon attaching it to a note inviting me to join him for dinner. I missed his head on the pillow beside mine; watching the glittering, glowing tower together.

At night, I tried to convince myself not to be stupid; that the lights on the Eiffel Tower sparkled as brightly as they ever had. But the fact was, they didn't. I tried closing the curtains. But that didn't help. As much as it hurt, I had to watch. Not watching was like telling the world I'd fallen in love with him. And, I told myself ninety-nine times a day, I hadn't.

Every Saturday morning, when I opened my door to take Baguette out for a walk, I found a large bouquet of roses mixed with other seasonal flowers. The concierge swore she never saw who delivered them. The roses were pink, yellow, white, or salmon colored, but never red, and there was never any card. Aunt Celeste said it had to be Honoré who sent them. I rolled my eyes and put that down to the fact that she saw everything through rose-tinted lenses.

Raphael Aragon seemed determined to win her heart, if he hadn't already, with old-fashioned all-out courting maneuvers. It was the opera one week, theater and late supper another. On the longest day of the year, it was moonlight on a private yacht on the Seine with a catered five-course dinner and dancing to a string quartet. She flitted around in her vintage tango outfits, more than ever like a hummingbird sipping nectar from sweet spring blossoms; loving all of it. I wondered what she'd do if he proposed. I didn't ask. I didn't want to think what it would be like if he came to live with her in her apartment above mine. Or if she went to live with him.

****

June dragged on and on, quietly—too quietly for my taste. Except when the Princess of Urbania, a minor principality even smaller than Monaco, came to Paris wearing a Burmese ruby pendant the size of a quail egg, which isn't all that large as eggs go. But a ruby, especially a Burmese, is another story.

She claimed it came to her via matriarchal succession of many generations. It didn't. She was born in Marseilles to a hard-working couple who scrabbled out a living on the docks, cleaning fish, scraping and varnishing boats, and informing on illegal goods coming in and going out of the country—before they disappeared following a big drug bust. I knew because Aunt Celeste wormed it out of Raphael Aragon, who seemed to know everything about everybody. Apparently, he still had ties to a couple of intelligence agencies in the Middle East.

The princess and her companion were staying at the Saint Francis, on the third floor. I mentioned it when our *Société* sat in the kitchen at Chez Gaspard one evening, tasting Robbie's menu for the coming week. As expected, André Dubillard tried to talk me out of going to get it. "I think you should stay away from there for a good long while. Your face was all over the news just a couple of months ago, wearing one of their flapper costumes. Going back so soon is too big a risk."

Aunt Celeste echoed him, and so did Robbie Gaspard. "I don't want to see you in chains, lass," he said, turning that fierce highland gaze on me.

But my poor parched soul cried for the thrill of placing a couple of chocolates on the pillows and leaving with a gem like that in my pocket.

"I have my own uniform for the lower floors at the hotel," I told them. "I will wear it, but actually, I shouldn't even need that. She's only on the third floor. No one should see me at all."

One night after I made sure the princess was at the opera, I scaled the wall, unlatched the window with a thin blade, and climbed into the room. She hadn't even bothered to put the necklace in the safe in the closet. It lay on the counter in the bathroom, surrounded by eyebrow pencils, lipsticks, jars of face cream, and a heap of facial tissues smeared with makeup. It deserved better care than that, which proved my point— she wasn't a real princess.

For a whole night, I felt myself again. The fact that all three of the other members of my *Société des Voleurs de Nuit* objected to my going in heightened the sense of risk and made scoring the ruby even sweeter.

It contributed a nice little boost to my account at Rhineland Bankgruppe, but it didn't fill the gaping hole in my heart. The glow had already subsided a couple of days later when July arrived and went on, as uninspired and uninspiring as spring.

Until one Saturday morning in the middle of the month when the bouquet left outside my door contained two dozen red roses and a peacock-blue silk bag tied with silver ribbon tucked into the middle. With shaking hands, I carried it to the coffee table and phoned Aunt Celeste. I left the door open and sat on the sofa and stared at it while Baguette stood on his hind legs and barked. Aunt Celeste arrived in cream-colored silk pajamas and robe, gave Baguette a pat, sat down beside me, and gazed at the bouquet. "Well, it's about time."

"Time for what?"

She gave me a one-armed hug. "Don't be dense, darling. Red. Red roses. What's in the bag?"

"I'm afraid to look."

She reached for it. "May I?"

"Please."

She peered into the bag and smiled. "I thought so. Hold out your hand."

I did, and the Queen of Persia tumbled into my palm. I slid it onto my finger and turned it to catch the rays of light from the window.

"There's a note." She fished a folded piece of paper out of the bag and handed it to me.

I should never have taken this from you. H.

Aunt Celeste hugged me while I cried. Then she made coffee, and I unblocked Honoré.

I phoned him, and when he answered, I said, "Thank you is not enough. It was very sweet of you to give me the Queen of Persia. In return, I hope you'll let me do something for you."

He hesitated. "Such as?" I heard a note of caution in his voice.

I took a deep breath. "This October, Bing Nashby, a self-made oil man from Texas, plans to show up in Nice with his mistress. He passes her off as an impoverished but noble kinswoman to the Hapsburgs. Actually, she's an exotic dancer he picked off the stage in Amarillo. But that is beside the point. She's been photographed wearing a tiara that I happen to know was stolen from a private collection in Zurich."

"You're telling me this because?" He sounded a lot more friendly.

"There's a nice reward for it, and I can help you recover it."

He laughed. "You speak my language. Dinner?"

****

As the Christmas season approached, Rhineland Bankgruppe gathered all the Paris employees for the annual black-tie dinner hosted by my boss, Monsieur Fischer. He sat at a table on a raised platform with his boss from Munich and their wives, who looked stunning in designer gowns, one white and one black, that even Aunt Celeste would have liked.

After dinner and before the dancing began, he called up the year's outstanding employees. While those who were not included pretended not to mind being left out, Monsieur Fischer gave each an envelope which everyone knew contained a nice bonus.

He called me up last of all. "To Mademoiselle Chloe Eugenie Duval I owe a debt of gratitude for unmasking Zachary Le Noir and saving Rhineland Bankgruppe the infamy of holding accounts that are still being investigated by legal authorities. Mademoiselle Duval did this at great personal cost. She persevered at exposing his ill-gotten gains even when I accused her of complicity and fired her. Mademoiselle Duval, please come up here."

Honoré squeezed my hand under the tablecloth and gave me a great big wink. Monsieur Fischer came down off his dais and met me in front of the head table. "*Merci, mademoiselle,*" he said and handed me a thick, sealed white envelope. I thought for a moment he was going to kiss my cheeks the French way, but that was too much for his stiff, proper soul. He shook my hand instead.

Honoré leaped to his feet, shouted "Brava!" and began to clap loudly. Monsieur Fischer flinched and the color rose in his face, but he kept smiling, so my colleagues had to stand up and clap too, whether they wanted to or not. I stifled a giggle, and as everyone sat down again, I kissed my boss, who, after an apoplectic moment, actually looked as if he liked it.

That night, as the lights on the tower subsided and before Honoré regained his energy, I took one last look at the Queen of Persia ring, then, before I could change my mind, I slid it off my middle finger and tucked it into his palm. I didn't care that he had given up his reward for returning it to the museum. If he could afford diamond cufflinks with Burmese rubies, he wasn't hurting. But I didn't like that he'd risked his reputation to give it to me. That didn't sit well in my gut. "I want you to take it back to the museum."

Chapter Thirty-Six

As the new year began, Robbie Gaspard, totally stoked, practiced his bagpipe at least four times a week, marching about in all sorts of wet, cold Paris weather. Annually, Alexander's Museum of Antiquities in Istanbul chose a different country and hosted a week-long celebration of that country's heritage. They planned cultural displays and events featuring that country and its enclaves in other countries around the world. And it was Scotland's turn to show off her traditions, so Robbie was preparing to play in a bagpipe marching band composed of individuals from seventeen different countries.

When she wasn't out on a date with Raphael Aragon, Aunt Celeste was busy stitching up replicas of the clothes a wealthy Scottish lady would have worn in the seventeenth century. Along with fabric designers from Canada, Scotland, and Italy, she would dress at least ten mannequins at the museum and construct a display featuring fabrication of Scottish tartans and couture across the ages. She'd conscripted André Dubillard to set up a computer program for individuals to see if a tartan was associated with their family names. And to make up for her neglect of Baguette, she'd promised him spiffy new vests and berets made from leftover bits of material.

Honoré made an appointment with the museum director to return the Queen of Persia to Alexander's

Museum of Antiquities a couple of weeks before the commencement of Scottish week. We'd decided on that day because it would be a year from the day I met him in baguette class.

I spent the bonus my boss had given me on a luxury cruise in the Mediterranean for the two of us. We'd go as soon as we saw the ring restored to its place in the glass dome on the third floor of the museum, and we'd return in time to take in the Scottish displays and watch Robbie perform in the bagpipe marching band.

****

It's hot in Istanbul. After two weeks of luxury cruising, I realize how primitive the museum is. No air conditioning. Only ceiling fans lazily stirring the air, steamy from too many bodies in a small space. Old-fashioned toilets with tanks on the wall and pull chains. Cold water only for washing. Except it's not really cold.

But it makes up for all that with its displays. Not the least of which is the Queen of Persia ring, perched on its pedestal against a black velvet background. It's as lovely as ever. I glance around the room, grasp Honoré's hand, and whisper, "They still haven't updated the alarm system. There are cameras on the main floor, but none up here. Only sensors on the doors and windows."

He nods without taking his eyes off the ring, or more likely, the way the glass bell that covers it is fastened to the marble pedestal. "You'd think they would have."

We stroll down the stairs to the main floor. Directly below the Queen of Persia, Aunt Celeste is taking her turn at the tartan display table, which is flanked by mannequins wearing traditional Scottish tartans. The table is long and wide enough to hold a basket of raw wool, a small spinning wheel, working models of three different types of looms, and samples of fabric, as well as the computer which faces the visitors so they can put in a family name and see what tartans, if any, might be associated with it. André Dubillard has been pecking at the keyboard, as if searching for a family tartan. As we approach, he turns and starts toward the entrance door. Honoré jostles against him and jabs an elbow into his ribs.

André yells, "Hey, dumbass!"

Honoré gives his shoulder a shove and shouts, "Watch where you're going."

The two face off, fists clenched and raised. A pair of guards leave their posts by the entrance doors, push through the crowd, and take each of them by an arm. I slip behind the table.

"Go," Aunt Celeste says.

I duck under the tablecloth and climb into the cubbyhole built into the underside of the table. It's hot. It's stuffy. The board under my back is hard. But I feel totally alive.

A word about the author...

I have studied writing in Paris and Seattle, and I write a monthly column for Pacific Yachting magazine. Murder Richly Deserved is my third novel of mystery and suspense, following Murder Unrehearsed and Murder Undetected.

I am a physical therapist, a foodie, a fanatic about good chocolate, and a private pilot. I lived aboard an old wood motor yacht for seventeen years. In my dreams, I'm a famous author, a pianist of renown, an acceptable water-color artist, and a globe-trotting yogini.

https://www.roxannedunn.com/

Thank you for purchasing
this publication of The Wild Rose Press, Inc.

For questions or more information
contact us at
info@thewildrosepress.com.

The Wild Rose Press, Inc.
www.thewildrosepress.com

9 781509 255573